COME, BOS

BOS

by Lucille Benoit

First Stillwater River Publications Edition

Library of Congress Control Number: 2018934097

ISBN-10: 1-946-30047-0
ISBN-13: 978-1-946-30047-8

1 2 3 4 5 6 7 8 9 10
Written by Lucille Benoit.
Cover design by Nathanael Vinbury
Published by Stillwater River Publications, Pawtucket, RI, USA.

Publisher's Cataloging-In-Publication Data (Prepared by The Donohue Group, Inc.)

Names: Benoit, Lucille.
Title: Come, Bos / Lucille Benoit.
Description: First Stillwater River Publications edition. | Pawtucket, RI, USA : Stillwater
    River Publications, [2018]
Identifiers: ISBN 9781946300478 | ISBN 1946300470
Subjects: LCSH: Dairy farmers--New England--Fiction. | Veterans--United States--
    Fiction. | Human-animal relationships--
Fiction. | Raw milk--Fiction. | Natural foods industry--United States--Fiction.
    Classification: LCC PS3602.E56 C66 2018 | DDC 813/.6--dc23

*The views and opinions expressed in this book are solely those of the author
and do not necessarily reflect the views and opinions of the publisher.*

———————

DEDICATION

———————

THIS BOOK IS DEDICATED TO BEE BEE,
the finest Bos Taurus I have ever had the pleasure to know.

U.S.D.A. YEARBOOK OF AGRICULTURE

1926 – PAGE 177

"From John T. Frederick's Green Bush"

Of this alone I can be certain: That love and knowledge of the earth, which means daily observations and acceptance of the facts of birth and death, of the puniness of man's efforts and the little meaning of his life, has brought me happiness, compounded of joy in simple things—pleasure in food, in wife and children, in beauty of flower and tree, of sky and water and the forms of earth, in the dependence and faithfulness of beasts, in freedom that comes from knowledge and acceptance of my weakness and of death.

COME, BOS

.

Chapter 1

DON'T BLAME
THE COW

DAIRY FARMING WAS ONE OF TWO LOVES of Jerome Duggan's life. The one he loved best was gone already and this day threatened to take the other.

Three notes of the top country tune were all he needed. Hitting the alarm and sitting up, he was instantly alert and aware. He untangled himself from the blankets on the daybed in the kitchen. Flopping there regularly was the norm.

Using a slant of moonlight through the window, he added a flannel shirt slung on the end of the bedframe over his thermal sleepwear. He stepped into a pair of workpants, all a uniform, faded style with bagged out knees, from the pile in a corner. Fingering under the bed for his boots, he felt for the socks tucked deep into the toes.

Crossing the kitchen, he opened the faucet and waited till the well pump brought up icy, cold fluid. Putting his hand in the stream, he caught mouthfuls lapping it up from the cup made of his thick, callused palms. A quick rinse and spit, a rub of his face with the wet fingers, he was all done with his morning bathroom routine.

Barely lingering a moment, he added a John Deere cap that substituted for a comb through his crop of wiry, grey ringlets. To complete his outfit, he pulled his threadbare barn coat from the row of hooks by the door.

He stepped out to a 4 a.m. world deeply asleep, at its darkest point before the dawn. This was the realm of cottontails, foxes and owls. He sensed the purity of the air as something tangible. His nose caught the aroma of early morning moisture strong with the scent of damp earth mixed with a topping of decayed leaves. A cool breeze with a warm promise caused him to hesitate in making a weather forecast. What wide swing of temperatures would this late, fall day deliver, he wondered, sensing the ache in his gauge, a long ago broken wrist.

The smells of the farm were Jerry's favorites, the hay loft one of his top picks. He sometimes found a few minutes to linger up there, sitting on a stack of bales, soaking himself in a sunbeam. The light added crispness to the hay's wildflower potpourri with an undertone of dirt. The nutty grain bin was nice, hinting of a multigrain toast but it paled in comparison to the strong corn relish odor of the silage. He had tasted all of them at some point, putting a touch of some especially tempting bits to his tongue through the years.

2

As he moved toward the barn, a short walk from the house, he enjoyed the feel of his body responding, revving up to the day's demands. With every step, he mentally planned his to-do list.

A running, continuously updated list was a hallmark of his father. Jerry had marveled at the never-ending chores his father wanted him to do. He avoided catching his dad's eye when he was younger. The list was not a suggestion but a requirement.

He'd missed some great days for hitting baseballs with the guys but acquired valuable skills. As a teen he learned to repair plumbing, weld simple joints, do straight forward wiring, caulk windows and shovel just about anything out of anywhere, developing core muscles that served him well for many years. He was well-versed in the list and its contents by the time he decided to make dairy farming his life.

After flipping on a series of lights in the milk room to guide him, he filled a dozen black, rubber feed bowls then put them in place in the milking parlor. Cold stainless steel equipment awakened his hands and fast work warmed them. The assortment of paraphernalia needing assembly was waiting to be flushed through with detergents and rinses. He connected the central milk chamber of the claw to the four eight-inch inflations and attached the equipment to the vacuum line to draw a disinfecting chlorine solution through it.

Then he headed out toward the pastures. The barn and house sat at the bottom of a circle of rising fields spiraling around the buildings with stands of large trees in the center and marshy woods left wild on the edges. From the top of the highest field, the view and air were the best.

There had been an urgency in his step when he was younger, always a half run he'd sustained for a long time. He wasn't sure when it had slowed just that in his sixty-eighth year, it definitely had and he was forced to accept it. Not without worry though. How in the heck was he going to stop a back slide of things? He had considered hiring one of his helper's "cousins" on a regular schedule but knew there wasn't enough in the milk check to make that realistic.

He was mulling those options when he came to a stop on the path that gave him his first look at the herd. They were the sight he lived for and they didn't disappoint. Those girls were as close as Jerry would ever get to seeing his late wife, Joan, again,

For more than three decades he had enjoyed the same memory at this point in his morning. He was leaving her warm side with a joke that he was off to see his girlfriends. When he'd mouthed those words he was living the heaven-on-earth period of his life. Those moments ended when the cancer took her.

"Come, Bos, come," he called. A number of golden heads lifted, the usual group that couldn't wait for their next meal, the first to respond to the call. "Come, Bos," Jerry repeated and the herd of Jerseys started moving toward the bar way. He lifted off the two cedar posts and the first few ambled through. They knew their way to the barn and he walked into the pasture to urge on the older and younger cows who both tended to bring up the rear.

All collected, he walked back down the path, still contemplating the need for new body parts that weren't going to ache so much at the end of a day. His girls ambled into the barn, all sporting trademark dark-trimmed, expressive eyes. His favorites among them never failed to say hello, even if it was just with a look. They came over to be petted like a pack of big dogs. The young stock were just getting the program under their belts and were all knees and wild eyed until they had settled down after having a few calves. But they were watching and learning and Jerry

4

knew he had developed an exceptional herd if for nothing else in the ease they gave him with producing milk. The farm was a calm, quiet oasis to him, a heavy lift, no denying but one that didn't feel like a yoke.

Among the many things the cows did without fight, was to submit to the equipment and handling of milking. The first girls dove their heads through the rectangular stanchions aiming at the bowls of grain on the far side. Jerry secured the latches before he moved to the milk room to check the levers on the pump.

Coming back to the milking parlor with a bucket of cleaning solution, he began washing the hooves and prepping the udder of the first cow. He stripped out some milk, checked it for thick, white clumps, a sign of mastitis, then attached the claw to the four teats making sure there was good suction.

He ran his hand over his first beauty, Ada, probably the best cow in the herd for her intelligence, temperament and production. He spoke to her telling her she was his favorite. He paid special attention to his task, feeling her udder from top to bottom, very gently just getting a sense of how much milk she had. He used the information to tell when she had given it all up and always made sure she had no hard spots when finished.

Nelson, his hired hand, had appeared. He was in charge of ushering in the cows four at a time, helping with the preparation, putting the milking equipment on then showing them the door so the next four could enter. Nelson was one of a few Guatemalans that had responded to the notice he'd placed with the Jehovah's Witness Kingdom Hall in Wakeville. That had become his source for finding help for the past 15 years. He'd chosen him based on the bright light of intelligence he saw in his eyes and hadn't been disappointed.

After three years of training, he had a very capable assistant who possessed the young strong back he lacked. They made a good team, synchronizing twice daily into a dance with this bevy of girls. The operation flowed smoothly through the 40-odd cows they were typically milking. During the process Jerry often formulated the rest of his day's plan, debating the merits of starting one repair over completing another half-done one. They went on with the work hardly conscious, moving in a pattern repeated now so many times, he wasn't sure he really couldn't do it in his sleep.

Almost finished with the whole herd, he saw the young heifer's back leg, bloody and tangled in a circle of wire. It looked like she'd stepped right into a wire trap. It would take cutters to remove it. Jerry came back with the tool and got in close to find the best spot to make the snip. He decided he'd try to cut at a section that was likely to quickly give him the result he wanted, where the band of wire could be unwrapped and removed. His body wore the badges earned at the hard end of a cow's hoof. He still sported some deep purple, gold-edged medallions that were sore to the touch and more than six months old. He positioned himself off to the side of the cow, at an angle where he wasn't likely to be in the path of a forceful kick if that was what she decided to do. He placed his left hand on her leg to transmit to him the first hint of movement and give him a chance to push back.

He pressed down on the handle and the brittle piece in the jaws of the cutters gave easily. It wasn't enough to get the wire totally free of the leg but encouraged by this progress, he studied where he might make the next cut and be done. He settled on a spot a little deeper into the tangle but he made sure to keep the cutters from catching any part of her leg. Needing both his hands on the cutters to get through the thicker piece, he took his left hand off her leg. He leaned in again and pressed down slowly and firmly.

The fury and strength of the young cow's kick was quicker and faster than he calculated. It caught the edge of his shoulder with good hard contact. Losing his balance, he flew forward landing squarely on his collarbone. The edge of the concrete flooring hit him at a right angle. He was lying face down, immediately nauseous and fighting to stay conscious, when Nelson, saw him.

Right away he sensed there was something broken and tried to form words to warn Nelson not to move him but the bulky arms were around his body and lifting him before he could get them out. The young man didn't know where he was hurt and didn't realize he probably shouldn't be moving him.

The floor space behind the cows was only about five feet wide so Nelson tucked Jerry up close against the farthest wall. Lying flat on his back on the cold cement floor he started shaking and felt the juggling of loose bone material—though he couldn't feel his right hand. As he fought off blacking out, he heard Nelson speaking into his cellphone in a panicked voice, trying to convey information in broken English.

He'd never bothered to ask Nelson much, just happy to have the reliable help on a cash, no-questions-asked basis. The thought of doing a fire drill in case of emergency was not something that would have been on Jerry's radar. He'd survived enough years of farming to believe he knew how to do the work safely and he'd been proven right by his track record of relatively minor injuries over many years. His skill and luck seemed to have just run out though.

Noticing him shivering, Nelson laid a coat from the collection near the door over him, helping to stem the shaking and the jarring of his broken body.

The local volunteer corps might not be too quick to respond at this early hour of the morning, Jerry thought. He went to his bag of tricks that hadn't failed him yet and tried to breathe slowly and deeply. The pain of his chest moving against his broken bones made that impossible. He didn't know if he'd be able to hold on to till the rescuers arrived.

He tried with what was left of his fading strength to tell Nelson to go back and pay attention to finishing the milking and to keep calm around the animals so they wouldn't get spooked by the tense situation. There were two cows whose machines should have been removed by now. They were milked out and needed to be led out so the last group of four could come in. Nelson understood Jerry's mumbling and turned back to finish the work. He saw also that where he'd put Jerry would mean walking the cows out along a path within a foot of him. He hesitated for a moment and then took hold of the first cow's collar and put himself between the sprawled human and the animal. Worse case he'd be the one to step on Jerry instead of the 800 pound animal.

Agnes, one of Ada's daughters, was the first cow to move. She eyed Jerry prostrate on the floor, stopped almost putting her nose to his face but gave no indication that she was afraid of the new position he'd taken. Mustering barely more than a whisper, Jerry told her everything was ok and she should just keep going.

She did, calmly moving by as Jerry said a silent thank you to her. Nelson got the next cow out with the help of Agnes' good example. He brought in only two cows instead of four and put them into the stanchions farthest away from Jerry. The activity was good to occupy Jerry's mind and prevent him from counting the minutes as he lay there.

The EMT's were blessedly quick to the farm given the distance from the fire station to this remote location and just as quick to give him something that besides easing the pain made it hard to keep his mind racing, thinking of all the problems his stupid rookie move had just triggered.

Chapter 2

MILK
IN A BOTTLE

FRANK MADDOX WALKED INTO JERRY'S KITCHEN, a place where time stood still. He hadn't been here in close to 15 years but virtually nothing had changed. He carefully put a quart size glass milk bottle down in one of the few open spaces on the table.

Seeing Jerry's left hand extended, Frank took it carefully and started trying to say a formal hello but was cut short.

"You aren't 15 anymore," the older man said with warmth and a wide smile. "and I'm not Mr. Duggan anymore, just Jerry. Thanks for coming over."

Without the benefit of his right hand, he struggled to lift stacks of items off the chairs but was defeated in the effort. Frank jumped in but quickly needed help finding an open spot to lay them back down. Not one inch of flat surface was available.

A guilty grin on Jerry's face and a nod of his head toward a small potential gap in the consistent clutter indicated a possibility and also that it didn't make any difference to him where the stack landed.

Frank picked up the bottle he'd brought and handed it to Jerry who looked at his father's name at the top in faint red letters, Charles Duggan, Fair View Acres. A drawing of a cow's head, encircled in a half moon with a rolling field formed the bottom of the circle. A few of these milk bottles were still around the place, Jerry recalled, but couldn't say that he'd laid eyes on one in the last 10 years.

"Lindsey, my wife, is always checking the antiques on "craigslist" for stuff she can repurpose, or rather I can repurpose them for her. She came across it and thought maybe you didn't have any left," said Frank.

"So this is an antique now," Jerry smiled. "That makes sense. Nice to be reminded."

The heft of the glass container was familiar, like the feel of his perfectly broken in baseball glove. Jerry had played with these as a kid, lined them up on a wall for BB gun practice. The quarter-inch thick glass shattered with a distinctly, satisfying sound. They were everywhere in the milk room at one time and just seemed to disappear over the years.

His mother brought in the few remaining ones, Jerry supposed. She used them for all kinds of purposes. If she had left any in a safe place, she could probably tell you where in this mess you could find it, he realized, but then again it wouldn't be a mess.

Looking around the kitchen that had become for all intents and purposes, his whole world, Jerry seemed to see the room's reality. The wallpaper was so old that it was becoming trendy again except for the layers of dust and grime. The colors and pattern had gone out of fashion and come back as a new retro look. Dark stripes from the failure of the gutter on the front of the farmhouse 30 years ago were perfectly clear in the flowery patterned design.

The furniture might be called antiques except they were bought when they first appeared, used for decades and not well-cared for or polished daily. They had acquired a patina but not one that sold in the finer antique shops.

Telling Frank to make sure he thanked his wife, Jerry put it on the table with a realization that it would only serve to increase his tendency to ruminate about the good old days.

It had been a month since the accident that had taken him out of the fulltime dairy business for the first time in more than 40 years. That one swift kick from a young cow created a grim picture. The accident had inflicted a neck and collarbone injury, the headfirst slam into the corner of cement flooring limiting the use of his right arm and hand and coming precariously close to snapping his neck. The extent of his injury was more than enough to make feeding, milking and cleaning up after a herd of cows out of the question.

Frank couldn't help but notice that despite his incapacitation, Jerry still appeared fitter than most men his age. He had agreed to talk to him about running the farm until he could get back on his feet. The lead contender for the job, he earned that rank during another life. He'd worked there as a teenager forced to either do that or face a worse fate.

Not even two days after Jerry's accident, the drum beats began in this close-knit country corner sounding out a call for a replacement.

The days of his youth spent at the farm held him in good stead to be recommended coupled with the fact that there were not enough reasons in Frank's life right now to refuse. Lots of folks knew that too.

He wasn't just a young kid with nothing better to do anymore looking for a way to expend energy at Fair View Acres. He was a better-than-average young man who had some of the makings of a future farmer. Jerry and others had seen it years ago even if they hadn't said anything to him.

Reacquainted with the lettering on the bottle, Jerry ventured to admit to Frank he wasn't able to stop kicking himself for his stupidity. Almost 100 years old, the farm now teetered on the edge, maybe lost from his misjudgment of a young heifer's clout.

The younger man started to argue the old-timer out of blaming himself, urging him not to be so hard on himself, tossing out a few more formal, "Mr. Duggans" until Jerry couldn't stand to listen.

"Did I tell you? We are eyeball to eyeball now and that means either I call you Mr. Maddox or you stop calling me Mr. Duggan."

Sitting beside him offering encouragement and possible solutions wasn't the kid Jerry remembered. He didn't look much like his father, Walter, who had been Jerry's best friend. Of the members of their teenage gang, only Walt, an eyeglass wearing, intellectual, had any interest in helping Jerry finish the mandatory list of chores, even lending a hand at some of the most important times like when they absolutely had to be elsewhere.

From the first steps his friend's son took into the house, Jerry's appraisal of the grown up Frank was that his father would be proud of him. His second thought was heartbreak remembering Walt and his wife, both killed by a drunk driver. Frank and his brother were fairly young men who could have taken that tragedy and used it to excuse any number of foolish choices. Neither one of them had.

Instead both turned to the military for a continuation of a sense of family with Frank picking the Army while Chris had gone to the Coast Guard Academy. The adult bearing of Walter's oldest son showed he still possessed the athleticism that let him hurdle the rail fences, pull chin-ups on barn beams and never tire no matter how much muck he'd shoveled.

A deep composure replaced the spark of constant energy Frank emitted years ago. He looked like a man who had been tested and passed. Jerry's only wish was that his friend could have been alive to see it. Looks-wise, he took after a previous generation, Jerry surmised. He didn't have his father's thick dark hair and eyes. Instead he had a sandy-colored crop of cooperative hair and more boniness than his dad to his well-shaped face.

His mental ramblings were interrupted by the realization that Frank was asking him a question. What was it he could do to help exactly?

"Everything would be best but I'm not sure how you feel about that or even if you remember what end of the cow to put the equipment on," he spit out.

He'd faced much harder tasks with less training so Frank confidently told Jerry he could. Good memories of working at the farm were fresh in his mind. He'd bet he hadn't forgotten anything even after all this time away.

The big fly in the ointment was going to be finances so Jerry moved right into that area. Truth was he wanted to come clean up front that he wouldn't be able to pay much cash money but he hoped maybe there were other things, like either equipment or wood from the lot, and all the free milk he could drink that might buy some of Frank's time. Not sure what he needed, Jerry blurted out the gruesome financial offer.

The reality of Frank's finances—his wife, the nurse, brought home most of the bacon. They lived mortgage free in his family's house with their 4-year-old daughter. Expenses were low and Lindsey's salary was adequate to allow Frank some leeway to continue trying to find his way. He'd served in active duty overseas and was still with the Reserves so he had some income but mostly he hopped from one small construction job to another with no guarantees. A garage was close to finished and weather permitting would be done in the next couple weeks, he told Jerry, and he didn't have anything firmed up after that.

Nelson was doing good considering he probably had a sixth grade education, only spoke some English and had never worked with animals until he got there three years ago, Jerry related to Frank. An assortment of relative or friends, not sure which, had been coming over to help out but that couldn't go on.

Just look at old Hank there, Jerry pointed toward a blanket of black fur sprawled under the kitchen table. When he was first injured the dog had lived on some stored layers of fat before anyone realized he hadn't been fed in days. He'd dropped 5 pounds, before his master came home and got him back to a daily feeding. No wonder the head of the big Lab mix, on hearing the tale of his own brush with death, came close and almost attached himself to Jerry's right leg.

He dreaded to think what the young stock looked like at this point and would lay his life that some of the milking cows had come down with mastitis. A pained look came into his eyes. He had let his girls down. They depended on him to keep them healthy and safe. He could only hope there was no major damage done in the short time and that with the right person things could be put to right.

Visualizing the actions of Jerry's hands, gently squeezing each udder to make sure it was soft and empty, Frank remembered how careful he was to always check that the cows were completely milked out, preventing as much disease and discomfort to his girls as possible.

Even if he had had the time for it, Jerry would never have imagined the days of his life coming to this point, suddenly and completely out of the bovine world. He had the feeling that he was missing his herd, not as a farmer, more as a member of the herd, as if he was one of them. He even wondered if they had noticed his absence and would usually come down on the side of yes. They would have sensed it, just like the loss of another cow but their wiring was such that the herd kept going. Loss or no loss, moving on without him.

"This place is a good farm, good land, raised lots of good stock on those fields. I just..." Jerry's voice trailed off, emotions overcoming him at the thought that it all could be lost.

Frank couldn't' find any words to fill the gap and just gave Jerry time to regroup.

Grandpa Duggan came out here just after World War I, Jerry finally added. He got gassed, mustard gas poisoning, in France. Doctors thought the fresh air would help his lungs. He did get a lot more years. Lived to almost 60.

The bottle and its timely design was from the days when the farm route was in its heyday. Fair View Acres had chicken and eggs in its product line. If any good land came available next door, his family put themselves in hock to buy it hoping the larger farm would lead to prosperity. The herd had up to 60 cows and the dairy business was good.

16

Plenty of customers appreciated his dad's jokes that came along free with the fresh milk no charge, Jerry added.

Vivid memories flashed through his mind on seeing the milk bottle, like seeing your life flash before your eyes except he wasn't dying, just wasting away.

Frank spoke up when the older man paused and they established he was willing to help for a while after the garage job was finished, not much more than a week.

Nelson will be disappointed, Jerry realized, knowing he hoped for a day off sooner but if that's the only sticking point, he will have to get over it, he decided.

They started to discuss the daily routine, more intense recollections forming in Frank's mind about how the process worked and what to look for during each phase of the work. Jerry was more than a wealth of information. He described some cows down to the pattern on her hooves and the size of her udder. He reminded Frank about learning the cows, their particular idiosyncrasies and needs, their unwavering habits. That would be one of the most important things to learn so that he could milk the herd without Nelson's help and give him a break. His mouth still worked fine so ask me anything, he joked, adding that he hoped those functions weren't starting to atrophy like the muscles in his hand and arm.

The farm was lost in time in more ways than the kitchen décor. Jerry had made some small improvements but a lot of things were being done exactly the same way as Frank remembered.

"You'll notice the little Farmall tractor still has that dent you put into it when you plowed into the corner of the barn," Jerry laughed, "and that old thing hasn't gone as fast as you got it up to in the cornfield in many years so don't even think about it."

The more they talked the more Frank couldn't wait to start.

"This farming thing though," Jerry stopped the enthusiastic exchange and turned serious, "it takes a tough toll. Don't make any mistake about that. I'm glad you want to help me but I hope you remember, it's far from all fun and games."

Chapter 3

CLEAR
INDICATIONS

FRANK MAY HAVE ONCE BEEN just the restless son of a friend, a kid who had been forced to keep busy working at the farm in his dangerous early teen years, but not anymore. He was back now ready to be a lifesaver. He walked into the barn ready to take over what Jerry could no longer do.

Though his dad and Jerry had been close childhood friends, he'd never asked his father to elaborate about their history. Maybe his dad carried him over to the farm in his arms, just a newborn, showing him off to his buddy. All he knew was that the farm had always felt like a special place, familiar and as good as setting foot inside an amusement park. Excitement swept through him now just as strong as his first recollections of the place. He'd made a show of disinterest when he was a teen. Truth was he felt he was being rewarded even back then.

His mom, Maggie, first suggested that he help Jerry after one particularly trying episode with a group of friends that ended with the police calling the house. Seems the guys had decided it was OK to remove a little lumber, floor tiles and roofing shingles from a construction site and convert it into a cabin for their own use.

He was 14 and much too lively to be left to his own devices, assisted by like-minded friends. His mom asked, more told, his dad to take him over to Jerry's, see if he had anything he could use up some energy on. There, of course, had been plenty. One potent first memory of Jerry's place was of a mountain of manure, piled up to his head. It filled a corner of the barn and spread out in all directions, tapering off to only a foot high at the edges. It needed to be shovel out.

Even that onerous chore hadn't soured him on the farm. He went back the next weekend, his mom dropping him off on a Saturday morning at 5 a.m. and not returning to pick him up until 5 p.m. He found the day had not only gone by fast but he'd had a lot of fun.

He loved the young stock, the babies, yes, but also the older ones, four or five months old, when their personalities became more apparent. Some were just made for vamping a young guy. His favorite had been a beauty that he could still see, little Adeline. She had a feather duster of a white mark on her forehead like a cap of Spanish lace. Add to that, she was not afraid to come over and beg for attention and keep it all to herself. If Frank stopped scratching her head, she bumped his hand as if to say, I'm not done with you yet.

He became the one in charge of feeding all the calves, mixing the milk replacer, holding half gallon size plastic milk bottles and trying to keep the nipples on the bottles as the young ones pulled and bucked. He learned how to get them to suck from the bottle, not choke the milk down, relax at the closeness of a human and respond positively to his touch.

Now he was getting a chance to return to the farm, twice as old, an adult with more responsibilities. From the minute he'd been asked to do this, he found himself remembering stuff he hadn't realized he'd learned. Like don't yell. He still could see Jerry's red face the day he'd scared a big, young heifer who was calmly entering the milking parlor. Instead, his loud roar, something about a great move he'd made during the last baseball game, scared her into the area of the bulk tank. She'd bolted through the double doors and dropped down a step to become wedged between the tank and the outside wall.

It had taken all of Jerry's patience, Frank knew, to keep his voice under control. Cows have no reverse in their transmission, something Frank hadn't realized until then. Jerry took a bowl of grain and kept it just back from her jaw, with Frank pushing on her forehead, finally talking her into backing up enough so they could shove her the rest of the way out.

Thinking about his 14-year-old self, the years of his first job at Jerry's farm, having some spending money of his own, being given responsibility for the care of the animals, making sure they had food, water, clean spots to lay down, Frank realized it had given him much more than an outlet for his pent up testosterone. He'd absorbed information and walked out a calmer, self-confident version of himself.

That was the man who had faced combat in Afghanistan. Grace under pressure was an offshoot of keeping the milking of the herd underway even as one piece of equipment failed or an injury of one animal was discovered and treated, while not causing panic in the rest of the herd. Funny similarities, Frank thought, but the Army certainly resembled a herd of camouflage-coated beauties.

He couldn't say he was not affected by the stint in the Army but he knew there were guys who had served with him that hadn't had the benefit of this youthful classroom. He had never put two and two together before now.

He also remembered the machinery, the times he'd been able to drive the farm tractors and the feeling of being the master of the field, out here spreading manure in the sunshine, the whirr of the engine making him feel powerful and free. He'd yell out a few epithets to friends while the tractor motor roared. They never knew they'd been dissed, those guys who were getting on his nerves on the baseball team because he'd screwed up an easy grounder that could have led to a double play. "Fuck you, Justin. You're a piece of dog shit, did you know?" Somehow telling the entire natural world felt really empowering.

When his driver's license gave him the means to do other things, though, he did. He wasn't super human. The guys were hanging out with the girls, not the kind at Jerry's farm. He left with barely a look back or a thank you to Jerry for everything he'd entrusted him with, the means to a lot of unseen ends.

The next contact Frank had with the farm was Jerry's sister, Tricia, calling 15 years later asking him to help her brother. As soon as he heard the proposition, he'd hoped Lindsey could support the idea because he didn't want to see the farm lost and because deep down, he knew there was a debt to repay.

Hi wife's craiglist searches were legend. She spent a part of almost every day making sure nothing was being sold she really should have. There was a huge assortment of pending projects in their barn, most "great finds" on the website.

When she came across the milk bottle, she'd been startled at first. Not many milk bottles were ever posted on the site. Clicking on the picture to make sure she was seeing the lettering correctly, she read the words Fair View Acres, clear as day.

A little tremor of emotion passed through her, one she'd felt before and cataloged as one more of those coincidences she'd decided were no such thing. They were destiny speaking and she was usually on the lookout and listening for them. She called the seller who was in the southern end of the state and drove out to buy it the next day. Once she had it in her possession, she broke the news to Frank.

He had to go help Jerry, she told him at dinner. Explaining why, she showed him the bottle.

Pretty cool, Frank thought. That's Jerry's place, no doubt about it, he replied. Some of those were at the farm when he was there as a kid.

"When you get a concrete sign like this, you have to be really blind to miss it," Lindsey said.

Frank had heard this kind of pronouncement from Lindsey before, always when she was looking for the right way to go, the right thing to do. She'd taken her current job at the nursing home, leaving the hospital work, after getting a similar sign. Her mother's best friend, Liz, had fallen and needed long-term care after a hospital stay and been admitted to the very place Lindsey was considering. She knew she was being asked to go there, not only to help Liz, and acted on that sign with certainty, never regretting it.

"Thank you for making it crystal clear what I'm supposed to do," Frank laughed at his own pun.

Someone enjoys sending out this stuff as much as they enjoyed getting it, Lindsey said with a quiet confidence.

They had gone right over to call Jerry.

Chapter 4

AFGHANISTAN

THE FIRST TIME FRANK TOUCHED DOWN at Bagram Air Field it was 104 degrees and the heat was the thing he noticed. On the third deployment, he shivered as the airplane doors opened to a frigid 12 degrees. He hated sweating profusely or freezing his butt off but now realized he shouldn't have joined the Army if that was the case. He was moving to voices telling him to offload, line up and be accounted for. He could already see his home for the next year, the beige tent city stretching along the perimeter of the airbase. Quonset hut construction served a basic function but had a few disadvantages like the fact that the sand came through unstopped.

A roller coaster ride was how Frank would consistently remember his tour. There was the sudden decent to reach the airstrip on landing and the rapid rise to clear the vast mountains of the Hindu Kush on the way out. Then there were the evasive maneuvers to avoid being shot down while landing in the countryside and the ability or inability of the pilots to keep an aircraft under fire aloft while loaded with what was approaching a maximum weight. He had been a thrill-seeking amusement park enthusiast, thankfully, or he'd have ended up like some of the others onboard, reaching for anything that might hold their last lunch.

There had been a high likelihood he'd end up here when he enlisted. The war in Afghanistan and Iraq was underway. Operation Enduring Freedom was a topic of discussion in his circle of friends either because others had already participated or they were talking about what their reasons were for not.

He hadn't had to sign up. He had become a 21-year-old orphan when Walter and Maggie, his parents, were killed just a mile from their home. Their death resulted in unintended financial stability for Frank and his brother, Christopher, who was just about to graduate from high school. Not that the emotional toll was worth it but his father's consistent years working for one of the area's largest machine shops and his mother's added income, first doing child care in their home for neighbors, then expanding that into a popular daycare center, had created a comfortable life for the Maddox family. Their conservative spending meant the house was not remodeled to the latest look but the mortgage was almost paid off.

There was life insurance too. That was something Frank knew his parents would not have been without. He and Chris had the proceeds from that policy as well as the accident settlement to thank for being able to take some time to find their way.

Chris had been accepted at the Coast Guard Academy and went forward with that choice after the accident. It seemed to be working for him. He'd graduated now from the Academy and moved to duty stations all over ending up on the West Coast for his latest tour.

Frank hadn't been as astute about finding his niche. He'd been working mostly construction but at a level that didn't involve much of his brain or much of his attention. So he had enlisted in the Army which offered him some other things, if not an increase in the use of his grey matter, at least more direction. He'd have to say he actually liked the comradery and the feeling of having a family again. He was tested as to just what he did have in the way of talents and had scored high on marksmanship, earning the Expert level. He also was finding a natural ability to gain respect and be a leader, something that earned him an appointment to specialist in short time.

His unit was being charged to do military duties halfway around the globe but he'd heard the real challenges in this "war" were the peace missions where they were charged to make friends and alliances with the Afghanis.

The features of the people were something Frank noticed almost immediately. They seemed ancient and suited these people who had been living in this area for far longer than anything Americans could lay claim to even in the old New England area he was from. He often was reminded of pictures he still had in his mind of the Bible stories of his youth, men and women in robes, dark eyes, sharp features and an intense passionate nature. The children were so striking, the eyes holding too much deep tragedy for their age. He had a hard time looking at some of them without staring. He was always being lured into emptying his pockets for them. They converged on him at every opportunity.

27

Add to that the Hindu Kush mountains were like nothing he had ever seen in New England. The snow-capped peaks gave Frank at least the semblance of cooling off, even as the temperatures at the base edged toward the triple digits.

Frank planned to catch his supper at the base Burger King today if only because it was quick and he wasn't homesick for good cooking yet. He found some of the others in his hut already chowing down and joined them, the nearest thing he had experienced to a family dinner since his parents' death.

By the end of his three-year deployment, he left with a feeling of regret that he hadn't accomplished much. He felt the Americans' repetitive attempts toward peace had never made a difference in the daily realities in Afghanistan. The problems in this part of the world were a tangle of centuries of fighting, bad leadership, outside intervention, all of it leaving the land in a situation that brought everyone who got involved here throwing their hands up in frustration. Nothing had changed, not just politically but physically in hundreds, if not thousands of years, Frank thought. The architecture reinforced that impression with evidence of the past crumbled into heaps on top of new destructions on an almost daily basis.

Frank felt his service had gained him a measure of personal pride. He'd survived, mentally and emotionally some of war's terrors, especially the mission nine months before he left, when his unit had lost three men in a roadside bomb explosion. Those were some of the same guys he'd been sharing a Whopper with a couple of days earlier. The sights and sounds of that day, he knew were coming home with him.

What he found back home was that his added maturity and new leadership skills didn't serve him well in an economy that had nothing to offer to veterans or anyone else. Between the circle of friends he had and some lucky breaks, he found small projects, construction work and what could only be described as odd jobs. He'd only barely stayed financially solvent without tapping into the insurance and settlement funds that he and Chris had agreed they would leave intact for now.

During this less than bright spot in his life, he'd thought he was in love with the likes of Alexandra Cesario, an unabashed flirt, self-centered and controlling yet demanding freedom. She held his interest and he might have thought that was what love felt like except for the little voice in the back of his mind begging him to remember love the way his parents had practiced it. She'd wandered off to find someone more interesting and someone whose finances were better able to keep up with her needs.

He hadn't taken that break-up well, trying to contact her even as she made it clear she had no further use for him. He just wanted to talk, to get a bunch of stuff off his chest and hear her say, just one more time, that she had loved him even if she didn't anymore. It had obsessed him badly enough to keep him from focusing on much of anything else including making a living.

During one temporary job he'd looked at his phone to find a particularly nasty text from Alexandra telling him to drop dead and soon. He felt his airways closing and his head spinning soon followed by a violent case of hives. He blamed it on the pineapple pizza from last night and left the work site, not returning again even though the company had been interested in putting him on fulltime.

There were nights of too much drinking and not always with friends who got him home. It was an unfortunate winter night accident that put him in the emergency room but ultimately saved him both physically and emotionally. He woke up in the hospital bed to Lindsey's face. There was no lying to those eyes, round orbs of golden brown that seemed to link right to her heart. When she asked him how he was feeling in the first conscious moments since the accident, he told her honestly.

"I feel fine," though the area of his feeling that related to that condition was not his smashed left arm, nose, black eyes and throbbing head. They were probably not winning her over on that first day but as he healed, she let him know he was not just another patient.

For her part, Lindsey had already taken notice of some of Frank's better attributes. His hands were the first draw. While attending to his blood work, she'd almost felt a jolt as she picked up the long fingers, well-entrenched dirt in some crevasses, but wide and strong and yet soft and sensitive. Her vision strayed up to the face associated with this hand and she was looking at clean cut features with distinctive shapes that made him stand out from the crowd and all topped by a short growth of fine light brown hair, like a little boy's. When he smiled for the first time, she was totally done in by the dimples.

He stayed in the hospital three days, spending a great deal of time on the lookout for the shiny auburn head to appear in his door. She made up reasons to go to his room to check on something. On the day he was discharged, they had already decided when to meet for their first date.

Before realizing the true cost of his accident, the hospital bills coupled with the loss of work and income while he recovered, Frank had decided this first date would be one Lindsey would remember. He had consulted with Chris and used some of the insurance settlement for his hospital tab but he tapped just a little extra to take her into the capital city where he'd heard friends praising a new Italian restaurant. The place was definitely not his usual date venue and he worried about his choice for days leading up to the night.

Lindsey insisted she would drive them. The pins in his left arm and elbow didn't make driving his large pickup truck easy. He'd argued about the distance not just to the restaurant but out to the countryside to pick him up. She wouldn't be deterred and he relented and gave her directions to his house.

When she pulled up he'd rushed to the window to see her exit the car in a blue dress, cut low and draping softly over her curves. The color combination with her auburn hair was not only striking but surprising given that all he'd seen her in before were scrubs. Frank was glad he hadn't changed their destination. He was feeling pumped to be the man walking into a nice restaurant with this woman.

Lindsey eyed Frank's attire and couldn't help but smile at its simplicity. No doubt his best Brooks Brothers shirt was recently laundered and ironed but with a man's touch. His black dress pants didn't fit him as well as the jeans she'd seen him leave the hospital wearing but that couldn't be avoided, she chuckled. He took in her look and threw out a defense.

"I have a jacket but I think I'll only be able to put one sleeve through with this thing on my arm. Do you think I should bring it anyway?" he asked.

"Sure, just in case you need it. You'll look quite suave and debonair with it draped over your shoulder," she laughed.

The reservation was for 8 but if they ran into a lot of traffic it could take more than an hour to get there, he predicted, offering to drive her car which was a little easier to operate.

She took his arm and turned him out to the street.

"No, I would rather keep taking care of you just a while longer," the nurse in her said.

Frank knew he was probably turning a shade of red at her compliment but tried to keep his feelings under control and not come back with a corny line he'd regret.

As they drove, her questions were typical nurse's inquiries— how was he feeling, did he have any more headaches, was he doing physical therapy, how much use of his arm had he recovered? Those conversation openers flowed into more and they found themselves talking with few lapses until they reached the restaurant.

She looked even more striking in the establishment's strategically placed lighting, Frank realized once they were seated. Her lipstick shade was chosen to make a perfect bridge between her hair and dress, something she knew but Frank wouldn't recognize. Its subtle effect was successful.

The menu had a large selection of standard seafood and Italian dishes but the specials of the night attracted them both, for her a salmon topped with citrus marinade and for him a grilled veal chop. She ordered only the entrée, said she'd never have room for the full dinner if she indulged in appetizers, so Frank reined in his appetite and decided he'd go big on the dessert course.

Nothing, not the appearance of beautifully plated food, questions from the waiter or even the act of chewing interrupted their enjoyment of learning about each other's lives, likes and hopes. The dinner became secondary.

Frank hadn't meant to discuss his tour overseas. He tried never to make that a topic of conversation with a woman but as they were waiting for the shared dessert they'd decided on, Lindsey's gentle touch seemed to hit a spring-loaded portal and he blurted out a description of a day in Afghanistan, telling her about the results of the brutality the people had endured over the years from different occupations and bombings. The accumulation of enough revenge-filled hatred to last for centuries had left one particularly handsome small child with a missing arm and lower part of his leg. A wooden crutch tucked under the small piece of the remnants of a shoulder and a very crude prosthesis on his leg let the child at least try to keep up with the others but he couldn't help but fall behind.

The face of that child was burnt into Frank's psyche and it was a memory that could elicit the feeling of being back there, working towards something he never quite believed would succeed. The problems in the country were too tangled, deep opposites too far apart religiously, ethically and everyone living on the edge of despair with little experience with happiness. Frank thought the real problem in the country might just be the lack of enough good to outweigh the bad.

Lindsey just listened as he spoke from deep in his soul. He'd hardly let anyone hear these stories and was a little surprised it had come out of him. Hearing Frank talk about his days in the war zone she felt like he'd entrusted her with a special gift, the gift of himself. She savored every word and hoped whatever had been the catalyst to make him feel she could be trusted with this information, she'd be able to tap it again.

They were slow to leave the sanctuary of the restaurant, not having made any plans for what to do when the meal was ended but they didn't want to say good night. She drove slowly back to the house. They'd stayed talking in the car until dawn. Somewhere during the night they realized they both loved the same kinds of movies, ones where good triumphed and someone could be a hero. They exchanged their favorite lines from all their top picks and talked about new releases they both couldn't wait to see.

He felt a little envious of her description of a large Irish family that was always making excuses to get together for food and celebrations. He'd been able to get a taste of what that was like while visiting some of his friends and though he loved his family thought his buddies awfully lucky to be part of that kind of circle.

He breathed a sigh of relief when it was Lindsey who said she wanted to know what day and what time their next date would be, as though she knew what he wished he'd had the nerve to assume. The blunt question brought out his dimpled smile and if she had any reservations about what she'd said or committed herself to, she lost it at the sight of Frank's face.

From that night they were never out of touch with one another for more than a few hours at a time, texting each other during the day, calling at lunch and finding their way to each other's side every night.

Within three months, Lindsey had moved into Frank's house and they were talking about the plans for the wedding.

Six years from that point, Frank had come a long way emotionally, with both the stability of marriage and the responsibility of a child. Lindsey's nursing job gave him some freedom to try to find work that wasn't low-paying and mind-numbing. The state had been hit very hard during the recession and opportunities had been scattered and few but things had improved and more money was flowing for the kinds of small home improvements that were Frank's specialty.

They'd made it through some lean years and Frank's income had been on an upturn just as Jerry's farm situation emerged. The phone call from Tricia caught him by surprise. She had made a quick introduction of herself and gone right into the reason for her call. It was New Year's Day and less than a month since Jerry's injury. Though he had been able to get some relatives and friends to help him, Nelson, the hired man, wasn't able to run the farm. They needed a man who could really do the work, understand the scope of what the dairy business entailed and be available to start immediately because the farm was already starting to suffer and could be lost before Jerry had a chance to get back on his feet.

Tricia made it clear she had decided Frank was the right man for the job. He remembered her somewhat but only vaguely, too distracted at the farm by plenty of more interesting things. She described Jerry's slow progress with physical therapy and how she was sure the animals were struggling and would be hard-pressed to survive the winter without someone stepping in to take care of things over there.

He saw in his memory the animals, the farm fields, the huge barn, old house and the man, Jerry's face, a man he'd come to like and give a youthful respect to. It didn't take long for Frank to get the gist of this call. They wanted to know if he could come and help, jump backwards to a time when he had done that before.

He saw again the Hindu Kush as she was explaining the problem and maybe because of or in spite of all he'd experienced over there, he wanted to jump onboard.

Chapter 5

CANCER
SIGNS

CELESTE STEPPED ONTO THE HARD FLOOR, testing, waiting. With less than a minute of consciousness today, she was already pretty sure it would be a better than average day. Not much pain in her stomach or legs, not much sense of nausea and a level of energy that indicated she might summon a bit of satisfaction, do a day of something constructive. Her mind jumped into action as she walked to the kitchen and the coffee maker. She probably would even drop a toast made out of that new cheese bread. That was an unusual start to a day, a breakfast that wasn't just a cup of caffeine.

It was a Saturday and a long weekend at that. Celeste had a mind brimming with wants. She was getting her energy back, something she had always prided herself on. Since her cancer, treatment and her road back with a healthy diet and exercise, she was on a climb of slow, small steps but a struggle punctuated by bright spots. She prayed for those bright spots to be more frequent and was being rewarded.

At her kitchen island she dared envision starting on a jacket she already saw complete. The bright zig zag-patterned, stretch fabric turned into a loose jacket, about hip length, three quarter length sleeves would be a comfortable fit but have a designer look. She couldn't wait to bring it to life.

Fueled by the coffee and the toast, she went to her sewing room, her favorite spot in the house. Stepping in, she first just enjoyed being there. It had everything she needed, a few different sewing machines, a serger, an old treadle machine and one that did embroidery. An ironing board stood ready in the far corner, the cutting table positioned smack in the middle and the stacks of her cloth remnants, backings, trims all stowed in an old multi-drawer cabinet she'd found at a yard sale.

In the windows were the valences she had made, embroidered with scissors, spools of thread, and other assorted sewing notions. Some other finds she'd made and hung on the walls were the pictures from editions of The Delineator from the early 1900's. The framed posters, almost a dozen of them hung on one wall, were so inspirational, Edwardian styles through to the Roaring 20's. The room's pale green paint with bright, white trim made the posters even more striking. The space had a calm but high fashion air which she had sought and achieved for her sanctuary.

She'd made a lot of things from this work space and loved when a new project was ready to be launched. Standing and working over the table, she began with a wrist snap, splaying the zigzag stripes across the top of the table and making sure the edges were even. Taking the pattern pieces from their paper sleeve she quickly found and cut free the ones she wanted.

The challenge in this project was going to be to get it right here at the pinning, she thought. If I don't place these pattern pieces perfectly, this jacket will be a mess. She noted all the lines for the fabric grain, the pointed marks for the match-ups and dared to insert the first pin. Moving slowly and carefully, she made sure she laid out the pieces so that the fabric would line-up once sewn.

Soon she was producing one of her favorite sounds, the "wrenk, wrenk" bite of scissors through cloth. The cutting done, she picked up the first two pieces to sew and checked the alignment of the stripes making sure she didn't create a jacket of sea sickness waves that undulated unevenly. She pinned the shoulder seams together. After making a bobbin of the project thread and dancing the thread through the machine, she was finally ready to feed the fabric into her sewing machine.

Gathering it up at the other end, she turned it right side up out, draped the finished side over her shoulder, and turned to look at her reflection in the mirror. The horizontal zigzag was a chancy decision that could have added 20 pounds. Not so, the navy, magenta, burnt orange and maroons colors of the waves didn't add girth. They added pizzazz, just what she was looking for.

She worked for two hours on the project before she noticed the time and her first thought was that she hadn't been able to do anything for that long for some time now.

The colon cancer diagnosis last year shouldn't have been a surprise. Her mother died of it 10 years ago but she thought she had taken much better care of herself. Her mother had never heard of broccoli or kale, much less eaten any for most of her life. Celeste, had introduced her parents to it when she started feeding her family the new "healthy foods." She began treatments fast and furiously, first surgery, then chemotherapy and now a finger-crossed, egg-shelled walk through life praying the cancer didn't return.

She heard before she saw Lorraine, her best friend, and could tell from the pace of her steps that she was on one of her many missions. Sure enough, the face appeared and the expression was obvious. Lorraine had a new idea, God only knew what and from where, but once found, had to be fully vetted and explored.

"Raw milk," Lorraine intoned, without any introduction. "I just read about how your gut can cure anything, cancer included. It needs strong probiotics."

She launched into a summary of an article in the latest healthy diet magazine she had just read. Lots of people had what amounted to sludge in their intestines, she explained, and once that is turned into a healthy soup of good bacteria, you're on your way to better health. An anthropologist whose young daughter had multiple health issues studied an African tribe where he was doing a dig and found they had no diabetes, cancers and heart disease. Analyzing their diet, he attributed it to the tubers they chewed that didn't break down during digestion but were intact and acted like roughage to push sludge accumulated in the intestines right out, or so Lorraine summarized based on her non-scientific understanding of the gist of the article.

The impression that this woman could move mountains had been Celeste's first and accurate impression. They both worked at the alumni office of the state university and started around the same time so they were the newcomers, initially sticking together to get their bearings but discovering they enjoyed each other's company.

Celeste Lefebvre, a quiet, French Canadian old-fashioned sort, and Lorraine Bell, a spark plug of mixed heritage who was adopted by conservative parents but didn't share their restrained personalities, were two unlikely comrades. Both single women in their mid-fifties, they had bonded and watched each other's backs, emotionally and physically, calling and receiving help on any given day.

While sewing was Celeste's favorite pastime, Lorraine's revolved around food, cooking and eating. The small deck of her condo was a garden during the warm months and then her living room was filled with wintering plants.

The memory of watching her grandfather dig up a small 8-foot by 8-foot square of lawn and transform it into a tomato patch had mesmerized her and allowed her to realize the potential had been there all along, just waiting for a smart guy like grandpa to make it sprout a delicious food. She was hooked on gardening from then on.

Her adult life hadn't turned out to include acreage instead it found her living mostly in an urban area with limited turf. She'd always managed to eke out a little exercise of her green thumb anyway and was a wealth of knowledge on how to grow most anything in a container.

Milk was a new area for her, though Celeste couldn't help but wonder if she planned to grow a cow.

Instead Lorraine speculated the farm on Dark Lantern Road in Fairford would sell them raw milk. It looked like a nice, clean place and there's a young guy working it now, she had already determined. Someone at work knew the old man and told her all about how he got hurt and then found a young guy to help him. That's probably a good thing for that place, new blood, she offered, and they could encourage him to keep a farm alive in this area. God knows we have lost enough of them," Lorraine thought.

She formed new attack plans daily typically drawn-up after discovering something in her relentless reading. A probiotics enhancement theory that pegged cancer and many other diseases to the state of your gut was no less probable than some she'd suggested.

Almost as soon as her friend was diagnosed with colon cancer, Lorraine started on her personal research project not just on cancer but food contamination. She'd filled binders with all the articles on food in the news in just the past year. Her first reaction had been to rail against the forces of evil that would do such a thing to her friend but then she got down to business. Celeste had not been asked to participate in Lorraine's campaign. There was no disagreeing with her strident, forceful personality topped by a crop of corkscrew curls that accentuated her every action.

Celeste had a real good flow going on her sewing project but hardly dared to say so knowing the energy level in her fiery friend didn't like baths of cold water. Lorraine was probably already planning that they were leaving shortly for the farm. It was a testament to the results of the attached pieces of fabric she had chosen for this particular project that stopped Lorraine from insisting she drop it.

"That's going to be fantastic," Lorraine commented finally noticing the project. "I could never do something like that," she added.

"That's why I'm making it for you," Celeste replied.

There was hardly a time in her life when she wasn't sewing, going back to her first dolls and the crude clothes she made for them by hand. One Barbie doll gown she made still survived in a trunk somewhere and she loved to look at it now and then just to marvel at the little girl who had always loved anything to do with handwork, sewing, knitting, embroidery. She loved it all and tried to do it as often as her life would let her.

Once Celeste felt good enough to get out to do some shopping, she'd headed to her favorite fabric store. Lorraine often complimented her on things she wore that were her own creations. She intended to try to repay her friend's work with some of her own. She could see how fabulous Lorraine would look wearing it.

What about tomorrow morning, Lorraine relented, if they tried to time it late enough so the farmer wasn't too busy, around 9 or 10 might be a good time to find someone over there.

"What are you planning? You think we should ask the farmer to buy milk right there? Is that legal?" Celeste wondered taking a mental detour to keep pace with her friend.

"Legal is whatever it takes to be healthy," Lorraine answered without any hesitation. She read yesterday about another recall, chicken, 2 million pounds. Not a company supplying chicken around here, thankfully, but just one more illegal, cut corners, make a bigger buck food vendor, she almost shouted. "It's time we take our food into our own hands, literally," she summarized in her not-to-be-argued-with voice.

She felt too good today to argue much anyway, Celeste smiled. Her best friend was an unlikely personality to be deterred by her quiet, thorough, calculating sort. This ball of energy had burst into her life unexpectantly. Their roles at the alumni office fund-raising arm used their contrasting talents perfectly, Celeste on the accounting side and Lorraine the rabble rouser bringing in the donations.

Celeste's two children were on the West Coast, her son enjoying the vibe in the Pacific Northwest and her daughter a mom of two young children with a husband whose family had a restaurant in Portland. She hoped to get out to see her grandchildren, something she dearly missed but first she needed to be strong and healthy.

How much damage could a glass of raw milk do? It might even work, if Lorraine's conviction on the magical effects of it were strong enough, she decided. They arranged to meet at Lorraine's house at 9 for the ride out tomorrow.

***

Up close the barn needed more work than the faraway vista promised. There was virtually no paint on the door, just a faint bit of white-wash on the walls, but Lorraine's impression of cleanliness and order was confirmed.

This old farm was not the resting place of multiple car remnants, old equipment rusted out in huge holey patches, mounds of tires and all of it with a vegetative covering. Those kinds of old farms dotted the area but real going operations were few and far between and Fair View Farm was the best bet.

News of someone bringing it back to life while the old farmer recuperated was also a factor. He must be somewhat up on the latest information on health, Lorraine hoped. She planned to convince him to sell her fresh raw milk. A tanker truck from a big co-op stopped there, she knew, but she was going after the stuff before it went to the processing plant.

Her research on what happened to that milk in processing was driving this quest. The raw milk got cooked quickly at an extremely high temperature, ultra-pasteurization. That made it thick and also killed all the helpful bacteria she was hunting for to fill Celeste's fragile gut with good microbes. There was also the homogenization process that she'd decided she wasn't keen on either. If you could shake up a bottle of orange juice, what was the big deal about making people shake up their milk. Instead the whole milk was separated, pulling out the cream.

Homogenization pushed the big fat molecules through a strainer so they were small enough to be absorbed. Her info indicated the fat would be best left large enough to flush right through a human's intestines. Then there was problem of time, how long it took to do all the processing and send it back to where it came from or to the parts of the country, like New England, that didn't make enough milk locally for the size of the market.

Maybe it wasn't as simple as that to summarize the milk industry, Lorraine dared to consider, but the fact of the matter was, she was bent on getting the unadulterated version of this stuff. Tampered milk was not good enough. She needs the real deal and I'm about to get it for her, Lorraine smiled at the thought.

They pulled up and to the right in front of the large barn. The pitted driveway made for slow going and Lorraine wasn't sure where it was safe to park, away from any incoming animals, tractors, trucks, and whatevers. It looked like a small door into an adjoining building afforded entry to a room where they might find the young farmer.

Jerry's old dog, Hank, called out the visitors. Frank had seen the two women in the SUV and saved them the problem of finding him. He stepped out of the milk room asking if he could help them.

Yes, Lorraine stepped forward, they lived in Wakeville and had come out to see if they could buy some milk.

Attempting to make a quick explanation of the farm's contract with the dairy co-op to sell them all its milk, Frank offered little hope.

"How would they know if you took just a little out?" Lorraine asked, determined not to go home empty handed.

Measurements are taken with every pick-up Frank said. The co-op knew full well how much milk every farm usually had and if there was a lot less, they would want to know why.

Not deterred, Lorraine dug deeper hoping to find a way around that initial problem, just like she always did when confronted with the impossible. Couldn't he give them a reason why that they would accept so that her friend here, who by the way really needs raw milk to live, could have just a little, like a half gallon even, she pleaded.

Curious as to the reason someone needed raw milk, Frank asked, what difference did it make.

There was an opening Lorraine could jump into with both feet, soon making Frank's head spin with her research mainly focusing on the theory that people who have had colon cancer need very good probiotics to keep their gut healthy. A healthy gut can prevent the cancer from returning and it can do that without drugs like chemo, she finished her summation.

Thinking to win the day with good old fear, Frank suggested they should be afraid to drink raw milk.

Levelling him with her eye, Lorraine asked him if he drank it turning that effort into a defeat for Frank. He did and had since he was a kid.

But his wife, the nurse, doesn't, he tried again, and she hadn't yet let their daughter drink any yet either.

A bull is not deterred from charging easily and Frank saw that same resolve in Lorraine when she shot back a "Why not?"

The raw milk didn't come with a guarantee it wouldn't kill her was as close to the truth as Frank could summon.

"Will it?"

"I'm not dead yet."

"Maybe that's because you're a big strong man."

"It's because all the cows have been vaccinated against things like brucellosis and tuberculosis and other things that would kill you from raw milk."

The standoff turned into more of a discussion of the evolution into today's pasteurization standards and how it insured no one would die.

"Ever look at the news lately and see how good that's working? In the grocery store just last week they had a sign up where the lettuce should be saying, sorry, some of this green stuff just made a bunch of people really sick so we recalled all of it. That's just this week. There's a new food item on the list every week. The weakest people die from eating that stuff," Lorraine laid out the scenario.

Reading food recall news articles was so far removed from Frank's literary preferences that he admitted he had no idea that was happening.

Bringing Lorraine full circle to her original question, she repeated, could he just let them buy some good fresh milk.

Maybe, Frank relented, but he'd have to make sure he could give the co-op a good reason for the shortage. Just a half gallon, that's probably doable, he decided. An appreciative Lorraine almost reached out and hugged him but drew back at the last second.

Celeste had watched and listened as her fearless, passionate friend convinced Frank to sell them raw milk. Now she piped up.

"I know Lorraine is a bit bullish," she laughed, "but I really appreciate you letting me try some raw milk. I've read some of this research she loves to quote and I think the less artificial stuff I put into my stomach, the better."

Taking a minute to consider these two and their quest, Frank said he hoped it would help. He added a warning to drink just a little at first. Milk being almost all water means the human body will react to the new bacteria like drinking any foreign water. The farm had a good, deep well but well water even if it hasn't been made into milk, can make you a little loose, he explained. It shouldn't take long though to get used to it though.

The women presented Frank with a screwcap gallon glass bottle whose last contents had been of an alcoholic nature so it was nicely disinfected. They watched him unscrew the bottom of the bulk tank and let milk flow out from a gooseneck tube into their jug.

The color of the milk was a creamy, pale yellow, not the bright white they saw on the grocery shelf. Shake it or you'll get all the cream when you first pour, Frank advised, it's not homogenized so it separates.

Promising to follow all his warnings, Lorraine added her own, that they would likely be back for more.

"Can we get more if this doesn't kill me?" Celeste asked.

"Sure, when would you be coming back?" Frank asked.

"How long will it keep?"

"We drink it pretty fast so I'm not sure. Maybe a week and a half or two," he estimated.

"We'll be back in a couple weeks, then. Saturday again. OK?"

"Sure, thanks for the warning so I can come up with a problem cow to cover you swiping this," Frank said.

After the women drove away, Frank went to tell Jerry what had just happened.

Used to be a whole bunch of folks around here came to get raw milk, Jerry said. "I never let the co-op have all my milk. People knew it was much better than buying that stuff they call milk in the store. Most of those people are dead now though," Jerry admitted. "But they didn't die of drinking milk. They died of old age in their beds."

This younger generation, he shook his head, hardly ever get anyone coming to buy raw milk anymore, he said. Nice to see the trend coming back into style, he thought, though those were no young kids. They were old enough to know what not to believe just because they got spoon fed a line from some big company or government bunch.

Frank listened and smiled. He'd been drinking raw milk for years due to his dad's friendship with Jerry. He'd brought home gallons of the stuff for him and his brother when he started working there, filling his family's bottles sometimes from his favorite cow, Adeline. The brothers diluted an entire box of Oreo cookies in a tall, cold glass on a routine basis. Boy that was good! His mother had a hard time keeping up with her two boys and their ability to down a serious amount of milk. It hadn't hurt their bones, spurring them both to their more than six-foot height. Frank had forgotten until he got back into the dairy farm business how much he liked it.

He had never thought much about where the rest of the milk went in those days but now he realized, as Jerry was confirming, no one bought raw milk much. The product in the commercial cartons in most stores wasn't anything like what he drank from the farm bulk tank.

The current tanker truck pulled up every other day. The driver tested the tank for any sign of contamination from medications, especially antibiotics, then attached hoses that drained the tank and added it to the tank's contents. The co-op was one of the largest in the country and Frank realized he hadn't bothered to find out much about it since taking on the farm work. Jerry still handled his finances and they hadn't touched on the topic of where the milk went or how much he was paid for it other than the underlying realization they both had that it had not been enough for a very long time.

"How long have you been selling your milk to this co-op?" Frank asked. "Has it been the same one for a long time?"

"Heck no, they keep consolidating all the diary businesses so they have us squeezed with no place to go. I used to sell to Cortland Dairy a long time ago. They were a small local bunch, processed the milk right over near Worcester. Not many of those small guys left and they have all the farms they need. Can't get in with them today. We're stuck with this big national group that has a whole division somewhere trying to find new ways to take money out of my milk check."

Frank didn't bite on the opening to discuss the farm's finances. He wasn't ready to know yet how financially untenable this operation was. He was just enjoying the farm, the animals the independence. Confirmation that he wasn't destined to do this for long was the last thing he wanted to think about on this beautiful morning.

He changed the subject to his list for today and Jerry gave him, as always, the benefit of his years. Instead of doing things the way Frank proposed, Jerry could always be counted on to tell him a better and easier way to do it. He came away from these conversations with an amazement of how deep Jerry's knowledge about his farm went and curiosity. How did something like that happen over time? Did it happen to anyone who devoted themselves like Jerry had to this little piece of farmland? In the bank of information Frank had accumulated in his life experience, Jerry was an exception, not the rule.

Running over to get a truckload of corn was next on Frank's list and he asked if Jerry needed anything while he was out.

"Nothing you can buy," Jerry sighed.

Chapter 6

TAURUS
MORNING

DESPITE TRYING TO IGNORE IT, Frank knew he'd been creeping towards admitting he needed some satisfying work. He was glad he'd agreed to do dairy farming even just as a temporary occupation. Standing in the barn ready to start milking, he was firing on all cylinders. Most of this was not much more than what he'd done as a teenager only now he was in charge instead of just helping. He was ready to take over unlike the young kid who had been glad to let the responsibilities fall on the older man's back. His deployment to Iraq and Afghanistan had not left him well suited to return to his old life. He'd been home for seven years, trying different things, working at jobs that he couldn't make believe he liked. This one fit for many reasons.

He assembled four stainless steel milking machines, cleaned them in a chorine solution, rinsed them thoroughly with the vacuum pump, prepped to be filled with white contents. The bowls of grain were put in place for the first cows. He tested all the water bowls to make sure the girls could quench their thirst while they gave up their milk. Many of them drank so much, Frank imagined they were trying to replenish their body fluids as quickly as they were going out. Some made a great splashing and gurgling as they drank.

Jerry's was an antique set-up. Most of the bigger farms had milking parlors with automated machinery. Fair View Acres still milked cows almost the same as 20 years ago with just a few improvements.

The milking area was consolidated into a small sectioned-off parlor in the mid-80's. The original barn was the type that was a fixture in its day, a gambrel roofed, 50-stall stanchion barn. The cows milled into the barn, counting off stanchions until they arrived at the one they knew to be theirs. They were milked right where they stood. For most of their life at this farm, the cows had stayed locked into the neck holds for the duration of the winter, a practice that had many drawbacks including the cows falling through rotted floors and being strangled.

Some milking parlor improvements were done with the help of the local agricultural extension office. The extension service had tried to talk Jerry into more "improvements" but he'd balked. He had been too heavily influenced at his father's knee and found he couldn't change his entire mind set. The parlor should be used to most efficiently get milk out of these animals, nothing else, according to the extension philosophy.

Not under the tutelage of Jerry's father. Milking at Fair View had always included serving a meal and a drink to the girls. The cows drank copious amounts of water while they were being milked and they also ate during milking which his dad told him was something important to notice because it was the first sign of possible trouble in the animal. If a cow stood and stared at a full feed bucket, she was having a problem, Charles Duggan told his son a thousand times. Rushing to get the milking process done and get out of the barn cost you in the long run. Take the time to look over the herd during milking. Make sure they're all fine and then send them out. That was Jerry's training and it had served him well, too well to make a drastic change.

His final concessions resulted in the girls filing into a new sectioned off four-cow milking parlor. They were still held in by stanchions, had a drinking bowl right beside them and were fed contentedly while being milked. Jerry's funding assistance hadn't been enough to install a rear gate which would have taken care of the other end of the milking process, the manure end. New parlors lowered a gate after a group had stepped in and not only could they not wander away, there was a gutter that prevented the cow lifting her tail and dropping her load on you.

That was one improvement Frank wished Jerry had made. There were some other things, though that he was glad hadn't changed. In this setup, Frank knew every cow that he was milking. He knelt beside the girl and even if he hadn't seen her face as she entered, recognized distinctions in her teats, the shape of her udder, sometimes recognized her by the shape or spots on her hooves or her stance.

He'd seen a few other parlors, checked them out online after he'd started at Jerry's, and the cows moved more quickly in and out. The drawback, to Frank's thinking, especially with a small herd like this, you didn't really get as close to the animals and interact with them.

Sure there were some cows, he hated to be near, like Susan, the old, cranky girl who still produced more milk than most of the others but kicked out fiercely before she settled down to giving it up. She had her reasons for being a bitch with a huge udder that Jerry told Frank to make sure to milk out completely to keep her from getting mastitis.

She was built all wrong, teats sticking out in every direction. The milking machine had to stretch to take hold of all four teats that protruded outward instead of downward. Her daughter, Sally, had inherited exactly the same udder and Frank could only hope she didn't develop the same bad attitude and that this would be the last of that line.

Another challenge was Greta, a big boned honey with an insatiable appetite. She was heading in, Frank noticed, and he knew to keep her away from the far end of the milking parlor. That was where a wheelbarrow held some extra grain. Greta and he had more than once tangled over just how much grain she should eat. Her way of thinking was as much as she could cram into her mouth and as deep as she could reach into the grain before she needed to come up for air.

The delicate size of Zelda was a sharp contrast to Greta and he let her into the stanchion closest to the grain. Sliding over the metal hinge to close the stanchion, Frank's thoughts turned to the positives as they filed in, all of them knowing the routine, stepping up to put their heads through the stanchions, digging into the feed bowls and letting themselves be held until the milking was done.

Dipping a wash cloth into a disinfectant solution, he began wiping down Zelda. Even if he hadn't seen her face, he recognized this girl. Every cow had a personality, Jerry had taught him, and the smart farmer knew his animals so he wouldn't get hurt and they would get the handling they needed. That was something he'd dredged up and back to the surface of his mind when he returned to the barn, the cows and all their similarities but more importantly their differences that let you know just what kind of animal you were about to deal with.

Zelda had two of the smallest teats he had ever seen, a result of frost-bite after she gave birth to her first calf. That calf hadn't lived and she almost hadn't either. The birth came during a bitter cold night and the wet tiny appendages had frozen almost solid. The vet saved her rear teats by cutting away dead tissue but left just barely enough teat end to keep the inflations attached. Frank knew to stay close to make sure they didn't fall off during the milking process.

Christy was next, one of a long line of knock-kneed girls, their back legs turning in at the knees making the machinery hard to attach. The claw mechanism was like a four-legged spider with tubes at the ends that attached to the four teats of the cow's udder. Once the vacuum pump started, the suction through the inflations grabbed hold of the teats and produced the impression of a feeding calf. At least it would seem to be doing that given that their moms let down the milk meant to feed them. Instead of a waiting belly, it was pushed into a stainless steel milk can.

Frank found himself more and more in tune with these animals as he stayed on, now more than a few months into this new venture.

Nelson appeared at the door, his black mat of a hairdo, bright dark eyes making contact with Frank's and his usual slight grin and head nod a signal to put the milking process in full throttle. The Guatemalan spoke a good bit of English and Frank remembered some Spanish from high school so they communicated pretty well. Gestures and shared mixed language phrases helped make do.

The milking got going into its familiar rhythm, a bovine entrance, identification of the next cow and her quirks, wash up, machinery on and then a perusal of the animal for anything out of the ordinary, loss of appetite, cough, cuts, even just a sense of the girl not "looking right." If nothing went wrong, no equipment failed, no cow thought up an unusual new trick, they could finish milking the 40-odd cows in just over 2 hours. Frank had a lot of plans for his day once the milking was finished. He had started his stint here just as the cold was bearing down for what turned out to be harsh New England winter. He had been limited to doing the milking through days when little could be done outside on the farm other than keep things operational, not frozen. March was just around the corner and with it spring air pulling Frank outside almost every day. Fences in the pasture needed work. They were falling over in places.

The rotational grazing plan, Jerry's latest idea, would not work without keeping the herd on a controlled movement across six sections of pasture, letting them eat it down to stubble and then giving them a lush new section. Meanwhile, the stubble could regrow, ready for a new rotation.

This land had the deep topsoil to support the plan. Not many acres in these rocky southeastern New England states had the deep glacial till that made for good farming. Most of the land was a deposit of what seemed to be a glacial garbage dump, rocks, sandy soil or hardened clay too thick for plants to breath.

Almost 200 years ago, someone very observant had recognized this as prime farm land. How the Revolutionary era farmers had done it Frank had no idea but he knew they were right as many generations of farmers before him had also confirmed. Native Indians were probably more important in that process than anyone had given them credit for, Jerry explained. They'd farmed, burning open fields to keep them clear. Once the learned Europeans showed up, all they had to do was take it over.

Frank didn't dwell much on the how but he was jumping right into the now and all the things he'd planned to try to get to. First things first, he headed to the calf barn. Walking in the door he was greeted by a hardy hello. Bawling calves knew his step and were not bashful to let him know they were hungry. Assessing the toll the night captivity had taken, Frank saw in a glance a manageable pile of manure to clear and no broken pen bars, the feeding troughs in relatively good shape given the energetic activity that happened twice a day around its perimeter and all animals standing and shoving, generally a sign of every one of the girls feeling well.

Filling the trough with grain, the little crowd of youngsters moved quickly into that area and Frank took up the shovel to clear the floor of muck. Some of the young stock took the time to gaze his way with a look that Frank could not help but take as a bovine snapshot fixing him as the "good guy."

Finishing his cleanup of the main part of the free pen, he took better stock of the heifers, new mothers in waiting, bred and due to give birth to their first calf. One, Merry, a stocky bulk of a heifer, wasn't participating in the feeding frenzy.

Taking up his observation post at the cow's backside, he saw the signs of labor, bulging of the opening tissue, thick, viscous liquid around the area and with this girl, a wild look in her eye, apprehension obvious over her unexplained condition. It had been two days since he first saw the signs of her calf's arrival.

Frank glanced over at the special birthing suite in the corner and saw it was mostly clean and ready. He took hold of Merry's collar and coaxed her toward the corner suite, talking to her encouragingly and assuring her the move wouldn't hurt.

The expectant new mom reacted to Frank's tone and moved with him to the pen, entering completely when Frank placed a nice, sweet smelling chuck of hay into the corner rack. She would need a visit later in the day to check on her progress and try to make an educated guess on what time of day or night her baby would make its appearance. The rest of the pack didn't register any special needs to Frank's eye so he opened the back doors and shooed the crew out to some green grass.

***

The striped, red welts on Merry's face were the first things Frank saw as he entered the calf barn in mid-afternoon, the first chance he'd had to get free. Angry and raw, they could have only been produced by her repeatedly banging her head into the metal bars of her stall. They travelled from the top of her face to her muzzle, bright bloody wounds. He could only stare, flabbergasted that the animal would injure herself so badly.

He walked calmly toward the stall using every warm tone in his voice to sooth her. He didn't really care what he was saying, just hoped he was making feel-good noises for her. Putting his hands through the bars, he gently laid them on her back and moved in a soft swipe toward her rump. She reacted with apprehension but he went back touching her again, a little more firmly, still giving his best imitation of a friendly beast.

Merry eyed him with a look that gave him an accurate sign of her mental state. The look registered with Frank. This is a woman in labor. Lindsey had the same look during the birth of their daughter, not sure she was up to the job, wishing it all away, getting wracked by a wave of pain and not knowing how to get relief until the contraction had ended.

58

His Lamaze coach training came back on instant recall and he uttered the important words.

"Breath, Merry, just breath, deep into your diagram," he said. "Do you have a diaphragm?" he added.

He instilled that important note of confidence he had used for Lindsey, telling her this was a path to something wonderful at the end.

Frank moved around to the metal gate, turned the round knob that moved the latch back. He stepped into the 8 x 8 stall and put his hands back on Merry's flank. She didn't move away which was a very positive sign she was willing to listen, allowing for the possibility that he could help her. He examined her progress toward the birth of her first calf. Panic was written in her expression as clearly as if she was doing her first screen test. This could be an imminent event, he guessed.

Doing a quick calculation, Frank also realized one reason she was so distraught had to do with the slow progress of this birth. Merry was just about at the end of her rope with pain and fear of an unknown. This was taking much longer than usual and though Frank wasn't an expert at this cow birthing yet, he already knew that anything out of the ordinary usually wasn't good.

After about five minutes of Frank's coaching, Merry dropped down into the sawdust and Frank followed her there, sitting himself in a corner up against the outer metal bars of the stall, within reach of her large head and face. He started to caress her neck keeping up a low-toned monologue. Frank told Merry about his daughter's birth, how his wife had seemed to doubt her ability to do this amazing thing but how it had all turned out just wonderful, a beautiful daughter, his wife a beaming, glowing proud mama and all really just a matter of breathing and relaxing, as best he could summarize.

Merry's reaction to his story was blunt and easy to read. She turned her head, levelled him with a soulful direct gaze and rolled her head deeper into his lap with an exhale and a sound of thanks. The actions surprised Frank who thought he had developed a pretty good understanding of these cows but this bovine's obvious message threw that theory out. She was clearly telling him thanks, showing her appreciation for the attention and giving him feedback that showed more intelligence than he had realized.

His favorite calf, Adeline, had "spoken" to him like Merry was doing but he had thought her the exception, not the rule. Adeline had been able to somehow let him know the water in the pail was old and warm and the hay had become moldy and she was not going to eat it. He just knew by some mannerism what his little favorite needed. He hadn't expanded that expectation of communication to include communicating with the whole herd but here he was faced with a new girl giving him the same kind of messaging.

He lost track of the amount of time he sat there with Merry but was roused from a seeming daydream he had gotten into when Merry rose to her feet. The time was here, her stance screamed and Frank moved quickly to her rump looking to see more evidence. He wasn't disappointed. Before too long, Merry strained with a contraction. About three of those later, he caught the first look at a pair of hooves heading in his direction.

Finding a length of baling twine hanging off the metal bars, he prepared to tie the twine around the hooves when they made their next appearance in the birth canal. Merry didn't disappoint and gave another strong push and he slipped the twine around the hooves and held the string taunt as they retracted back into the cow's body.

A few more contractions mixed with Frank's pulling on the twine at the right moments as they came forward, and a big, bull calf made his appearance in the sawdust at Merry's feet.

The surprise of his arrival in a whole new world was clear on the little toro's face. Merry turned her head to look but didn't get the gist of what to do next. After giving mom and baby both time to adjust to the new situation, Frank moved the little guy close to his mom's mouth and Merry's instincts, till now somewhat lacking, kicked in. She started to lick her newborn. He responded with attempts to stand on skinny legs.

He had witnessed about 10 births so far at the farm. This one was the first when he had played such a key role and he couldn't help but feel a little proud of his obstetrics work. The creation of a new life was still a time of heart-filling emotion for him, coming in direct contrast to the killing he had witnessed in the war.

It didn't take long for the patting-himself-on-the-back session to end. The sound of Nelson's voice with an urgency ended his moment of luxury and contemplation. What broke now, he wondered.

He went back just before leaving for the night to check on the newborn and his mother. She would need a bottle of calcium, Frank realized, and went to get the assortment of items required to administer it. He hoped this young heifer, who already had shown herself to be a little nervous and tense, would cooperate as he tried to stick her with a needle and get a bottle of life-saving fluid into her.

He decided to get Nelson to help, just in case Merry had a few more things to show him today besides her obvious appreciation for attention. He wasn't close to being comfortable with the administration of calcium bottles to the cows yet. He worried about putting the needle in the wrong place, at the wrong angle and doing more harm than good.

He was glad for any chance to talk with Jerry or the vet about the whole process and would have liked to see either of them in the barn tonight. Not likely, he realized, so he bucked up and went at it.

Merry was standing, the first sign that she was not in bad shape. Her body's calcium levels had not dropped to the point of bringing on a condition called milk fever. This was exactly what this dose of medicine was designed to prevent. She eyed him but not overly suspiciously. Frank was doing his best imitation of calm and hoping Merry's distraction with her baby would help keep the astute animal from sensing his fear.

He jabbed the needle into her shoulder with Nelson suspending the calcium bottle over her head. Releasing the clamp, he saw the blessed sight of bubbles and knew the drip had started. Waiting out the emptying of the first bottle, he administered a second based on Merry's size.

Finished, he dragged himself through the clean-up, putting all the equipment back where he could find it next time. He straightened up as he finished sweeping the floor. Breathing in a deep slow breath, he realized it had been a day when he hadn't followed his own advice and drawn anywhere near his usual number of breaths.

Chapter 7

AT
THE EDGE

THE FIRST TOUCH OF THE WARM WATER on his tired body was welcome relief to Frank. He stood in the shower getting wet and relaxed. It had been a busy day with tons accomplished but always at a price. His legs were done, he realized. He'd hauled two pickup beds of shavings into the storage shed, repaired about half a mile of posts and electric fence, done a major cleanout in the loose pen area of the barn, scraping the floor clean and spread new shavings throughout. That was between the milkings that had blessedly been pretty uneventful.

Warmer days of late May had led him to don short sleeve shirts but he was realizing why he didn't often see Jerry wearing them. The places where splattering manure had reached were pretty high, up around his armpit, and he laughed at the thought of Lindsey stepping into the shower after him if she should find out about that. He made a mental note to leave lots of hot water running after he was clean and doing a systematic swiping of the walls to make sure it was thoroughly rinsed.

Soaping up he thought about his next move tonight which was to return to a world he had all but abandoned. It was his belated 30th birthday party. He had refused the entreaties from his old gang to get a stretch Hummer for the night and do Boston for this big milestone.

He was meeting Lindsey at The Edge, their favorite hangout before dairy farming dominated his days. They hadn't been there in months and Lindsey had promised she'd get him down there. All his friends had insisted he celebrate 30 whether he was a dairy farmer or not.

He toweled off and headed to the bedroom where he hoped to remember where some decent clothes were, ones that weren't worn, plaid and full of stains. He found a pair of jeans and realized they were loose on him so he hadn't been packing on the pounds in his new career. His favorite dress shirt, the Brooks Brothers light blue twill, was a little wrinkled but nothing anyone would notice under dim lights.

The clean clothes and smells of something other than a barnyard were a good transition for him. He was making a determined effort to shift himself out of the realm of cows and milk and back to a guy who used to like to go out, especially with his wife. She loved to be with friends, came alive at a party like he didn't always see at home. He hadn't obliged her need since he started the farm work until one night when she'd finally just blurted out a comment something to the effect that she really needed to go do something other than listen to his report about udders.

Despite his preparations and intentions, as he opened the door at The Edge, he felt a little uneasy, like a stranger in a strange place. He was glad to see Lindsey was already there. Brian, his childhood best friend, and Melanie, his current girlfriend, were at the table with her and Frank saw a couple of other friends lined up at the bar.

Brian gave him the usual "Franko" shout as soon as he saw him and Frank smiled and relaxed, back to a form of himself that apparently wasn't gone.

He gave Lindsey a kiss and a squeeze and sat on the stool next to her. Brian yelled over to Greg and Matt at the bar, "Birthday boy is here. Get Franko the usual."

Cold glass steins were soon taking up most of the space at the small table and it was off.

"How's that cow thing going?" Brian jumped right in. Frank had fully expected it from his friend, the one who never shied away from being nosy and speaking his mind. They'd had some discussions before Frank started the dairy work and Brian had all but told him he thought it was a waste of time and a stupid idea.

"I like it," Frank said. Watching Brian make a face, he knew, here it comes.

"What part do you like, smelling like manure, getting up in the middle of the night, working till sundown or the fact that you're more broke now than you've ever been and getting broker?"

"All of it, I think," Frank countered. "Is that what you dragged me out here to tell me, like I need you to state the obvious? There is a lot to it and it's interesting."

"EB is interesting, building submarines. I could get you in there tomorrow and you'd be making great money in no time," Brian said.

"Making money isn't everything," Matt chimed in. Frank turned him an appreciative smile. Always could count on Matt to go head to head with Brian. "I'm in that office building I work at all day and I'd give up some money to get out in the fresh air a lot more. How is it working in the great outdoors all day?"

"Definitely that's part of what I like most," Frank said. "I don't mind the animals and you can't smell the manure because your nose goes numb about five minutes after you get there."

"Is the old guy coming back, or is he all done?" asked Greg.

"It doesn't look good. I think the doctors told him he'd never be able to handle all the lifting with the kind of break he had in his neck and collarbone. There is a ton of work just hauling stuff at that place."

"You're never at the gym anymore, guy," said Brian. "Don't need it by the looks of you."

"You want a work out, come over to help me on a day I clean out the calf barn. There's a metal bucket about five feet long, two feet deep. It rides on a metal ceiling rail the length of the barn. You lower it with a chain, fill it with shit and pull it back up. Push it out of the building where the manure spreader is waiting under the rail and dump it. Do a few reps of that and you're all set for the day," Frank said.

"We got a load of Canadian hay coming, next week about 500 bales. Any of you guys want a cheap workout, feel free to come help load that into the hayloft."

"So you get a free workout everyday but you can't pick the muscle groups to work on," Brian jabbed. "It's always all of them, right?"

"Whatever, it's not going to kill me," Frank said.

"How long you thinking of doing that?" Matt asked. "Are you thinking of taking over the farm?"

"He probably is because he doesn't realize every girl I know is lactose intolerant and we drink more beer than milk. The kids in school are even getting sow and almond milk these days," Brian said.

"I thought I was coming out here to have my life celebrated not get grilled like my wife would be doing if you guys weren't so all over it," Frank said.

"Let's dance," he said, and grabbed Lindsey in one fell swoop. They headed to the dance floor where there was barely any elbow room to move. Lindsey pulled up close to him and put her fingers into the place at the base of his neck.

"Old gangs don't change just because you stay away," she joked.

"I knew they'd all be on me about the farm thing. I just wish they'd let me kind of work it out before they trash the whole idea."

"Just dance, that's what we're here for, not a therapy session with poor counselors," Lindsey laughed and stepped away so she could follow her own advice. They stayed out on the dance floor for the entire next set. As soon as the last song was done, Lindsey headed to the ladies room and Alexandra was standing beside him almost before the bathroom door closed. He hadn't seen her but she had obviously seen him. She was her usual brash self, making no bones about wanting his attention.

"Rumor had it you had gone to the dogs, no the cows," she said. "Glad to see that wasn't entirely true."

"How are you?" he responded on auto pilot.

"Not bad, but nothing exciting going on in my life right now."

Frank didn't want to take the bait, ask about the rich, promising guy she'd dumped him for so he looked away.

She offered up the answer anyway.

"Rich just wasn't my type. First of all, he was too possessive. I could barely leave his sight and he was so needy and immature, not at all like you," Alexandra explained as though Frank wanted to know.

"Too bad," he murmured.

He left her standing on the dance floor and moved toward the table where his friends were all eyes, yet not one of them coming over to save him. They knew he was probably squirming like a bug. They all lived through his heartbreak when he had been convinced the only woman he would every love was Alexandra. That was so many actual and emotional years ago and he'd come such a long way, he realized.

"Hope I see you around more often," she tossed out like a challenge. "Not," he mouthed as he headed back to the safety of the gang at the table.

The guys ran out of manure jokes after the second round. The night turned into the old format, ball games bets, job searches, who saw who and guess what they were doing. Frank and Lindsey were well saturated with relaxation and a good buzz by the time they left.

At home, Frank paid the babysitter, and drove her the short ride home. When he got back, Lindsey was cuddled under the blanket half asleep, just the state he loved her in. She opened half an eye confirming his assessment but surprised him with a whole sentence.

"Where do you think you'll be in five years?"

"Would right here with you be the right answer?" he ventured.

"Good try," she smiled. "I mean, do you think we'll live here, you'll still be working the farm, Aubrey will be a big sister to a few brothers and sister? Things like that."

"Now, you want to talk about all that now? I was hoping to get some sleep before the 4 a.m. wake up call."

"Right, not now, but soon. OK? And as for sleep, The Edge isn't the only place that we never seem to visit much anymore," she said, placing her hands tightly around his chest and covering his lips with her soft inviting pair.

He thought he replied but wasn't sure he'd been able to or needed to. They were deep into kissing and touching each other in a way that Frank felt melted them into one big, new, single unit. He didn't love Lindsey just because she was a strikingly beautiful woman. There had been a few of those in his life. He loved their love, how she made him feel and he hoped, how he made her feel, like the rest of the world didn't exist or matter.

He once thought a woman like Alexandra was the only one for him, had cried for months about her leaving him. When he needed them most, his friends pulled him through though not until he'd wandered around lost for months. He couldn't find a way to knock her out of his thoughts. Then an accident that could have killed him, instead gave him his angel, Lindsey, the ER nurse who knew when she first saw the broken man that she was the one to mend him.

When he finally laid his head on the pillow sleep overtook him quickly. These days, he didn't last long on the horizontal. He woke to the country station playing the latest Tim McGraw, Always Stay Humble and Kind and the sight of the number 4 on the hour. As if I could be anything but humble and kind with a woman like that in my life, was his first waking thought.

***

A week later, Frank stood in the farm driveway figuring if only two or three guys showed up it would probably be enough. He had just gotten the phone call from the driver of the Canadian tractor trailer. The farm was a little off the beaten path and the driver was closing in but trying to make sure he was headed in the right direction.

Brian, Matt and Greg had promised to help unload the 500 or so bales today in response to his throw down of a challenge. He'd feed them afterward, he promised, not to mention include the beverages. They'd said they'd show up but so far, not a sign of anyone and the truck was about 15 minutes away. Figures, Frank thought, this will be a long day.

He scrolled through his contacts looking for the name of someone he could call who might actually show up. His contact list of names was pretty much at the X, Y and Z's before he heard a truck approaching that indicated Brian Black and his souped up Big Wheel. Inside were Matt and Greg. Frank stayed rooted to his spot when what he felt like doing was running over to hug those guys.

"So, I was just calling real friends to get over here to help," Frank said, as the crew exited the cab.

"We're here so where's this big hay loft and hard work? Let's get to it," Brian said.

Frank pointed to the hay bale elevator lying beside the barn door. "Two of us have to get upstairs and the other two stay down here. Let's put the loader in place. The truck's almost here, he just called," Frank said, wasting no time in putting these guys in motion.

"What did you say, 500 bales? That will take no time," Matt offered.

"We'll see," Frank countered. "If that doesn't hold us till the pastures are ready for the cows, then I'll be sure to call you for the next load too."

"No problem," Matt slapped him on the back. "Show me the way."

They climbed upstairs into the 20-foot high hay mow. Both ends were topped with a small window through which an indirect shaft of light was shining. To Frank, it was churchlike, a cathedral-size space with a grandeur in the workmanship that humbled any thought he had of being a competent carpenter. The men who built this barn were leagues beyond any ability he had or that of most of the better carpenters he knew. Ten-foot 2 x 10 beams rose at three angles to the peak. They were spaced every two feet. The barn roof framework stood on a floor of polished planks that Jerry told him served as a bowling alley whenever time allowed. A set of bowling balls were still tucked in the far corner of the huge building. Matt worked in a large office building but even he saw the hay loft and wowed.

"Can you imagine building this thing?" Frank asked him. "From what Jerry tells me, it was just his dad and a few friends put the whole thing up in no time because the old barn had burned down."

This wasn't even one of the largest barns that had dotted the countryside, Frank knew, and just in his lifetime, he'd seen quite a few of them lost. One big fire at a barn near the high school had been the most excitement he'd witnessed as a kid. At the time, all he remembered thinking was how cool it was to see the flames shooting up that far.

At the start of the winter in the old days when the herd had been at its largest, Jerry told Frank he had this loft stuffed with almost 8,000 bales. By April, every one of them were gone and he was scrambling to find hay in early spring. The Canadians were doing something right because they could always be counted on to have some available. They were still delivering but the price was high.

Frank had asked Lindsey to come over and count the bales as they were loaded, making sure they didn't get charged for more bales than they actually got.

He opened the hay loft doors and shouted down to Brian and Greg to lift the hay elevator in place. He and Matt grabbed the edge and secured it at the door opening.

"We'll stack the bales starting in the corner here, a bit back from the first and second drop holes," he explained to Matt. "Start the first row in this direction and the second level will go the other direction. Try not to let the bales break open. It's a mess to throw them down if the baling twine is half off or completely broken," Frank explained.

He grabbed two hooks and handed them to Matt.

"You can use these, if you want," he offered. "They help to move the bale if you get the hang of them. I can unload and you take them over to stack, OK?"

"How are these things made?" Matt asked, picking up one of the bales. "I've never seen one up close."

"They're pretty involved. There's a whole lot of individual sections in those bales that come apart and make it easy to feed. If they all come apart in the air on the way down from the loft, though, that's not good."

"How do they get tied with the string?" Matt's interest was real and gave Frank a chance to talk with someone about how much there was to this farming work.

"Making hay is like an art, if you listen to Jerry talk. He used to have a hay field across the street, did it for most of his life but then he got into the rotational grazing. He made the hay field into a pasture for the cows to have another spot to move to. He doesn't cut hay on that field anymore but he sure knew how to do it in the day," Frank said with obvious admiration. "You have to be a good weather forecaster. You need at least three dry, sunny days in a row or the hay will get moldy before you even get it baled. There's one day to cut it, the next day you have to fluff it around. They call it tedding. You're trying to get it all dry and then you can make bundles of it and try to have the baling equipment not break down in the middle of it all," Frank smiled.

"Probably not likely, right," Matt astutely added.

"There's a lot of moving parts. Jerry's got the old equipment in the garage out back. The whole thing has to work perfectly, scoop up the bundles, pack them into bales, lash two strands of baling twine around it and spit it out the back," Frank said while pausing in his work to do a pantomime of the equipment operating. "That plan can go to hell every step of the way and Jerry will tell you when it does, it's because a storm's on the way and you have to hurry to finish."

"Sounds like another real fun job," Matt said. "Where did you say this stuff came from?"

"Canadians have this hay making down. They always have a lot of hay available. It's amazing really, their winters are worse than ours but they must still have a lot of farmland up there. Never really gone up that way to see it but I think I might do that... if I ever get a weekend off," Frank laughed.

"I hope I get a chance to learn how to hay," Frank added. "Jerry said it's one of the best things to do but you have to like riding around in circles in a wide open field. I remember spreading manure when I was a kid and I loved it so I'd probably be a sucker for haying."

Below, the other guys were looking at the elevator, working out the operational plan.

"I see how this thing works," Brian called out. "Those rotating spikes grab the bale, it rides up the elevator and you guys catch 'em. Piece of cake."

"Tell me that when the bales are all up here and we're sitting around drinking a cold one," Greg said.

True to his prediction, the cool temperature of the day didn't keep the guys from working themselves into a heavy sweat before the first 100 bales were off the tractor trailer. They did get the hang of the work but that didn't lighten the weight of the 50 or more pound parcels they were wrestling up and over with a continuous pressure to keep up with the pace of the elevator and the challenge of the friendly competition of the ground crew against the loft crew.

Lindsey had taken her spot near the loft doors but out of the way of the guys. The comradery of the group did make light work of it. A constant harangue of insults and jokes flowed despite the distance from ground to the loft. They had logged 527 bales put up by noon, according to Lindsey's count. Frank paid the driver and looked at his friends. At least they were all smiling, he saw.

"Thanks guys. That went great."

"You have got to be kidding, doing this on a regular basis, man," Brian said, pulling bits of hay off his face, out of his waistband and hair.

"Guess that means I shouldn't call you next time," Frank suggested.

"Get a regular job, one where you don't work your ass off for peanuts, is all," Brian replied.

"I guess," Frank said. "I kind of had fun doing this but I have noticed it's not for everyone."

Hay and the associated work was one of the many worries Jerry had expressed to Frank. People who had the know-how, the equipment and the hay fields were disappearing as fast as the farms. Jerry had just lost a friend who supplied a lot of hay for the farm in an equipment accident. He had no alternates waiting to replace him and the price of buying Canadian hay instead of local was huge.

It was just one of the areas of the farm world falling by the wayside making the remaining farms struggle that much more. A longtime grain distributor had closed up shop about two months ago also. That meant now he was getting grain from the next closest dealer who was about 10 miles farther and more dollars away.

"Farms can't exist in a vacuum," Frank told his buddies. "If I didn't have you guys to help me, I would have done this with Nelson. Jerry's told me stories about bringing in hay by himself, loading the bales at the bottom and running up to move them after a few start to stack and threaten to fall back down. I know that couldn't have been fun but he just did whatever he needed to do, year in and year out."

Frank knew it would have taken him and Nelson three to four times as long and he probably would have had a hard time moving tomorrow. He hoped at least a few of these guys might come back for another load but he was finding that what he called fun was not the same definition as most.

Chapter 8

BABY
ANGEL

THE LITTLE FORM was only barely visible on the far side of her mother. When she poked her head up to see the intrusion on her first day, Frank saw the definite shape of a heart on her forehead, not a lopsided substitute resembling that shape but a very well-formed symmetrical white heart against a dull auburn coat.

Her mother had white markings on her head so this was not unexpected but the obvious shape made Frank blurt out "Angel," her new name.

Daughter of Ada, she was already on her way to being special. The genetics in the A-girl lines were some of the best, intelligence and even-temper being their strong point but hardy, good milkers and problem-free were traits in the genetic pool.

Frank grabbed his phone out of his pocket. Jerry would love to see this, he knew.

Angel didn't seem to mind having her first baby picture taken and turned obligingly so Frank could get a good picture of her unique markings. He took a few, including the ones of her feeding from her mom some of the colostrum that would give her a great start on immunity.

Turning to Ada, Frank was glad to see her eating hay and looking energetic, no sign of milk fever. After checking the water bowl was functioning and Ada and her new girl were all set, Frank headed to the door of the duplex.

"Just dropped," he said, as he opened his phone and showed Angel's picture to the old man.

There was no denying the good looks of this new calf, straight back, bright eyes and the signature marking but the smile on Jerry's face was a sad one.

As though warning Frank to stay away from the wrong kind of woman, he counseled, "Those girls get to you with those damn eyes. After you fall head over heels, raise her to have her first calf, bring her onboard as a milker, proud as a parent, then the price of milk will be go into the toilet. The government will tell you that you have to sell her for slaughter or ship her out of the country, if she can survive the trip."

"A few years ago, there was one just as cute. I remember you spoiling her great grandma, Adeline, when you were here as a kid. I can see you're going to fall for this one too then the US government will decide they don't need as many dairy farms and they'll try to get farmers to sell these beauties. Here I am, an old man with nothing but debts, regrets and a new bunch of nice cows nobody knows if they do or don't need anymore."

Frank had seldom heard this many words come tumbling out of Jerry at the same time. The program on the TV caught his attention and he realized Jerry had been listening to the news and the presidential election campaigning, depressing in the endless bickering and the lack of inspirational candidates and ideas.

He was being given a chance to run. He'd helped the farm survive the winter, stayed on now into spring and the weather was improving and he was showing no sign of leaving. If anything, he and Jerry had started to discuss plans, things he might do to make the place better.

The discussion about the future of the farm was hanging heavier over them with each passing day. Jerry's medical prognosis wasn't improving. He had gotten a pin removed in his shoulder and was taking physical therapy three times a week but the best that was likely to produce was a little more range of motion so he could do everyday things, like cook and care for himself. There was no fix to bring back strength to his right side, the kind needed to be a dairy farmer.

Getting more serious about the farm and making a commitment to that work Frank knew was a talk he was fixing to have with Lindsey first. It would be time soon, though, to have that talk, maybe decide to fully commit or let Jerry know he was not the guy to keep this place going. There were no others waiting in the aisles but there were some other options, vegetable farming, selling to developers who were seeing some activity in the real estate market especially for new homes, even just selling the place to a gentleman farmer who could afford the price of open spaces.

Frank shut off his phone and looked at Jerry, moving back to his chair and his resigned retirement. He and Lindsey had to have some serious discussions and soon.

Later that afternoon, checking on Ada, he found her a little slow to eat. Her udder was bursting with milk, the strain of which, on these fragile Jersey girls, always made their calcium levels drop to a dangerous level. If he wanted to make sure she didn't come down with milk fever, he was going to have to get a few bottles of calcium into her tonight or face the prospects of a dead mother in the morning. He pushed through his own fatigue and got a needed surge of energy from the sight of the newborn's face. Finding the calcium gluconate, needle and tubing in the store room, he attached the items and headed to the house to confirm with Jerry just how to do the calcium drip. He'd done it about half a dozen times already and definitely was more confident after his success with the temperamental Merry but was still a little apprehensive, not especially fond of the need to be a large animal vet.

"Stick the needle in her neck, not too deep but get it in so it stays, make sure you see bubbles in the bottle so you know it's moving through the tube. Be calm around her. Take your time and make sure you put two of those totally in her. It would be a real shame to lose her," Jerry explained. Frank had heard the stories of Jerry outside in a blizzard giving a cow calcium, doing what he was apprehensive about trying in a clear, dry barn with the lights on. He resolved to make this the last time he showed Jerry the wimpy side of his farming abilities.

Ada cooperated fully, making his job easy. She stayed standing indicating the calcium in her body wasn't so depleted by the milk her body was making that it had fallen low enough to stop even the muscle of her heart from working. It was slow going though. Frank pushed past a really deep exhaustion, cleaning up afterward and putting things back so he could find them in the morning if need be.

When he finally got home, he told a very sleepy Lindsey who'd gone to bed an hour ago, about how well it had gone. He hoped she heard about his beautiful new baby and that she really meant the "good job" she murmured.

Chapter 9

BREAST
FEEDING

NELSON RARELY WAS SICK so Frank knew he felt really bad when he found him lying on his side on a bale of hay in the calf pen. He sent him in to his rooms on the other side of the duplex where he lived and took a deep breath. The night milking would be a long one. He was operating on just a few cylinders himself, probably a touch of the same thing affecting Nelson.

He texted Lindsey, knew she'd worry if he was much later than usual. Her first thought would be panic that he was hurt. She phoned him as he was tucking the phone back into his pocket.

"Nelson isn't here to help me tonight. I sent him home. He looked awful. I don't know what time I'll get done without him."

"How about I come down and help?" Lindsey offered. "Aubrey is staying at my mom's. The two hadn't had enough time together yet, they decided. Mom just called me about an hour ago. She's only bringing her home in the morning. It would be too quiet here all night alone. I'd rather be of use. I'll be there in five minutes."

Lindsey had never volunteered for milking duties before but Frank realized she had been asking him more questions lately about what it was like to work with the cows. He probably hadn't been paying enough attention to realize she wanted a chance to see for herself what he had gotten them both into.

She walked into the milking room looking very much the milkmaid, her head topped with a gingham kerchief, plastic calf high boots and by the looks of it, some of his old clothes.

He'd already cleaned and assembled the milking equipment and gotten the pump working. He showed her how much grain to scoop into the first feeding bins and where to set them out on the far side of the stanchions.

"The biggest thing to remember is that every cow is different so let me see which girls we have and I'll tell you what to look for. We have to wash them and dip their teats before we put the machines on. I think you'll get the hang of that easily. If you can get them prepped, I'll be able to keep moving with the machines," he said.

Her eyes were a mix of excitement and nervousness, he thought. "Are you afraid to get up close to the cows?" he asked her. "Really, a little," she admitted.

"They're wired to be so much more afraid of you than you are of them," he laughed. "These herd animals are on the defensive all the time, ready to run for it, just remember that. They won't hurt you on purpose, except for grumpy Sue when she has mastitis, then look out for her kick but I won't let you get anywhere near her," Frank promised.

"Let's go," Lindsey said. "We won't find out what kind of bedside manner I have until I get my hands on my first teats."

Two of the first girls in were great ones for Lindsey to get initiated, Kitty and Kelly, mom and daughter, both interested in eating, and letting go of their load. Frank dipped the wash rag into the disinfectant and no sooner had the heat started to warm her udder, Kitty was dripping milk onto the floor. He finished washing all four teats and wiped them dry.

Then he took a small metal cup with a strainer in the cover and pulled gently on each one of the cow's teats. A little squirt hit the cup's lid. He checked for signs of thick, lumpy output. Seeing none, he took the claw into his hand, flipped it upside down and listened, checking that the apparatus had started pumping. He flicked the inflations into place and Kitty was on her way to a saggy bag. He brought Lindsey over to Kelly and the genetic similarity of mother and daughter produced almost an identical result, a little warm water, a flow of milk and a quick install of the milker.

Every cow isn't as good as these two, Frank cautioned her.

Anxious eyes were on Lindsey, every cow aware of a stranger in the mix. The older, wiser girls showed less concern, Frank noticed, taking that as a sign of their trust in him.

Lindsey really was ready to get to work. She'd listened long enough. It seemed to her she'd been in the barn some days hearing Frank talk about this ritual. She stepped up close to Ada.

"That's the mother of the baby," Frank pointed out to her. "The one I told you has the heart on her head."

Lindsey knew about Angel, a baby with the distinct white shape right above her eyes.

"She's beautiful too," Lindsey said, looking at the cow whose description she'd heard from Frank so many time she felt like she already knew her.

"She's a great milker too. She is one of the clean girls. I swear if she gets any dirt on herself it's because some other cow splashed her. She must only lie in a spot of clean and dry pasture because she never needs much washing."

"You told me that about the cows, how some are neat and tidy and others love to be messy," Lindsey said.

"You'll see for yourself," he said. "Just notice Ada and how clean she is and remember all these cows have been in the same pasture all day."

Lindsey asked to try milking the cows into the strip cup but her attempts brought nothing.

"What am I doing wrong?" she asked. "It seemed so automatic, like just squeeze and the milk comes out."

"It's really a little harder than that. The motion is more of a roll of your fingers from the top near her body down to the tip. It's not about squeezing harder. Part of it, I swear, is getting the cow to cooperate."

She tried again but got only a tiny stream and Frank stepped in coaxing out a strong stream with what looked to Lindsey to be the exact same thing she was doing.

"It takes a little while to get the right touch," Frank said. "Don't worry. If you keep at it, you'll be able to do it in your sleep like Jerry."

Lindsey was quickly washing and drying udders, dipping teats and stuck to those jobs. Frank found he could move the milking along at a good pace. Towards the end of the milking, Lindsey asked to feel the cows' udders like she had been watching Frank do all evening.

"Why do you handle their boobs so much," she asked. "I'm not enough?"

Frank grabbed her in a bear hug to make sure she felt like she had no competition from the much bigger busted crowd he saw on a daily basis.

"Their udders are hard and full when they come in because they made milk all day. You need to make sure it's empty and soft when they leave or they'll get mastitis," Frank explained.

"I know all about that, smarty," Lindsey retorted. "I've been pumped out and milked, you know. How do you think your daughter survived her first year of life?"

"I loved the feeling of being a cow," Lindsey laughed. "Being here, doing this, I'm remembering all those feelings of nursing Aubrey. Giving birth was awesome enough but thankfully it was over fairly quickly. When my milk came in, that was mind boggling."

"Yeah, I do remember your shape was a little unbelievable, like you'd just had a serious boob job gone wrong," Frank laughed.

"I would have never believed my body could do something like that," Lindsey admitted.

Greta was the last girl and Frank placed Lindsey on his side and brought her hand up to Greta's loaded hard udder.

"Feel how hard she is now?" he said. "After the machine has been on for a few minutes, hopefully, she'll be all softened up. This girl has a hard time of it, though. She doesn't always milk out good. She seems to want to keep her milk for herself."

"I had a few times when I felt like I had milk that wouldn't come out of me," Lindsey said. "I'd have some days when I felt like I had a rock in my boob and I needed to have Aubrey nurse so that she would suck it out. Maybe I could have used a super pump like this contraption," she said, grabbing hold of the claw.

"Really, I don't remember you telling me about that," Frank said.

"Yeah, it wasn't often but sometimes I felt like I got stuck full of milk and it wasn't getting out," she added.

Frank felt Greta's quarters and paid special attention to her left front where he knew she often stayed hard and full of milk. Sure enough, she wasn't milking out good and he hated to think of her needing to be treated for mastitis again. The machine had done all it could to convince Greta to give up her load.

He took off the milking inflations, hooked them on the pipe hook and started to hand milk her problem quarter. This had worked sometimes in the past, giving her a little more pressure and massaging her udder as he worked the teat, he had gotten her past some close calls before.

Lindsey watched, her head almost resting on Greta's side, feeling like a nursing mom again herself, trying to get that food out of her. She saw a small amount of milk being coaxed out at first and as Frank worked the combination of massage and squeeze, the amount increased and Greta gave up a nice stream, unfortunately wasting it on the floor.

Just about then Lindsey more felt it than heard it but she sensed Greta exhale and relax, just like she had felt when Aubrey finally found just the right place to suck and that hard rock spot on her boob had loosened and emptied.

"You got to her rock spot," Lindsey told Frank, "She must feel a lot better now because her spot was much bigger than any I ever had," she laughed.

"Do you really think this is just like what you did on a much bigger scale?" Frank asked, a little believing yet skeptical. "I've never heard Jerry say anything about humans and cows milking the same but then again he didn't have the chance to have kids and live with a nursing woman either."

"Totally," was Lindsey's confident reply. "Why wouldn't it be? The biggest hurdle I had convincing my friends to try breastfeeding was to prove to them they were just like any other mammal and could do this. Now I'm standing here trying to convince you that I'm just like that cow?"

"I guess I forgot," Frank said. "It's still pretty amazing to put two and two together like that, though."

"Remember my friend Kate who wanted to give up in the first few days. She didn't believe her little boobs would make enough milk. She ended up loving how she filled out a sweater once she got going and her little boy, Julian, he was a fat pudge," Lindsey reminisced with beginnings of a thought that maybe she'd get to do it all again. "Greta's got hard spots just like I used to get and there probably are just as many ways to help her. I used to make sure my bra wasn't too tight, but that's not an issue here. She needs plenty of water to keep her flowing, I would think, just like I did. I remember downing those big glasses of ale especially in the first months."

"I haven't heard of a brew for cows but I do check those water bowls before every milking, make sure they're all working," Frank said.

They moved to the four remaining cows and the conversation languished as they both lost themselves in thought. Frank looked over at Lindsey as they put the last milker on and decided again he was crazy in love with that woman, hoped she would stay in love with him forever. He kind of hoped Nelson would be sick a little more often too.

"I don't get it," said Lindsey said once they got home and started eating anything and everything in sight. "Why do you give some cows less food and others a lot?"

"It depends on where they are in their cycle. They get pregnant, have a calf, make a lot of milk at first, get pregnant again and then slack off and get dried up," Frank explained.

"So who were the ones getting less food?" Lindsey persisted. "I heard and saw them trying like crazy to get more food and you were pushing them out. That doesn't seem right. Shouldn't they get enough food to be satisfied?"

"There were two cows I hardly gave any food to. Those two need to stop giving milk, stay dry for a couple months and then they'll have a new calf and start milking again," Frank said.

"So what does that have to do with food, more or less of it?" Lindsey wouldn't be put off until she had the whole picture.

"They stop milking when you stop feeding them," Frank said, expecting that to be the end of the discussion.

"That's crazy," Lindsey shot back instead. "They're pregnant, about to have a new baby and you starve them?"

"I'll start giving them grain again a month before they deliver their calf," Frank said, pleading for this to be the final point.

Lindsey took a deep breath and Frank knew this would be a major shot across the bow of his dairy boat. He waited to get the question right so he could get the answer right but was thrown a curve ball again, one of many Lindsey was throwing now that she'd had her first stint in the barn.

"When Aubrey stopped nursing, I didn't miss a meal. Why would you have to starve the cows to make them stop milking? Just milk them less, like when Aubrey started running around all day and couldn't care less about nursing, not to mention, she was always anxious to try new things to eat. My milk just stopped without any special 'drying off.'"

That was not one Frank was ready for. As far as he knew, Jerry had always dried off the cows just like he was doing, reduce the grain, milk less, yes, that was part of it, not leaving the milkers on very long, just enough to keep the udder empty. Were cows like humans and they'd dry off by themselves?

"What would happen to a cow if she wasn't a dairy cow," Lindsey went on, clearly not finished with this issue. "Wouldn't her calf just go its merry way and stop nursing and the mom would stop having milk, just like a person?

"I have to say, I think you might be right but dairy farmers all do it this way," Frank defended himself. "You could take your sweet time to stop milking, I have to have that cow dry and ready to give birth and start milking again. That means I have to stop her fast, and feeding her less grain works."

"That's not fair." Lindsey kept up the cow defense. "She's eating for two and if she's anything like I was, she's starving all the time. That baby is just sitting there getting fat at the end of the pregnancy and you have to eat to let it put on weight. Tell me that isn't true of a baby cow."

"Really, I'm not sure," Frank admitted defeat if for nothing else to get on some other topic. "I'll ask Jerry about it."

"Thanks, babe," Lindsey cooed. "And thanks for listening. I feel like a have to stand with my fellow milking moms and figure this out."

Frank's smile was one of slight regret for involving Lindsey in the dairy operation at all and one of love for a woman so easily absorbed in taking care of things, not just him and Aubrey, her patients at the nursing home and now some cows she had just met.

Chapter 10

GOATS, PIGS
AND OTHER UNWANTEDS

PULLING UP TO THE DRIVEWAY of the farm, Frank caught sight of something fuzzy and alive. Getting closer he realized the two objects were young goats tied to the barnyard fence with dog leashes. They were eating every bit of grass they could reach but otherwise looked fine.

Only slightly startled, Frank realized the farm had once again become a dumping ground for someone's unwanted animals. This place had been a magnet for that for many years. Smiling, Frank remembered all the times he'd meet Jerry at the local donut shop early in the morning collecting day old donuts. Those were the main diet of two enormous pigs Jerry acquired in just the same way. He'd fed and raised those two brutes for years, topping them out at well over 500 pounds only to let them die of old age and bury their carcasses in the farm cemetery along with numerous cows.

Nothing in Jerry's character would let him make bacon out of those pigs. When he called them, they came running for a scratch behind their ears so no amount of common sense would translate into making a meal out of them, not in Jerry's world.

Frank already knew he'd be similarly inclined, not able to butcher and eat the livestock he'd cared for. It was a definite drawback, that soft heartedness, not one that helped with the farm finances at all.

He untied the two goats and happily found they were trained to be led. He headed to the main barn and put them temporarily into the birthing pen until he could figure out a permanent place. One thing was for sure, they were probably going to stay, seeing as the demand for young goats was not strong. Maybe he'd get lucky with a craigslist add offering them for free.

Climbing into the hay loft, Frank started dropping bales through the openings spread along the length of the barn. He was just letting go of one bale and not able to stop himself in time. One of the many kittens roaming the barn was directly under the drop hole and the bale was headed for a direct hit.

Jumping down the ladder, he lifted the still bouncing bale and found just what he thought, a very dazed little black and white kitten. He picked her up gently, expecting the worse. Miraculously, she was stunned but barely hurt. A little blood on her mouth indicated a broken tooth maybe.

He carried her to her mother's side and mom immediately started tending to her baby, licking her gently and the little one snuggled up and let herself be tended. This baby belonged to the best mother cat in the barn. She was an excellent mouser and her babies were healthy which he couldn't say about all the felines found on any given day in the barn area. Some of them were regulars, some occasional visitors, all found their way to the feeding station which was filled twice a day with fresh warm milk. Even Hank, Jerry's large mixed-breed dog, lapped up as much of the warm milk as he could. He was more than 14 years old but more spry than most dogs his age. Frank had never heard of milk as dog food but if Hank was proof, maybe it should be.

The cats earned their keep killing mice. There was no denying the reciprocal benefits of giving the bottom of the milk can leftovers to cats who patrolled day and night against vermin entering the grain bins. The signs of their work were usually easy to find, a carcass or two every week of many assorted sizes of rodents, some tiny babies, others 10-inch long rats. The little injured kitten was now purring at her mother's side. It's determination to not only survive but to thrive brought Frank up short. He allowed himself to think back to his days in the battlefield of Afghanistan when men all around him were doing the same thing. It was an empowering thing to survive a tough fight and a bitter pill to swallow when the results were different.

He wasn't sure if he liked the intensity of the emotions this farming business brought out. There was a closeness to primeval things that was unavoidable. When things went well, and thankfully there had been a lot of those days, Frank felt like a million dollars, something that nothing else short of a great day with his wife and daughter, could approach.

When things went bad, and there were so many ways for that to happen, most of them unexpected, unavoidable and undeniably sad, Frank had initially been inclined to turn and run from it, but more recently he'd found that inclination losing ground to the sense that he was getting all in with this farm, and he'd better make some decisions on how that could ever work long term.

His friends would bully him, try to talk him out of it but he'd been at the farm now for more than five months. Without a nurse for a wife, he knew, he would have never had the opportunity to do this kind of work for one month. Lindsey's salary, his Army Reserve income, a few construction projects he'd been able to squeeze in, a roofing job on a small ranch, the new porch on a friend's house and others like that had kept them afloat though not making any financial progress.

The Reserve weekends away and the upcoming days when he would have to be gone to fulfill his annual commitment were made possible by Nelson who could still be counted on to find a friend or relative to come in and help for a short time. That hadn't been without issues. Every Monday morning when he returned from his time away he found things that weren't done, or at least not done right, water pails dry as a bone, calves sinking in deep manure, cows who had suddenly developed mastitis because they weren't milked out completely. Then there was the equipment, put away haphazardly, some of it hard to find, nothing replenished.

That was the price to pay for being away from his charges for even a short time. A conversation with Jerry was coming to mind, Frank recalled. He had turned down an invitation to get away on a cruise with his sister and her family. They had booked the trip, paid for Jerry's fare, were in the driveway waiting for him to get in the car and he flat out refused.

He'd been pushed into going by people who thought they were doing him a big favor, letting him get away, relax, have fun, stuff they thought he needed more of in his life. When the fateful moment came, Jerry described his behavior like that of a panicked animal, seeing himself torn from the safety of his herd, feeling vulnerable and lost without them.

That would be his fate, Frank thought, if he stayed. He needed to start talking about the possibility, though. He wasn't one to plan these things but he decided to be on the alert for a good time to bring up the subject with Lindsey.

She had lived a long day at the nursing home. Frank could tell with one look when he walked into the kitchen. She was doing what she usually did when that happened, sitting at the table, reading and regrouping. She gave Frank a weak smile and reached for him for a re-entry-to-their-world kiss.

"Who was it that rocked your world today?" he asked. "Helen try to escape again or was it a new noro virus outbreak?"

"Nothing like that," Lindsey said. "Mrs. Dagostino went to the hospital. She fell, probably broke her hip and wrist. At 91, I'm not sure she'll be coming back. She was such a sweet lady."

"The problem is she didn't have to fall. They should fire that CNA on the first shift. She doesn't know how to work with the patients with dementia. She was rushing her into the shower. She should have been getting her to cooperate not pushing her along too fast."

"What do you have over there, a herd of cows?" Frank couldn't help but see the similarity. "That sounds like exactly what I have to do with my girls, get them to cooperate by talking nice to them and moving them slowly. Maybe there's a future for me as a CNA."

"You have your hands full with your own patients, I think," Lindsey replied. "I could use someone who does their job like you though. There's another aide that thinks I don't know when she hasn't cleaned the patients' beds, leaves them lying on wet sheets on their way to bed sores."

"My patients tell me right away when something isn't done right," Frank noted. "I swear it's like they're talking to me telling what needs to be done and nagging me to get going on it."

He moved over to the stove and lifted the lid on a pot of what smelled like chicken soup almost putting his hand into the hot mixture and taking a taste. That's when he realized he hadn't taken a lunch break. There had been a few distractions.

"We had a couple goats show up at the farm today," Frank said. "I hoped Jerry hadn't seen them and maybe I could advertise them on craigslist, find them a nice new home somewhere else. But no, Jerry moved his big armchair over by the side window where he can oversee everything. He probably could tell me the plate on the truck that dumped them because he has a hard time sleeping and watches television all night. He hates to lose a patient too so I'm sure I'll be learning all about how to care for goats real soon."

"Nothing wrong with having a big heart," Lindsey answered as though cued to give Frank a segway into the question of whether to make a long term commitment to the farm or cut his ties with it.

"A big heart doesn't pay the bills," he said, to try to open up the discussion. "Just like I'm not helping pay the bills now with this farm project. You've been taking all the weight and I can't keep letting you do that."

"Have you taken a look in the mirror lately," Lindsey said. "Don't you know the man I see now every day is so happy, I have a huge payback?"

The words, spoken so quickly, without hesitation, were like a revelation to his heart. He hadn't been happy before the farm, and he couldn't deny that the place had made him feel good. His hands were calloused from all the shoveling. His knees were aching when the milking took especially long and he'd been forced to kneel on a cold wet surface. He saw stuff that needed fixing every day and never saw enough daylight to make a dent in most of it. He had barely taken Lindsey out even for a quick Friday night fish and chips in months. Aubrey seemed to love the farm and his stories about what happened there. That didn't make up for the many nights she was already asleep when he got home or the fact that every morning, he was gone long before she got out of bed.

What was making him happy about this situation, he wondered. Lindsey answered for him.

"You are moving to your own rhythm, being independent without some boss man ordering you around. You were never really keen on that, you know. Making something of that farm would be something you could be proud of. Maybe it's in your blood to be a dairy farmer. I'm not sure why, but I know you are in the right place," Lindsey said.

"How could we every really make a go of that place?" Frank countered. "I mean the kind of life where Aubrey actually gets to go to college if she wants to? We have a nice place here without a mortgage, enough acreage to have a few animals, even a little herd of cattle if we wanted. This place is my land, my parents' and grandparents land before me. I'm not sure I can love Jerry's farm as much as I love this place."

"Here's the bottom line. There is no future in dairy farming in this area of New England." Frank added. He spat it out, the big obstacle. He had gotten himself involved in something with no future, a business tangled in governmental regulation, national politics and mired in the smell of manure in a society of processed, sanitized food and operating pretty much the same as it did thousands of years ago when humans first domesticated cows for milk but trying to exist in a day of space-age ideas.

"Did those women from the city convince you yet to look into raw milk and selling it right from the farm?" Lindsey countered. "There's a future in that kind of thing. People want farm fresh, local sourced and you can do that with a good return for that investment."

"I would have to study that more. I don't know whether I would even want raw milk from any cows other than Jerry's," Frank countered. "I need to know they are cared for like we do."

"I can support you in this," Lindsey said. "Not half-heartedly, but we should be talking about this with Jerry before we get any ideas in our heads that he would never go along with. He may be hoping to get back into the barn and send you packing."

"Right," Frank breathed out. "I heard him make some remarks though when he got back from his last doctor's appointment. He does have the idea planted in his head that he may not go back to dairy farming. His break was really bad. There's only so much that therapy can do to give him full use in that arm. He probably won't ever get the strength and motion back to normal."

"That must be such a hard thought for him to even remotely entertain," Lindsey sighed.

"Jerry is a great guy and the last thing I would want to do is anything that would prevent him from taking his farm back."

"You're not doing that. You're giving him a chance to keep it operating when he might have just had it all go away the day after he got hurt."

"Did I do him a favor or would it have been better for him to have the Band-Aid torn off and be done with it?"

"I happen to know that you were sent back there, not just for Jerry but for you. The force likes to do that, you know, get a two-for-one out of these kinds of things."

Frank knew Lindsey was very serious when she started involving her beliefs and the workings of the unseen. She had a faith he admired even if he couldn't quite match it.

"Ok, I hope I am up to the mission in store for me," Frank offered.

Lindsey quoted a line from one of their movie favorites, a line they both loved about moving forward with conviction.

Frank put his head down at the words and absorbed the reminder not to let doubt defeat him. He made a promise to try to keep a beaten tone out of his discussions with Lindsey.

"By the way, is that soup edible?" was his next thought.

Chapter 11

GLYPHOSATE

"GLYPHOSATE," LORRAINE INTONED in her usual bleacher-reaching soprano. She had barely gotten two steps into Celeste's kitchen.

Sure this was a long explanation, Celeste nonetheless bit and asked about the battle cry.

"We have to find out where Frank buys that corn he feeds his cows," Lorraine said. "I think it's Round-Up Ready seeds and that's full of glyphosate."

Now, she's going to start telling him what to feed his cows, Celeste had to smile. Last time they were over there, the mission had been to tell Frank how to run the farm business, go raw milk, make ice cream, attract the health food crowd. She saw him as a young guy who was not afraid of hard work and getting his hands dirty but no crusader for pure food. She wondered how much he was listening to any of Lorraine's foolproof ideas.

If he read a little more, he would understand, Lorraine argued as they drove home.

Time on his hands to do the mandatory reading on all this stuff was hilarious, Celeste calmly explained.

"Not a problem, I'll be happy to fill him in," Lorraine retorted. "The thing is, if you open your eyes and do some research, there is so much information out there that is not getting to the people. This Round-Up Ready stuff, where everything we are growing has to be doused with pesticide and the crop we eat survives it. Not what I want to eat, not that anyone is asking. That's killing us!! Did I tell you I'm going to join the CSA that's run by the school. They're growing things I can't do in my limited space and they're using a lot of heirloom seed varieties."

"I know this is way off course but I am trying to get this vest finished so that I can wear it to work Monday."

"Sorry, I will tone it down a tad but listen, when can we go back out there for a little more of a serious talk with Frank, help him understand the opportunities he might not be seeing. I know he actually listens to you more than me because you're the one showing him how good that raw milk has been," Lorraine said.

She'd had her first colonoscopy since the surgery, coupled with blood work, all results were better than average, her doctor reported.

"I have been feeling really good and optimistic, having way more good days than bad and not dreading waking up in the morning. It's not just the raw milk, though. I wouldn't be here without the operation and chemo but I am so cautious about everything I eat, like it has to pass a test. I hate worrying about whether I'm sending something through my gut that will bring the cancer back."

"The problem is, you can't find stuff that's safe," Lorraine almost shouted. "Why would anyone who makes food want to kill the people who eat it?" Does that make any sense? There are big food producing companies destroying their own customer base, did anyone notice?"

"I probably had a bowl of cereal this morning laced with growth hormone," Lorraine added. "We all get a free hormone replacement program even if we haven't started menopause."

The rest of her tirade involved disparaging even her favorite dish, chicken as loaded with too many harmful ingredients.

"I, for one, could use a dose of hormones," Celeste joked to try to tone down the level of agitation Lorraine had worked herself up to, "but I think it's probably true because I've had a lot fewer hot flashes these days than usual."

"So you know I'm right," Lorraine jumped right back into it. "Imagine what that stuff is doing to the young kids who are eating it over a much longer period of time. The girls are getting an early start to their periods and I don't want to even consider what the impact is on a young boy. It makes me want to scream that no one is paying attention to any of this. I read a report about the level of hormones in chickens being very low but what about the fact that the low level is in about half the food we're eating from the butter on my toast to the milk in my coffee?"

"So, how about we go out to the farm today? I have a whole plan for that farm. There are people who will buy his milk because I don't think he has any bovine growth hormones in those cows and we just have to find out about the corn he's feeding," Lorraine's plan poured out of her. "They could do what this farm in Wisconsin did and pasteurize and distribute their own milk if they don't want to go the full raw milk route. I would prefer Frank took that plunge but he's not buying it yet."

"I love going out there. Just being at that farm makes me feel good. Seeing the cows, those beautiful faces, I'm in," Celeste agreed.

They talked about the herbicide information Lorraine had recently hunted up as they drove to the farm. The highlights Celeste caught as Lorraine kept up a heated condemnation of Round Up Ready crops was that they end up not having the same nutrients as "real" plants grown naturally. The Round Up pesticide ends up in the plants and in the consumer. Lorraine was livid that this stuff would be slipping onto plates without anyone knowing about it.

It was a little too much drama for Celeste to jump on this bandwagon right away but when Lorraine did her homework, she was usually eventually proven right. She caught the fringe research early then followed as it became mainstream. This line of investigation was pointing to what she calling "organized criminal fooding." She would ask Lorraine to leave her some of the stuff to read and try to get a better understanding when she had the energy for it.

***

The now familiar blue Subaru pulled up but not on its usual day and time, and the women's' visit couldn't have come at a worse time.

Frank was waiting for the vet to arrive. He'd spent a long morning already and had no extra time for anything. One of his best milkers, Laura, had a cough yesterday. The cool night air had turned that into something much worse. She was running a fever of 106, high enough

103

above the normal 101 that was the point he needed to put in a call for help.

The sure sign of major problems with Laura was the wretched smell from her diarrhea. Frank's nose was immune to the smell of "good" manure. He'd noticed before that when a cow had more than normally loose stools and they smelled really bad, it all pointed to illness. Laura's pungent, sour and eye-crossing smell indicated the possibility of a serious illness.

The vet advised them to hose her down until the fever went below 104 and he'd get over there as soon as possible. Frank and Nelson had taken turns for an hour this morning keeping a gentle flow of cool water coursing over Laura as she stood in the stanchion. She had thankfully been standing in the spot closest to the floor drain so the run-off wasn't too hard to handle as long as they monitored the flow.

The morning clean-up was way behind schedule and Frank could hear the bawl of the calves who knew they were overdue for breakfast. He thought it was just a raw milk pick up but Lorraine, true to form, didn't waste any time getting to the point of this unscheduled visit.

"Do you buy Round-Up Ready corn?" she asked almost before even saying hi.

"I'm not sure. I buy what Jerry told me to buy and we haven't really ever talked about what kind of corn it is."

"All the seed comes Round-Up Ready, according to what I'm finding out, and that's full of glyphosate," Lorraine expounded. "You shouldn't feed them that stuff."

Frank was usually not short with people but Lorraine's timing for this assault was way off.

"I'm sorry but if you don't want to buy any more milk, that's great. You're really making me do something I'm not comfortable with anyway," Frank blurted out. "I have a very sick cow I'm trying to take care of, a bunch of young stock that think I forgot about them today and I'm sure as hell not of a mind to discuss any of their food right now."

He turned and walked toward the calf barn without even asking if they wanted a jug of milk.

Lorraine had met her match, Celeste couldn't help but notice. Frank's direct response and Lorraine's capitulation were the first time she had witnessed her friend back off, let a plan go and admit defeat.

"Let's go," she offered. "We need to give him some warning before the next visit, I think."

"I was trying to help him and this farm," Lorraine said, rather mildly for her. "I can see he's got too much going on to listen right now. Did we ever get a phone number from him? I'll try calling or maybe just a text to let him know we're coming next time."

On the way back to the city, they couldn't help but pull over for a yard sale at an older home not far from the farm.

The design on a warming tray caught Celeste's eye and she unburied it from the pile of odds and ends on the table. It looked like it hadn't been out of this box for many, many years, maybe around 1950 something. That was a good thing, she thought. There were few moving parts so it probably still worked fine.

She'd started making her own yogurt from the raw milk they were buying at the farm but the batches were small in a pint-sized crock pot. The tray was just what she'd been looking for. Someone at work had described the process she used. It entailed setting the heated milk mixture on a warming tray to transform into yogurt. It not only sounded easy but inexpensive. The process used barely any electricity and took about 4 hours to make a thick yogurt, she'd been promised.

She found the yard sale table owner and paid the $2 for her warming tray without insuring it worked. It hadn't been worth the effort to find a cord and outlet for the price and she was feeling lucky anyway.

They both picked up some other great finds. Lorraine snagged a two bowl set of mixing bowls from about the mid-1940s that had a dated red, yellow and green design of a rooster and hens. Celeste found a vintage Anne Adams pattern envelope, one of the older designs she loved. Boy, they knew how to design them in the old days, Celeste thought. She wished she had lived during the days of the pattern's popularity because they must have been a joy to bring to life. Her plan was to try some of these old patterns in the new fabrics of today, stretch knits and textures that weren't available back when. She hoped to spark a new popularity for something like this with just a bit of ingenuity to select the right material. Happy with their finds, the women headed to Celeste's house and jumped right into cleaning and testing the warming tray. They plugged it in and were rewarded with a quick heat emanating from the surface.

Homemade yogurt from Frank's milk was a daily ritual now in Celeste's day. Vegetable quiches were another addition to her diet. Simple meals were probably the best description of what she tried to eat, straight forward meals made out of chemical-free ingredients. She had dropped back into some old eating habits, grabbing a fast food lunch with a friend a few weeks ago, that showed her how much her food choices had changed. The chain restaurant favorite she'd ordered on instinct reeked of foreign tastes she had never noticed before. She'd wanted to stop eating it, even throw it away but had put down a good amount and just acted like she'd enjoyed it to keep from ruining the lunch. She knew there wasn't going to be another lunch at that place if she could help it.

Almost on a daily basis, Lorraine sent her food contamination messages telling her what products had just been announced as tainted with e-coli, listeria, or found to have dangerous levels of something harmful. If a food was being outed as less than perfect, Lorraine would be the first to know and the first to spread the word with Celeste at the top of her notification list.

The foods she'd allowed herself to eat were starting to make a difference. That difference was in what she tasted and how she was finding certain food she had liked now had a new nuance and not a good one.

Macaroni and cheese for example. She always loved a creamy, commercial version. It had become too salty lately and not as appealing as the one Lorraine had talked her into making. The cheese sauce began from scratch, a roux made from the farm milk, with real butter and unbleached flour. The cheddar cheese was a small Vermont brand, pricey but sharp and flavorful. The result had been nothing like the boxed dish. Add to that, Lorraine's homegrown cherry tomatoes and the crusty seeded wheat bread to swipe up the last bits of cheese sauce and Celeste was completely off the old version. She had to admit it seemed there were tastes she had been missing out on that Lorraine was introducing to her palate.

If nothing else, the amount of fruits and vegetables Lorraine kept pushing into her made her very regular, more of a vegetarian for the greater part of the week. A feeling of vitality, lack of pain and maintenance of her weight were all things Celeste liked and wanted to retain.

Lorraine had insisted on doing a taste test when they purchased the first gallon of raw milk. She'd bought two commercial milk cartons, one from the small local dairy processing plant and the other from a major national brand. She poured out glasses of all three and conducted a blindfolded taste test so she couldn't see a difference in color or texture. She went first, putting on sleep goggles and telling Celeste to put the three different milk products in identical glasses and set them on the table in front of her. Guiding her hand so it securely picked up the glasses without making a mess, she sipped from each and then made her decision on taste, texture and anything else she noticed.

Both women had done the test before they announced their opinions and the results had been very close to identical. The farm milk left no mucous residue in their mouth. Once it was swallowed it was gone and there was no lingering feeling of needing to rinse your mouth clean. Both commercial brands had the famous milky residue.

The national brand was the unanimous choice for worse. It even tasted burnt compared to the farm milk. It had a multitude of additional flavors mixed in with the faint taste of milk. That difference was highlighted against the simplicity of the farm milk flavor. The local dairy was a mix, better on the flavor front but still with some of the mucous residue and some added tones of additives.

Once the less than scientific test had been completed, the women agreed they would try to stick with drinking and using as much of the farm brand as they could reasoning that if the basic ingredient was better the final results couldn't miss.

A few quiches bore out the theory. The creamy texture and milk and cheese flavor didn't fight with the assortment of vegetables they'd experimented adding. Spinach and broccoli were the most accommodating to the mix but they'd tried fresh tomatoes, squashes and every kind of pepper Lorraine grew which went from sweet to burn-your-mouth hot. All had been a success.

They planned to add more homemade yogurt to their food production as soon as they could find a better process. Celeste's co-worker had finally provided it. Armed with the new warming tray they could now execute experiments in yogurt making.

Reading over the instructions, they filled a thick Dutch oven with a gallon of the farm milk, heated it to 180 degrees checking the temperature with a candy thermometer. Once it had reached the right point, they removed it from the burner and took turns stirring the pot to cool it. It had to come down to about 115 degrees before they could add the live yogurt culture. They'd bought a high-end brand of plain yogurt hoping to maintain a good viable culture for a long time.

After they'd added the yogurt and made sure it was dissolved and incorporated throughout the milk, they set the Dutch oven on the warming tray. They set a timer for four hours, the minimum amount of time for the yogurt to spread and create a full pot of yogurt. They didn't do a repeat of the milk experiment with their yogurt, just dug into the finished product the next day after they'd refrigerated it and added a little strawberry sauce and granola to it. The homemade yogurt, like the milk, tasted fresh. It had so little interruption in the consistency of the taste or the simplicity of it.

It soon became a staple in Celeste and Lorraine's diets. About then it occurred to Celeste she probably could never go back to a commercial substitute. It just wasn't going to taste good anymore. At least the cost of making her own yogurt was low and the time was well spent.

She had days of feeling she had too much time and days of a fear of not enough. She hadn't been able to get out to the West Coast for a visit with her grandchildren. She really missed her owns kids too and had so much to talk about with both of them. She was planning on bringing them up to speed on all the things she was doing with her diet, hoping they'd listen. Maybe she should have fed them better when they were young. Too many trips to the easy fast food places, she already had admitted mea culpa to that. What if they were going to develop the disease and follow her down the path to colon cancer?

She had seen blood in her stools and that had been the catalyst for her colon cancer screening. Thankfully that had detected the tumor early and at a treatable stage. She was optimistic she had gained more time. Her life didn't feel like it was ending. Often lately, she felt like every day she was beginning not just to feel better but to be better.

Chapter 12

A
SPECIAL PLANET

THE TIMING COULDN'T HAVE BEEN WORSE. Aubrey's babysitter called to say they had a family medical emergency and she couldn't watch her today. Lindsey's mind raced. It was 5:30 p.m. and she was due to work tonight at 7 filling in for a nurse who was out this week. There was no one to watch Aubrey she could think of on such short notice.

Before she realized what she was doing, she'd called Frank. He'd already gone to the farm to start the milking but she hoped his mind was functioning better than hers and could come up with a solution. She blurted out the problem the minute he answered and waited.

"Bring her here," Frank said. "Bring something for her to do, like the IPod, maybe a coloring book too. I can put her somewhere while we do the milking and I'll watch her. Maybe she can even go in and see Jerry and watch TV with him. We'll figure it out as we go along."

Lindsey's first reaction was to deep six any chance of Aubrey being hurt at the farm with Frank distracted by the farm duties. When he persisted, she relented with a long list of "make sures" that he promised to abide by.

She broke the news to Aubrey as soon as she was dressed. Mommy has to go to work tonight, she said, so she was going to go stay with daddy at the farm.

Aubrey was distracted by her current fourth viewing of her favorite movie and only slightly acknowledged what she was hearing.

She added the part of the plan involving taking things to do, like the IPod and a coloring book. Daddy will find a safe place where you can play, she explained. They packed a few snacks and rounded up the necessary parts of the emerging puzzle and headed out the door. Frank was in the barn with the milking process underway when they walked in.

Lindsey was glad she'd had a chance to see what the milking was like before she had to leave Aubrey there. She didn't feel worried about the cows hurting her baby, just that Frank might become distracted and Aubrey would wander from her appointed place in the barn.

"Don't go anywhere in this barn except with daddy, you hear," she told Aubrey. "There are a lot of things a little girl can get hurt on in there. Stay right where daddy tells you to stay,"

"I will," Aubrey promised and Lindsey trusted her good child to live up to the promise and said a silent thank you that she was already so mature and trustworthy for a kid.

An upturned pail waited at the far end of the barn. Frank brought Aubrey over and gave her the same lecture.

"Stay over here, sitting on the pail or call me but don't get up and wander around, you hear," he said.

"I know, mommy already told me," she said.

"The cows wouldn't try to hurt you but they are so big they don't realize what they could do to little things like you."

Nelson was smiling to see the little visitor and Frank wondered for the first time about Nelson's personal life. Did he have kids, a girlfriend? He had never made any comments or talked about anyone but he was a young guy, good looking and not likely to be disinterested in having a personal life. That might not be the case, Frank realized, as he struggled in this new country that was supposed to offer so much but was probably just sapping his youth.

"Where's Angel?" Aubrey asked. "Can I see her after?"

Frank had talked about the beautiful heart-shaped new baby so much at home he realized it was no surprise that Aubrey would ask to see her.

"I'm going to give her a bottle of her mommy's milk as soon as we get her mommy in here," Frank said. "You can help."

"Oh, yes, thank you daddy, thank you daddy," she cried.

That promise triggered a question every time a new cow walked into the barn, "Is that Angel's mommy."

Frank finally was able to say yes and Aubrey jumped off her pail. "No, stay over there! Her mommy hasn't given me her milk yet for her baby."

"How does she do that?" Aubrey's eyes were huge saucers.

"I put this machine on her and it sucks the milk out of her," Frank proceeded cautiously, trying to avoid a longer, more in depth

113

explanation. When you were a baby you used to get milk from your mommy too, but you were the little machine that sucked it out, he thought but didn't dare say out loud.

"Does it hurt her?" Aubrey asked.

"I try to make sure it doesn't," Frank answered. "As a matter of fact, I think she feels better after it's done. She gets so full of milk, she wants someone to get it out of her so that's what we do."

"Why does she get so full of milk," Aubrey went on.

"That's what mommies do. They get full of milk for their babies to have lots of good food when they're born."

Here it came. He had stepped into the trap despite his best attempts to avoid it.

"Did my mommy do that for me?"

"Yes, she did and she helped other mommies do it too because she really liked doing it and she wanted every baby to have good milk from their mommies. It's the best thing for babies."

"Angel's mommy's milk is the best thing for her?"

"Yes, for sure," Frank explained.

"Good, I'm gonna help give it to her, right?"

"Yup," Frank promised.

"Yeah!!" Aubrey shouted.

Somehow, Frank earned a period of silence while Aubrey pondered everything she had just learned.

Ada's milking went smoothly and when he finished milking her into a stainless steel milk can, he filled the large plastic baby bottle for her calf. It was nice and warm, like her mom's body, just the right temperature. Frank asked Nelson to get the next two cows so he could go over to the calf pen area and feed Angel.

"Aubrey, look, I have the baby bottle for Angel," he said.

"Where is her mommy?"

"That's her over there with the little bit of white on her face."

"She's big."

"Yes, she's a grown up mommy cow. Angel will get to be big just like her and be a good mommy too."

"How fast will she get big?"

"Not for a pretty long time. You're almost five now, you'll be seven when baby Angel has a baby, I think," Frank quickly calculated.

"I hope I can see baby Angel's baby too," Aubrey said.

"Well let's get her fed so she can grow up fast," Frank offered in an attempt to get moving.

The feeding went well because Angel was a good feeder, taking the large rubber nipple and latching on, sucking with consistency and vigor till she had drained the entire bottle.

"Did she have enough?" Aubrey asked.

"I think so."

"How do you know?"

"Well most of the baby cows have a bottle and they're all set."

"Maybe she wants a little more," Aubrey said, sounding just like her mother, Frank thought.

"I don't have any more to give her."

Luckily a kitten scurried by and distracted the next "why" out of Aubrey.

"Stay right here. Don't go running after that kitten, hear me?" Frank cautioned. "I'll be right back."

He went into the milk room to drop off the baby bottle. Nelson had things pretty much wrapped up, equipment torn down, washed and disinfected, hanging in wait for the morning milking.

The night was slated to be an especially warm one and Frank had decided to let the cows pasture out overnight.

Walking back to where he had left Aubrey, he took her by the hand and walked to the back doors of the barn. The herd was clustered in the free stall portion of the barn, probably hoping for just this move on his part.

He latched all the outlets to the rest of the barn and pushed the back door along the metal rail sliding it over to one side. The cows were ready at the first sight of the greenery outside. They amicably ambled out.

Aubrey caught sight of the evergreen woods behind the barn. She was quieter than normal just lost in gazing at the landscape out the back door. She finally offered up her impression.

"It looks like that movie, the one with the little bears who live on a star."

The description wasn't registering with Frank who had a million other things on his mind.

"You know, the one where the big man that's all black with a big mask and he talks funny and makes breathing noises? Remember one of the little bears died. That was so sad."

Frank had it now, the movie she'd finally gotten a chance to see when she feigned insomnia one night as Frank and Lindsey were doing a marathon night.

Looking at the farm fields laid out till they reached a tall stand of pines, the sweep of the Earth's horizon close up, he agreed with

Aubrey's description, it perfectly matched the movie—just needed an extra moon.

"I think you're right, baby. This might be the very same place." Frank answered.

His clear-sighted little girl recognized this scene as the lush, forested planet of the movie. He had to agree with her assessment. They lived in a place full of feisty, little fuzzballs too and they were under attack from a high-tech enemy that seemed to have a big advantage. He saw himself as a character in that same kind of drama, standing with his only weapon, the stick end of the broom he was leaning against.

Ingenuity was on their side and he could bring some of that to a fight but victory for this place was probably just the stuff of theatre and not reality, he feared. Not that his warrior heart didn't warm to the lure of the battle.

Chapter 13

JULIE

FRANK HAD NEVER SEEN IT HAPPEN but he knew what he was looking at as he got close to Julie. A large bloody mass stretched from her body and an enormous calf stood nearby, looking petrified. Another day starting with a lurch of his stomach, he thought, but didn't dwell on that long. He walked to Julie's head and bent over putting his hand on her, trying to make reassuring noises. She was splayed across the floor and his words were wasted, he realized. He was not going to be able to do anything for her. She was gone.

The size of her calf had strained her uterus and it had prolapsed, coming out as she pushed to expel the large baby. The old timers called it "casting her withers." It was often a death knell, even if Frank had been there and could have gotten the vet here quickly.

Julie was one of the best producers in the barn. Her milk outlay was always five gallons per day at the height of her cycle. He had been counting on that wonderful influx of milk to boost the farm income. Looking at this beautiful animal who had already given so much in all her milking days and now was giving up her life trying to do it again, he felt the lump grow in his throat, the burning pain in his nostrils as he struggled to hold back tears. What good would that do, he argued with himself. It was not worth the delay in getting to all the rest of his load.

He moved slowly toward the calf. She looked healthy and also looked about a month old, one of the contributing factors to her mom's death, Frank realized. This old cow should have been bred to a bull with a history of small calves. He was glad to have the new girl in the herd but trying to calculate the loss of Julie right now was beyond anything he could think about. He reached for a length of bailing twine that was hanging nearby and tied the calf's neck with it, attaching the other end to a barn post.

With the baby secured, he walked slowly to Julie's head, kneeling beside her and placing his hand on her face. Her markings were recognizable, dark stripes around her eyes, against a light cream contrast coat. Frank thought about all the days he had seen her approaching and realized he'd been happy to milk this girl. Her even temperament, easy letdown reflex, she'd given him few issues, not a memory of her having mastitis. It had been easy to take her presence for granted, he thought, lulled into thinking she was immune to vagaries of genetics and age coupled with bad luck. This day was one of those when he wasn't sure he wanted to be involved in dairy farming. It was filling some primal need in him but also sucking out of him deeper emotions than anything he wanted to feel. He collected himself and forced his thoughts to remedies for her loss and more scrambling to try to keep this farm afloat. A few promising heifers that Jerry had bought almost two years ago were going to probably be the saving grace, Frank thought, thankful that he was following in the footsteps of a very good farmer who thought ahead. Jerry couldn't have been planning on losing Julie when he made the decision to buy young stock but it was looking like a great call in hindsight. It would take a few first calf heifers to offset Julie though, he said, a belated compliment to her by way of a farewell.

Frank went in to break the news to Jerry.

"She was a great cow," was about all Jerry could muster.

They talked about how she had been bred to a small Jersey bull that was supposed to produce smaller than average babies. Although confined to the house, the old farmer was teaching Frank so much and in the area of breeding he was an encyclopedia of information. Julie was an older cow and he had tried to pick the right bull so this kind of disaster didn't happen. The problem is so many factors are at play, Jerry told Frank, you can only do so much and then fate steps in with an iron hand.

The science of genetics is integral to dairy farming but no one keeps a bull on the farm any more, Jerry said. They all use artificial insemination on their cows picking bulls from a list of their statistics, male vs. female offspring, calf size, and the daughter's milk volumes. Nothing is certain but you make your best guess and hope you're right.

Frank had been noticing how strong the mothers and daughters shared genetic tendencies, like their coloring, stature, conformation and even personalities. He mentioned how he had noticed some things while milking Caroline. She had a stance that was just like her mother Cloe's. It was a knock need kind of tilt to her legs that made it hard to put on the inflations. There wasn't much room to get to each teat because both these girls acted like they were trying to cross their legs, maybe to keep from getting pregnant, Frank couldn't help but jokingly consider.

He wondered if Jerry was aware of it. Right after he said it, Frank knew Jerry had noticed that and lots more that he had yet to see.

Jerry's face was sad, like a man with no place to go but a yearning to get there.

"Cows are animals you're working with to make a living," he said. "They aren't supposed to get under your skin and they aren't supposed to become your pets. It's not going to make it any easier for you to be a dairy farmer," Jerry said, "but I envy you. You're noticing things it took me years to realize."

Frank was still in the dark about exactly what Jerry meant but he knew there was more about to pour out of this usually quiet guy.

"You don't have to notice anything to get milk out of a cow, except where the teats are." Jerry said. "Put the milkers on, get them done and out the door. If I hadn't done that for most of my years, I wouldn't be here today talking to you about this."

"Somewhere along the line, though, I slowed down, had fewer cows to milk. I saw new things I had been missing about these animals. Like those very strong genetic similarities from how fast they eat their food to how they stand. You're absolutely right about Caroline and Cloe and I would put money on Chrissy being the same as soon as she's old enough to calf.

There were a few girls who caught his attention, Jerry recalled, that was the beginning of it. They became his special cows and they seemed to sense it. Usually he fell for the pretty face, the markings and the look in their eyes. The smart ones with a striking face, he started paying more attention to them, maybe out of boredom after all the years of seeing them all as one big group. Next thing he knew, he was noticing more and more things about the cows and catering to them like kids.

"Do you think I should stop looking so closely at them," Frank asked.

"It's up to you. I can't see that it makes this business any easier but I can't stop it now that I've started. Don't know as you will be able to either."

"What's the harm?" Frank asked. "It does slow me down a little but I was thinking it might come in handy to be a little more aware of each cow's quirks, so to speak."

"The problem is the dairy industry," Jerry said. "It's not a cow daycare or nursing home system. It's a use-them-up and call-the-knacker when-they're-through business. This isn't about having happy cows and keeping animals that don't earn their keep. It's about making money from a product that people want that these cows make, the white creamy stuff they would be feeding to their calves."

"Maybe there's room for happy cows," Frank offered. "There are a lot of people like those two women who buy raw milk. They'd like nothing better than to have me tell them all my cows are happy and that makes happy milk."

"They'd only pay so much for a gallon of happy milk," Jerry countered. "Even the most crazed animal activist still has a limit on what they think a gallon of milk should cost."

"Just how much is that and just how many people are there out there who want only a high quality glass of milk not a store bought brand?" Frank wondered aloud.

"What do you think? People seem to be drinking less and less milk, probably because it tastes so bad from the big dairies. Maybe if it tasted better, people would be willing to pay more," Frank looked at Jerry for an answer.

"They probably won't stop needing milk. Pizza cheese isn't going anywhere from what I can tell but that cheese isn't produced from good quality milk. They can make that cheese out of all kinds of low quality milk and people aren't any the wiser," Jerry offered.

"Cereal comes to mind. People do like a little milk on their cereal. How about milk or cream in your coffee? Even if they drink fewer glasses of milk with a sleeve of cookies, my personal favorite, the world can't exist without milk so it has to be a good line of work to be involved in," Frank persisted.

"Milk can be made for the entire country from a few huge commercial dairies. They can process the living daylights out of it so it barely resembles the original thing, maybe even powder most of it or do God knows what new iteration to it. The important thing seems to be that the right people make a ton of profit selling the junk. There's nothing in this business that has anything to do with happy animals," Jerry's treatise ended.

"I'm pretty sure that what you're saying is true for the majority of the country but I'd like to think there is some small bunch of milk drinkers who don't want cows and local dairy farms to all become extinct," Frank countered.

"The truth is we've already let so many great cows genetic lines become extinct, I can't image where this will all end," Jerry said. "The government's been no help. Swear all they care is that someone who's a big campaign contributor is making money from the dairy co-op system so they stay in office."

"I'm sorry," Jerry said. "I just let you hear a side of me I don't usually listen to or let anyone get a glimpse of. It's the side of me that's developed a bad case of resentment over how dairy farmers have been treated. Most of my friends are long gone from this business. They told me to get out hundreds of times over the years so I have no one to blame but myself for staying. I never could and I don't want to start trying to figure out why I couldn't do it. It's too late for that."

"It's very obvious to me, Jerry, that you've been a good dairy farmer and that you have loved doing it," Frank cautiously offered. He didn't want to try to counsel this man on farming or life by any means. He had never been inclined towards doing anything like that with anyone but he couldn't keep quiet letting Jerry think his life's work had been for nothing, for his farm to reach a dead end.

He wasn't sure yet that he would keep it going. He was sure this farm had already played a special place in his life, from his time learning years ago to now when he felt he was coming into his own sense of purpose being here every day.

"There has to be dairy farms and cows," Frank said. "I want my daughter to see cows here when she's all grown up and I want them to be on this farm."

"Wishing it won't make it come true," Jerry said. "but I hope more than anything that you get that wish. Wishes can only become realities with support and a plan and New England dairy farms have neither."

"There's supposedly some suits sitting around USDA offices in Washington mulling the question of how to keep farms in New

England," Jerry almost choked as he said it. "At least there's some feeling that there is someone in this country's government whose job it is to keep good, fresh milk flowing. I certainly have never seen any good results or ideas coming out of that bunch. They've never even set foot in a barn much less been up close and personal with a cow," he said. "What they decide has to be something than can be factored into a computer program."

"I think someone should consult with the USDA about what it's like out here in the trenches," Frank said.

"You and me both but that isn't likely to happen. I've been in this business all my life and it's a number of incredibly stupid decisions that have gotten the dairy farms of today to the place we're at, fighting what seems to be a losing battle against mega dairies somewhere far away. Government help is the biggest reason this industry is a mess and government help won't get us out of it," Jerry stated with finality.

Frank called it a day and headed home, hoping for the comfort he counted on to soothe the day's stabs.

Once he had described Julie's death to Lindsey, she insisted on Googling a prolapsed uterus in cows. The YouTube video was pretty graphic, showing a uterus completely hanging outside a cow's body. That animal had survived it and the farmer had been able to clean and reinsert it quickly.

Also, that cow hadn't severed the veins and arteries that Julie had severed and that had killed her, bleeding to death. Lindsey's medical background still didn't make it easy to view now that she had started coming more regularly to the farm to help Frank. It didn't seem to her to be much different from losing a patient at the nursing home, especially the sweet ones.

She walked over to the small cabinet in the corner of the kitchen and took out her favorite after dinner tonic, Chambord.

"Can I get you some Bulleit?"

"Yeah, and we'll toast her. Julie was worth the price of good liquor."

Chapter 14

BOVINE
EQUITY

WHAT LOOKED LIKE A CHECK STUB was laid open on the kitchen table, obviously waiting to be shown to someone when Frank got into the kitchen for breakfast. He was curious and interested but scared at the same time. The information probably was going to confirm his worst fears, that there was no future in dairy farming.

"This is what they call the net proceeds due us this week. Farm gets two of these every month for about the same amount," Jerry said. "It ain't pretty but I thought you should know sooner than later."

The check was for just under $5,000 and even though Frank had been warned it wasn't going to be a lot, he did a double take at the number.

"We can barely pay for the grain and hay with that," he said.

There would be a little more, that would come in a separate check, for the butterfat, Jerry added. Thank God the girls were big on making butter-fat because it's the only fat around here, he sighed.

"How have you been even keeping this place going?" asked Frank. "What have you been using to keep the lights on in that barn?"

He thought maybe he was being a little too nosey but the question had been asked before he could take it back. The problem of finances had started to loom over the farm more and more since he and Lindsey had begun seriously contemplating either buying the farm or at least making a more permanent arrangement with Jerry.

"It sure ain't this check," Jerry admitted. "Did you see the price of milk per hundred weight is down to almost $15. My father was getting almost that back in the '50's. The highest I've ever seen it get up to is a little more than $24. Do you know of anything that hasn't doubled in price in 50 years?"

"Then of course you have to deduct the fees and charges from the co-op. There's the membership fee, marketing and government assessments for all the dairy research they're doing on our behalf. Don't forget the transportation charges. I was paying less than $2 a gallon for gas this past winter but do you think that fee went down?"

"I got insurance through this bunch, but don't try to collect on that either. When the silo was damaged in a bad storm and I tried to get the insurance to pay for it, they said it was an act of God. I said, not the God I know but that didn't change matters."

"If my sister wasn't well off, this place would have been sold already," Jerry admitted. "She's been sending over supplements, so to speak. Not that I want her to but I couldn't stop her. She knows what the situation is around here."

Tricia had found a great guy, he said, a man who had the brains for these new things called computers. That was back in the late '70s' early '80s. Her husband, Denis, had seen a future in the new machines and moved them out to California where they were really taking off back then. His career in computers had taken off too and they had wanted for little since the early days of their marriage. Jerry was glad for Tricia. If ever there was a woman who deserved a great life it was his big sister. She'd been not only sister to him but even a little like a second mother after their father died. He'd been a thorn in her side sometimes, he remembered, but she had loved him to pieces even when he didn't deserve it and their bond was rock solid, built of cement that they both knew nothing would ever shake, not even the distance between the East and West coasts.

It didn't really surprise Jerry that Tricia didn't let the farm finances out of her sight. She demanded and got a periodic update and even 3,000 miles away, always identified just about how short he was going to fall. The checks were always in the mail shortly after the update had been provided. Without them, he fully realized, he'd have gone out of the dairy business long ago.

The writing on the wall for the future though, was that a new farmer might be in the works, one who didn't have a well-off sister. Jerry figured he better come clean to Frank about just how awful the financial realities of New England dairy farming were.

"This check isn't going to go up. Milk is likely to drop under $15 in the coming months," Jerry went on. "Did I mention there was no money in dairy farming?"

"I did get the warning up front," Frank could only half smile at the attempt at humor. "Really though, how can they get away with paying you so little for this milk? The price of milk at the store hasn't gone down, why are you getting paid less? Every one drinks milk. We're making something that everyone wants."

"Somewhere in California, I heard, they're probably making as much milk as we make in a year in a single day," Jerry said. "There are farms with 10,000 cows making more than anyone can drink."

"What good is that to people on the East Coast?" Frank said pleadingly. "That's only about 3,000 miles away. Even in a refrigerator truck, that stuff can't be anything great when it gets here."

"You don't have to go that far. New York has some pretty huge dairies too. Those farms are major industry, even pollute the air around them like a factory, I've read. Doesn't matter how they make the stuff, as long as there's a lot of milk being made somewhere, they just process it and move it, ultra-pasteurized, dried, made into cheese. It doesn't matter if there's fresh fluid milk in close proximity to where people live anymore," Jerry explained.

"The government made a show of caring about keeping dairies in business across the country so fresh milk would be available without trucking it 1,000 miles but that went by the wayside. They haven't had any real legislation that does New England any good in years. This area is probably drinking mostly New York and Pennsylvania milk, a little local stuff but not even 2 percent, I'd guess." Jerry came back.

"Doesn't the government regulate milk production in some way anymore?" Frank asked.

"Now you're getting into a minefield. The government's involvement is probably the biggest reason this milk business is such a mess. They started out acting like they were trying to make sure the whole country always had plenty of fresh milk but once every politician in the last 60 years had gotten his hand in this thing, it's become a nightmare."

"Doesn't seem like they're making sure there's fresh milk over here," Frank said.

"Mostly, the USDA is only concerned about the big farms and whether the country has too much or too little milk overall," Jerry said. "They've had as many programs to kill off dairy herds as they have stuck up for them. The first one I remember was back in the 80's. I knew some farmers that took advantage of it. Land prices were sky high and that's when the developers were hanging around at the door of a farmer with a nice flat, open field that made for cheap land development."

Jerry described how quickly the subdivisions were cropping up where once there were open fields. The pace of suburban sprawl in the 1980's produced a transformation of farmland to housing subdivisions. He estimated that he personally had seen 10 farms in his small corner of the world lost to development in that short frenzied period. It had been at just about that point that the government added an enticement to get farmers to help reduce the country's overall milk production.

"I had some of the best cows I think I had ever bred. They were almost all great milkers, healthy, good dispositions. It had taken me years to have such a wonderful herd. USDA offered the dairy herd buyout because they thought there were too many cows and the only way to fix the situation was to turn off the spigot of milk, like there's a faucet on them damn cows."

Frank had never heard about the program and almost found it hard to believe that the government would be urging dairy farmers to get out.

"You had to either send the herd to slaughter or send them out of the country and stay out of dairy farming for five years if you participated in the buyout," Jerry explained. "I would have rather cut off my right arm than do that to those girls. Do you have any idea how much great dairy stock was just destroyed as though the genetic pool of those animals was garbage? We've lost that pool and we will never get it back. It's extinct."

"They just had another buyout in 2009 but I stopped even looking at those programs after that first one. All it showed was how little those suits understood about what dairy farming, good dairy farming, was all about, where the cows and the milk they make are a thing to take pride in and fight to preserve."

Jerry had been getting stronger, moving around the house, doing some chores but this conversation sank him into his chair like the day he'd come home from the hospital. He took a sip of the special tea he'd started drinking every day, a brew of honey and lemon maybe mixed with a few other ingredients.

"So, I wanted to show this check to you and talk about some way for me to pay you back for everything you've been doing," Jerry changed track. "You can see there's no way I can give you real money, but I thought maybe I could sign over some of the cows to you. Depending on how long we keep going like this, you get a new cow for every month or so you work here. They're going for around $1,000 a head these day. You showed up in January and it's already June so I already owe you six cows."

"What am I going to do with the cows?" Frank shot back.

"They're yours to sell if you decide you aren't interested in milking them," Jerry replied. "That will pay you back for your efforts at least a little."

"Who would I sell them to? I can't sell them to the cattle dealer and sleep at night any more than you would be able to," Frank admitted.

"Then we're both fools," Jerry sighed.

"If you were my son, Frank, I'd tell you to hold onto land, as much land as possible," Jerry said, offering advice, not something he did a lot so he had his attention. "The land is what made America a great place, some place worth fighting for ever since the first settlers set their eyes on this."

"Yeah, they probably couldn't believe their eyes," Frank offered. "So much of it not a bunch of desert or ice blocks. The forests must have blown them away with giant trees like nothing they'd ever seen."

"Land holds its value, I can tell you that," Jerry offered. "When I was about your age, the price of real estate around here doubled and tripled in value in about five years. I talked with my mom about selling to the developers. They were just about killing each other to try to get their hands on this place," Jerry said.

"Why didn't you sell out?" Frank wondered aloud.

"I'm not 100% sure exactly why or that we were right not to," Jerry smiled. "At the time, I thought the land would keep going up and wanted to keep it so we'd make more when the right time came."

"How does it compare now to what you were offered back more than 30 years ago?"

Jerry started mumbling numbers like, $100,000 and now maybe $800,000 or $900,000. He remembered the conversations with his mom about what they'd do with the money they were being offered back in 1980. The farmhouse and 80 acres could have brought them almost $150,000 which seemed like a million back then.

His mom's health had long ago been compromised by her sacrifices for her family. She'd missed so many nights of sleep the deep circles under her eyes were old news that Jerry had stopped noticing. She was still more active than most but she knitted less, strained more to open and close handles and started finally falling asleep with some unfinished chore held in those hard-working hands.

She had been the one to put up the stronger protest against selling out. Her words came back to Jerry now as he heard himself throwing out advice. She did not want her son to lose this land, a good patch of farmland that once paved over for driveways and rooftops would be lost forever. "My mom saw the value of keeping farms around back then and didn't let it go," Jerry said.

The bottom had fallen out of the real estate market as the years progressed so the window of opportunity to cash in closed almost as quickly as it had opened. There weren't as many people fueling the suburban sprawl of New England now or developers with new plans. Many of the last proposals to hit the planning departments during the boom years were more than 20 years on the drawing board before finally seeing completion, Jerry told Frank. Real estate values did rebound eventually so the decision to hold on to land had been a wise one, he added. He doubted it would ever be a bad investment.

Farming though was a different issue, figuring out how to support a farm business when the only thing really going up in value was the land the farm was on. Jerry had watched farm after farm go by the wayside as the value of the land became the only remaining asset.

States, natural conservation districts, private land trusts even national preservation associations put together financial packages that lured the best of them out of the farming business, Jerry said. The many vagaries of life dealt people situations where illness, deaths or some unimaginable other tragedy led to a deal to sell out.

"If I didn't know better, I would almost think there was a conspiracy to take land away from all the old timers, the families who grabbed hold of as much land as possible when they first got to this new place, America" Jerry said. "We're heading back into the kind of world where really wealthy people own land and the rest of the poor suckers just get to have the sheriff come and collect the taxes, like in Robin Hood."

"I remember that story from the Disney cartoon. I loved how Robin Hood let the Sheriff of Nottingham have it," Frank joked. "What do you mean, heading back into that kind of world?"

"We've had hundreds of years of a lot of little people owning enough land to sustain themselves, maybe even make some money, like growing crops or having cows. That era in America was the best one. It's pretty much gone."

"I think you're right, about trying to own land, a good size piece and one that gives you a chance to make some money from it," Frank said.

"Well, good luck trying to do that in your daughter's generation. She'll be living in a world where a lot of this country is tied up tight by a small bunch of very rich people, I'm afraid."

"I don't want to see that for her," Frank said.

"Don't give up on this place, then," Jerry asked. "We could come up with some way for you to farm this place and make a go of it. I wouldn't tell you that if I didn't think we could find a way."

Frank felt a wave of energy run up his spine and his brain shook with the blunt statement from the old pro. He wanted to sit down right there and hear a plan that he could then run home and talk about with Lindsey. They'd thrown out possibilities of how they might make the farm work but this was the first time Jerry had offered to advise them on what he saw.

"Gee, Jerry, Lindsey and I would really want to sit down with you and talk about that," Frank finally blurted out.

"Let's do it."

"Is now too soon?" Frank laughed. "I'll get Lindsey's schedule and we'll try to figure out a good time, OK?

"Don't wait too long," Jerry quipped. "I might do some other stupid thing and put myself even further out of commission."

Driving home, Frank devised his whole delivery of the news, like "You'll never guess what Jerry said today!"

He ended up getting home to Lindsey down with something that had the look of either food poisoning or a bad stomach bug. He didn't bring up the farm at all just took over care of Aubrey, giving her a simple quick grilled cheese dinner, reading her a story and telling Lindsey just to try to relax and feel better.

The plans to thwart the bad guys from taking all the land away from the little guys would just have to wait.

Chapter 15

FLOWER
GIRL

LINDSEY'S SISTER HAD BROKEN THE NEWS to Aubrey almost a year ago. Her services were needed as a flower girl. Leah was marrying Rob after a long test period of living together. The news was not totally a surprise, more likely an indication that Leah's clock had struck the hour and the next news would be a new niece or nephew for Aubrey.

The announcement hit Aubrey just as Lindsey had expected. She excitedly bounced like a beach ball up and down. At just five-years-old, she knew friends who had done this and they all had shown her pictures of their beautiful dresses and flowers and the wonderful places they had been to for the big wedding party. She couldn't wait.

Frank had known for a long time about this event too but couldn't have predicted where or what he might be doing when the big day finally arrived. He found he wasn't able to join in with the exuberance of his daughter. His initial response to the news that he and Lindsey were also being asked to be bridesmaid and usher had been low key.

Once she reminded him that the day was approaching and they had to start making more arrangements for fittings and rehearsals, Lindsey had expected more enthusiasm from Frank but his reaction had grown closer to terror. The expenses were not exactly a luxury he could afford, but the time away from the farm that the wedding would require was the bigger hurdle. He already hated to leave for the Reserve weekends knowing what the price was.

This was not negotiable or something he could politely turn down. His daughter would be a flower girl, dressed like the little version of the bride he better start preparing himself to have in the future. And it wasn't that Frank didn't like Lindsey's sister and Rob. Her big, close family of four brothers and sisters was something he envied.

Frank's brother, Chris, was somewhere on the West Coast patrolling for minisubs full of drugs. The two kept somewhat in touch through e-mail, but they hadn't spent much time together since Chris' graduation and commissioning. They had reached a point in both their lives when they didn't need to huddle together as tight anymore. That hadn't been true before the accident.

Frank had an efficiency apartment at that time but moved back to the family home almost on the night his parents died. The brothers wandered through the aftermath of their parents' death, paperwork for insurance claims, death certificates, funeral arrangements, two young men so far removed from any familiarity with this kind of duty it might have been comic to someone with a twisted sense of humor. They formed a team, bouncing all the questions they had off one another in the hopes that the other one had some information on this topic.

Losing even one of their parents wasn't on their radar. His mom and dad had been in the prime of their lives involved in all kinds of things, community organizations, part of a social circle that included friends from their youth or the latest newcomers in the neighborhood. The wake had been somewhat easy given how many people came and the positive distraction of all their comments, their memories of the good times as well as the lavishing of praise for the people his parents had been.

Chris's life moved on quickly after their death. He had already been accepted to the Coast Guard Academy and moved out shortly after to start school. He'd been a good cadet too, maybe more so due to the fact that he had grown up quickly just before starting. Now he was on to the next chapter, serving in the Pacific.

They both knew they were definitely there for each other but neither of them was the needy type that made a distress call easily.

Lindsey's family, the Keanes, on the other hand, were made up of frequent Facebook updaters, a sort of uni-family always checking on one another and involved in everything they were doing. Frank and Lindsey's wedding had almost exploded the capability of the internet to handle all the postings. This one would be no different.

Leah would be planning a unique but lavish bash, Frank laughed, because she was the baby of the family, the princess. He thanked his lucky stars again, that he had gotten the oldest daughter, a more realistic woman who hadn't insisted on the most expensive of everything for their wedding. Even with all the advance notice, Frank was a little surprised at the time frame that Lindsey laid out for him. The big day was now one month away. The spacious backyard at his in-laws home would be turned into a formal dining room, complete with lighted tent, dance floor, ceremonial arch etc. The choice of location for the wedding gave him some comfort. He knew how long it took to reach his in-law's house, two and a half hours unless it was the middle of rush hour traffic, which this wouldn't likely coincide with. He optimistically hoped he could enjoy this party with Lindsey's family doing something they did well, celebrate each other's milestones. He was due at the tux rental chain next week for a fitting. By then Lindsey and the girls would all be putting the finishing touches on their ensembles from head to toe.

He started to formulate the plans for leaving the farm work to Nelson and whatever cousin he would bring in. He would be able to give him some warning and let him line up his helper this time and Nelson could bring the guy to the farm so that he could meet him and maybe even give him some training.

Worse case, he thought, it will be like a practice session for the looming week away he was going to have to take to fulfill his annual Reserve training. He'd done six weekends away all with some variation on the same result. He returned to work undone, or done poorly. Farm work attracted few except those who saw it as a way to escape a life of poverty south of the border. They didn't come with a lot of schooling or agricultural experience but they had strong backs and worked cheap. He was happy to have them because the alternative was doing everything himself then he'd never be able to get away.

Arriving home one night he found the girls talking about the wedding. Aubrey was old enough to understand her role and young enough to still be the perfect picture of innocence. Lindsey was more excited to see her daughter in the wedding than her own part but she was happy for Leah and also praying for the niece or nephew that would be coming along once this step was taken.

"How are the bridesmaid and flower girl doing?" he joined in.

"Daddy, I can't wait. My dress is purple like mommy's and I'm getting a little basket to hold. The flowers are going to be in pieces and I'm going to throw them out of the basket."

"You are going to be the best flower girl ever," he told her, scooping her into his lap as he lowered himself into the kitchen chair.

"You smell poopy," Aubrey reminded him. He'd only taken off his boots at the door but still had the day's farm clothes on his back, fully stocked with aromas.

"You better start now, daddy," Aubrey offered. "If you wash up real good every day, you won't stink for Aunt Leah's wedding."

***

The light went on almost exactly as the minister pronounced Leah and Rob man and wife. Frank's blood went cold as death and he didn't even smile along with the rest of the wedding party, something that was captured clearly in a picture the photographer snapped.

He had to get in touch with Nelson. A cow he hoped would clear up a lingering case of mastitis was taking a turn for the worse and he had treated her with antibiotics last night. He tried to steer clear of using the medicine on the cows. If a cow had any trace of antibiotic in her system, it would be in her milk. If it was in her milk, that milk had to be totally discarded, not even fed to her baby.

The consequences of doing anything else with milk from a cow on antibiotics were dire. The entire bulk tank of milk could become contaminated and have to be thrown away. And even more drastic, if the bulk tank contained antibiotic tainted milk and the co-op truck came to pick up the milk, the entire tanker would be contaminated and the cost of throwing all that milk away would fall on the farmer responsible. Every pickup included a sample of milk that was tested at the plant. Any problems with milk from a number of causes and most especially, any trace of antibiotics, and the farmer whose bulk tank was the source of the contamination was readily identified and charged for the loss of the whole load. That kind of financial crisis could wipe Jerry out, Frank knew.

He had heard it a thousand times from Jerry, be careful. Make sure you know which cow you treated and make double sure her milk is discarded. He was already blaming the chaos of the pre-wedding preps and the fact that he had decided to drive home, do the morning milking and then drive back to his in-laws. He had pushed the envelope and now there could be a huge price to pay.

His first problem was getting away from the happy moment. Everyone was forming the receiving line and he knew Lindsey was trying to catch his eye and have him move over to stand beside her. He had his cellphone in his pocket and had promised not to take it out during the entire day but this was an emergency. He tried Nelson's phone, a text that he hoped would be a quick end to this problem. He would tell Nelson to throw away Eva's milk until he got back. He really shouldn't have started the antibiotic without being there.

He went over to Lindsey and she gave him a "look" about having the phone out but he summarized as quick as he could and she understood. He'd read her the same riot act about being careful which cows are treated and discarding all that milk.

Nelson didn't respond and the minutes each were a painful ticking like a time bomb that he couldn't' disarm. He survived the entire receiving line. Before he joined the rest of the wedding party to be introduced and seated he had to contact someone to get the message to Nelson. He hoped Jerry might answer his phone but that was a long shot. The man ignored most electronics unless he had a compelling reason not to. Another obstacle was going to be that Jerry was only just getting mobility. He would have to go out to the barn and find Nelson to tell him.

He rang the house and of course no one picked up. An answering machine was attached to the phone but usually it was full and Jerry didn't worry about deleting messages. He could only hope he'd have a small window of message space still working.

Someone finally had taken his side. The machine picked up and offered, "Please leave a message at the tone."

"Hi Jerry. Frank calling. Please try to tell Nelson he has to dump Eva's milk. I gave her a dose of penicillin. He can't dump her milk in the tank. I tried calling him but can't get him to answer. If you can call me back, I would appreciate that and I know, you told me a thousand times. I am so sorry."

He tried to participate in this beautiful day, his daughter's radiance and his wife looked amazing too, something he was in danger of forgetting since they got out so seldom. Lindsey had her auburn hair up and littered with small white flowers, and the dark plum sateen dress was short and formfitting. He knew the other women in the party were wearing variations of the same dress but to his eyes, no one looked as good as Lindsey and he hoped to tell her and show her.

Angry with himself and almost distraught with worry, he stumbled through a lot of the functions, gliding into the tent with both

Lindsey and Aubrey on his arms, somehow stuffing some food into his mouth to make it look like he could eat and his stomach wasn't in a knot, even holding Lindsey for a slow dance but he was only half there. His head was in the barn.

Jerry was only half awake but the tone of Frank's voice on the answering machine stirred him. He was saying something that was a problem, he could tell even in a slight daze. His stiff neck and shoulder slowed him down as he moved to pick up in time. He reached the phone table and replayed the message.

Disappointment in Frank only crossed his mind for an extremely brief moment and then he felt a course of adrenalin kick in like in a previous life. His farm was in the crosshairs and he was needed. It didn't matter that he'd only walked out to the barn with help so far, he was going to go find Nelson and hopefully in time to stop disaster.

Looking at the time Jerry gauged that Nelson had started milking the cows but probably only a handful so far. Hopefully Eva wasn't one of the hungry girls tonight, one of the ones pushing to be first. He strained his brain to remember where she usually fell in the order, not a forced order but just a natural one the cows seemed to agree to impose on themselves. Eva came in with her sister Edith, he thought, and those two would be at best in the middle of the pack, not the first or the last. He believed he could make it.

He hadn't gone out to the barn much since his injury. Inside, he was cautious to hold onto furniture and counters but he would need to make the wide open space of about 40 feet between the house and milk room. His strength to move just about anything heavier than a feather was disgusting him by the time he pulled his jacket on. He was breathing hard and sweating. He forced himself to calm down for just a moment before he tried the stairs. Falling and getting hurt again was not going to help anyone, he told himself.

His injured right side needed to be the last part of him down each step. He tried to hold the side of the wall and edge over the stairs slowly, making sure he kept upright.

He pushed open the outside door and called out as loud as he could, "Nelson!!!!, Nelson!!!,"

No answer but he didn't really expect it. He eyed the most direct path to the milk room, started to maneuver over the rough dirt driveway, calling Nelson's name with each step.

As he got closer, seemingly after an eternity of time, he heard loud Spanish music which explained why no one had heard phones ringing or his screaming. He fell against the door and yelled again. This time he got a response, a sound that indicated someone had heard him.

Nelson's surprised look was cut short by a bark of Jerry's voice. "Eva, did you milk Eva yet?"

His young helper looked like his brain had frozen and no answer came out. Jerry kept up, "You have to remember if you milked Eva yet. Frank treated her this morning. You can't put her milk in the tank!!"

Nelson's face showed the reality—he hadn't been paying attention to which cows he'd milked. To him they all blurred together. He'd gone through the right process technically but not with the kind of attention to each cow that Jerry and Frank continued to try to get him to understand. That meant they had to find Eva and examine her to see if she had been milked. Her coat was a roan red like a lot of the other girls so she didn't stick out readily. She had some unique marks, though, like a white blaze on the top of her neck and she had a small knob of a horn left on the right side of her head. Jerry knew he wasn't up to moving into the herd to try to find her.

"Nelson, get Eva. I need to see if she's been milked and if her milk is in that tank, we're dumping it."

The wait to see Nelson returning with the cow in question was almost more than Jerry could stand. He gripped the wooden doorframe, not just to keep his balance but also to squeeze strength out of the very structure of the sturdy building. He'd been in this position of his own making so he had nothing but sympathy for Frank. The farm was a wonderful combination of so many interesting puzzles to solve, challenges to overcome. It also was a mountain of information to keep straight about machinery, supplies and the long list of things related to the cows.

The wait was interminable and Jerry found himself thinking back on the night of his first anniversary. Joanie had done something very pretty with that shiny, blond hair he loved so much. It was kind of up and things were tucked in to make it swoop. He was sure there had been a name for the hairdo, but dammed if he had any idea what it was. They had agreed to have dinner in the big city at an Italian restaurant. She had called to make a reservation, trying to make sure they got in and out quick enough for Jerry's small tolerance for being away from the farm.

They'd ordered and the appetizers had arrived when he stopped chewing and just looked at her. He didn't remember the exact chain of events after that but he definitely remembered leaving with most of a chicken dinner in a doggy bag. They got back in time to stop the possible calamity that night and he was saying an earnest prayer that he could call Frank soon and tell him the same result.

He knew Frank didn't make this mistake on purpose but that didn't make it any easier. Another day in farming, with a life and death sentence hanging over your head, he had almost started to forget.

A bovine face appeared at the milk room door and Jerry quickly looked to the right where a knob of horn bone should be and then to her upper back for the spot of white. They were there and now he dared to look below at her udder. He bent over to make sure he was right. Her udder was pulled tight over a full load of milk waiting to be taken from her. He thanked Eva for being slow to get into the barn tonight.

"Maybe you knew, even if Nelson didn't," Jerry intoned in her ear.

Frank hadn't stopped looking at his phone even as he tried to be present at what was a very nice wedding. He had particularly tried to make sure Aubrey's big moments weren't missed, the walk into the tent splaying just the right amount of rose petals, her photo shoot with Leah and the entire wedding party. She had been the perfect wedding party member, waiting her turn and smiling for all she was worth.

His phone finally toned and Jerry's name appeared. He almost didn't want to know but answered.

"Jerry, did you get there in time?"

"Yes, Nelson hadn't milked her yet. He made sure to throw her milk out," Jerry said. "Don't be too hard on yourself. Truth be told, I'm guilty of doing pretty much the same thing and lots worse."

"I am so sorry, Jerry," Frank started.

He was cut off, only because Jerry needed to go not only sit down but lie down.

"Tomorrow will be here before you know it and you'll have another chance to either screw up or get it right all over again," Jerry said.

"Thank you for caring. Have I told you that you're doing a great job and I am so glad you are working my farm? Well I am and now go have fun for what's left of that party."

Chapter 16

FARMER OF
THE YEAR

WHEN JERRY ENTERED THE BARN after such a long time away, the fact that he was back was not lost on his best girls. After the wedding day crisis, he realized he was better than he thought and needed to re-enter the world of the living. The turn of bovine heads to the sound of his voice, the familiarity without the skittishness of a newcomer were all the signs he had hoped for. He thought they would remember him after all the days he'd been their main caretaker but he'd never been away from them long enough to test his theory.

Putting his hands on a soft, golden coat was therapy stronger than anything he'd been receiving from the professionals. He couldn't get enough of the interaction, his hand sucking energy from their flanks.

He was glad he had lived to see this day but then his eyes focused on this familiar place as though he was a stranger here.

When had those thick cobwebs begun to hold up the corners of the milk room? How had that pile of grain bags, bailing twine, paper towels ever gotten that high. Where were the coats of paint he had imagined were still complete on the walls and trim?

He knew this was none of Frank's doing in the last months. This was his doing in the last 40 years. Everyday he'd done everything until he had nothing left to give and he was seeing, almost with new eyes after his hiatus, just how far that had taken him. Nowhere near where it needed to get, he sighed.

Frank was right by his side not really helping but making sure Jerry's strength didn't suddenly wane. He had gotten the doctor's blessing to come out if he promised just to walk around and stay clear of anything that could hurt him. Just watch. Jerry promised to do that but hoped he could get out there and find himself more capable than the doctor was predicting.

Instead he felt weaker. The sight of so much to do and the realization of just what it would take to do it—that he knew better than anyone—it was exhausting to look at.

He moved away from the cows who were clustered on the far side of a gate that protected Jerry from what was sure to have become a welcoming shoving match. He and Frank moved toward the milk room doorway, Jerry moving slowly, a slight shake of his head apparent every now and then to Frank. He stopped completely at a dust-covered wall hanging that Frank had never really paid attention to before. Jerry lifted it from the nail and wiped it on his shirt sleeve.

"Outstanding Young Farmer of the Year," was clear now to Frank and the seal of the Farm Bureau, the insurance company most farmers belonged to. He leaned forward to get a look at the year but Jerry obliged him with the information.

"Joanie and I were running strong in '72. We were doing so many things here we were nonstop, sunup to sundown. So young we weren't feeling it. I had installed the pipeline that year so we stopped having to lift the milk jugs into a dump station. That took almost an hour off the milking time, a little longer on the clean-up, but well worth it. We were flying through milking some days."

A beautiful girl, his Joan, slim build, bright yellow hair, sparkling blue eyes and a slightly crooked smile that nailed him. She had settled Jerry down pretty fast when he got back from his years in the service. She was a friend of the bride's at a family wedding. He never repaid his cousin for that introduction.

On their second date Jerry piled a picnic basket and Joanie onto the seat of the John Deere. They rode a lazy zigzag through the pastures, Jerry pointing out the towering hemlocks, the mountain laurel in bloom, explaining how well the farm was laid out to take advantage of the sun and yet sheltered from the north winds.

They reached the highest pasture and Jerry positioned the tractor pointed toward the million-dollar view overlooking the barn and house, the fields spread out flat in the distance dotted with golden specks of bovines. He laid a tablecloth in the grass and they enjoyed a simple feast of chicken salad sandwiches, his mom's homemade grape juice and brownies.

It wasn't too much later that Jerry had just blurted out what he'd known when he laid eyes on Joanie, that he wanted to marry her. She hadn't hesitated a moment in saying yes. They married and settled into one side of the family duplex.

Joanie was a spitfire of activity and interested in everything. She'd dug up all kinds of scattered little areas and planted rows of peas over here, strawberries over there, a bigger spot for the tomatoes, peppers, zucchini and anything else she could find time to grow.

She learned the dairy business and took on the responsibility of dispensing medication. Jerry had been so proud of her, glad she had relieved him of his least favorite job. Their life was a continuity of early rising, non-stop chores, short food breaks where they'd quickly tumble out all the challenges they were facing and give each other a pep talk before moving back into the fray. Jerry had known even as they were living that life, it was the best days he'd ever experience.

They thought they had a lot of time to start a family but breast cancer took her only five years into their marriage. There would never be anyone else in Jerry's arms.

"I remember Joanie bought me a new shirt the night of the annual district meeting," Jerry said returning to the present. "like maybe she had been given a tip-off. I almost busted out of those buttons when they ever called my name and you're the first person I've ever admitted this to, I thought I was maybe at least up for consideration because we had done so much with this place. Back then there were a few of us, not as many as in my father's day but at least we still had a small group of farmers, all of us competing in our own little corners of the world. That annual meeting was a chance to compare notes but also to see how the district thought everyone shook out."

Jerry smiled remembering how Joanie had wanted him to hang the plaque in the parlor but he wouldn't hear about it. He stuck it on the nail, right on the most travelled route to the milk room so that he could see it and be reminded he was a good farmer. He sort of figured the girls could read a little too and they'd see it and be proud of him.

Somewhere a long time ago, he'd forgotten it was there. He wasn't sad about how he'd decided to spend his life and he wanted Frank to know but didn't want to say anything that would give the youngster any idea that he was advocating he make the same decision. There'd be no award banquet for the best farmer in this part of the country anymore. There weren't enough of them around to fill a small room, let alone a good size banquet hall like the one where he had stood and been recognized by his peers.

The loss of almost all the farmers around meant a loss of not only plaques from their walls but sources of information maybe over breakfast at Katie's Place, always a good cheap eat to head to after the morning milking had been finished. You'd find a good five or six farming types in there back when this plaque was printed. He'd liked and needed the conversations even the needling each other that his cronies liked to dish out. He knew where he could go for help if needed and it wasn't that far away.

Frank would have none of that if he kept this place going, Jerry realized with regret. Farms existing in isolation just didn't have as good a chance, he thought. Everything a farmer needs can't be in short supply and far away. People these days liked to say it takes a community to raise a child. He'd heard that and his take on it had been to turn the concept to farming. It takes a community to raise farmers and support them.

They looked over most of the places Jerry had been dying to get back out to see, his milking cows, the young stock, especially the new ones that he'd never laid eyes on like that special one he'd seen only in a picture, Baby Angel. He proclaimed her as cute as everyone thought she was.

It demoralized him only for a little while, he found as he continued his tour. The place shouldn't be scrutinized with an eye to perfection, he decided. It should be felt and Frank had established a good feeling in this barn, all around this farmyard. The animals were exuding a sense of well-being, contentment that was the real measure of this place. He'd had it to. He knew then even without being reminded by a plaque on the wall covered in thick dust. When they went back to the wall that held the plaque, Jerry wiped the rest of the loose stuff off the glass, dropping it to mix with the sawdust under his feet.

"I think I'll take this in the house now," he said. "It ain't going to do you any good and don't wait for anyone to hand you one. Look around at what you're doing here and listen. The place will tell you if you're a doing a good job."

Chapter 17

FRANCIE

EVERYTHING ABOUT THE LOOK of the young heifer was wrong. She was standing so Frank could see the profile of a gaunt face, a row of ribs and a stiff posture. All together they spelled a very sick cow, he thought, but he wasn't sure what she might have.

She was far from the herd. They had moved up into the higher pasture and were feeding on a very good new pasture section he'd just opened up to them. Not only was she not happily grazing with them but she was not even chewing her cud, just staring blankly out as if in a trance.

This girl was one of the cows Jerry had bought a few years back. They were part of his plan to bring the farm production up to a sustainable level. He'd named her Francie to help him keep track that she replaced Freida. So far he had seen nothing out of the ordinary in her.

She was on the small side but well-shaped, firm high udder and a good intelligent look in her eye. She was due to calve in about a month and Frank was already counting on her production to put some much needed cash into the farm budget after the loss of Julie.

He approached her and took hold of her collar, urging her into the barn. She resisted which Frank took as a good sign. He left to fetch a small bowl of grain. Returning with the prize and putting it under her chin, she responded and followed him. Once she was tied into a stanchion, he added a chunk of fresh hay to the handful of grain and she started eating, another good sign.

He took her temperature which was normal and looked at her more closely. No visible injuries, she was eating well but she seemed to have melted away before his eyes in the last few days. He couldn't believe he hadn't noticed it. She previously had some meat on her, now she was close to skin and bones. She seemed to be a fraction of herself.

He decided calling David Cooper, the vet, was the only option, hoping his schedule would have a small opening where he'd be able to swing around today to see her. Back in the farmhouse, he mentioned Francie to Jerry.

"I had hoped we wouldn't have any issues with those new girls. I was trying to grow the herd and I've done it by buying from cattle dealers before but only when I really had to. I've always preferred to raise all my own stock," Jerry said. "Buying cows from even the best sources is always dangerous. I know, that's a little bit of news too late to do you any good now," he apologized.

"They were all tested and up to date on shots. I have all the records you got with those cows," Frank replied.

"Some things aren't easy to detect, even with tests," Jerry said.

The vet arrived just as Frank was finishing the night's milking. He'd moved Francie over to the calf pen area, tied to a post. She hadn't seemed to mind. Frank described her background, coming from the auction house, clean health record, seemingly fine in every way until today.

The vet's posture and gestures were making Frank nervous. "What do you think is wrong with her?" he asked.

"I'm pretty sure she has Johne's," David said.

"And what is that?" Frank asked.

"I'm seeing it more often and the fact that she wasn't raised here makes me a little more sure of that diagnosis. There's a lot of Johne's around and unless your herd is self-contained, it's highly contagious. The only way to keep your cows from catching it is to keep them far away from cows from other farms."

"How do you treat it?" Frank ventured, hoping the expense was not going to bury the farm further.

"You don't," David said. "You cull this cow and probably any others you bought unless you want to watch this disease run through the whole herd."

"Are you saying there's nothing you can give her, nothing to cure this Yo... what?

"It's spelled J-O-H-N-E-S but pronounced like a yo-yo with knees." David explained. "This cow is not able to feed herself. She can eat all she wants but she'll seem to be always hungry. The reality is she's not processing the food to feed herself, let alone, make up a bunch of milk to feed a calf or to contribute to a dairy farm output."

"You need to cull all those cows you bought. Any of them calf yet?" David added.

"Yeah, one did and she had bull," Frank said.

"If he nursed from his mother, he needs to go. Most probably has Johne's too," David said.

"He headed to the cattle dealer before he was a month old," Frank said. "I had made sure he nursed though so he'd get the colostrum," Frank injected with a pained looked. "You mean he could have caught it that fast?"

"Johne's spreads by contact with body fluids like manure and even mother's milk," David explained.

"Your whole herd needs to be tested and even if some come up free of Johne's today, you have to keep testing because it may not register at first."

"And if a cow has it, I have to kill her?" Frank couldn't' believe his ears. "I can't do that."

"Now that you've had them exposed to this disease, you can't afford not to do it," David said.

Jerry wasn't an expert on the disease but his constant reading of every dairy publication he could get his hands on made him at least familiar with it and its incurable nature. He had been a dairy farmer for a long time, and had never seen anything like this terrible disease in his herd or anyone else's around here.

Frank promised to do some research with the help of his more than capable wife. Lindsey had a real interest in the physiology of the cows, always finding the comparisons to her human charges. She would research the disease and find out all about it, he had no doubt.

He got home early enough to find her at the computer, something she did when she had a little more energy left. He looked at the screen and saw she was looking for his next repurpose project. They'd decided to change the vanity in the upstairs bathroom and Lindsey had set her heart on some kind of ornate dresser turned into a bathroom vanity by adding a granite top. Hopefully, she said, it would be long enough to accommodate two sinks. Frank's challenge would be to pipe a double sink through the base of what used to be drawers full of underwear. He had to admit, he did like the challenges she threw his way.

He put his lips to the side of her face and stayed there, smelling her and relaxing. She'd long ago accepted that his little exercise did him a lot of good so she obliged him. Once he could pull his face away from her cheek, he asked if she had the time to look at something else, a disease that a cow had come down with.

The Google search screen was up in an instant and Lindsey was looking for a word.

"J-O-H-N-E-'-S" Frank spelled out for her. The choices asked in cattle or dairy and she clicked on the dairy info. A national Johne's information site came up.

"Says it's a bacterial infection, a relative of tuberculosis," Lindsey read. "That doesn't sound good. Is there just one cow that has this?"

"Just one I found today but it's hard to really know. The disease can be in a cow and there is no test that is sure to catch it. The cow might not show any symptoms for years. They can catch it at birth from their mother if she was infected," Frank repeated what he remembered of the vet's information.

"What is the doctor going to do to treat her?"

"He's telling me I have to 'cull' a nice word for 'kill' her."

"No way. That can't be the only solution!"

Lindsey had taken this news worse than he had, Frank realized. She was not a good one to be deciding the fate of dairy cows that she had put her hands on. It was like they were all becoming her patients. He wasn't nearly as bad but just the fact that he understood how she felt was a sign that he had a little of the pet cow mentality. Jerry already had admitted this weakness but swore he had it under control and had proven it many times over by doing what needed to be done, regardless of his preference to run a cow retirement home.

"The vet said I have to get this cow and the other one Jerry bought out of the herd before more cows get infected. The disease spreads through their manure and right now, that manure is all over big, shared open fields. I can't even tell you what a problem that already is but I can't let it get worse."

Turning her attention back to the web site, Lindsey saw a description of the size of the threat Johne's was in a herd. The iceberg effect, it was called and it suggested that for one animal with signs of a late stage of Johne's there were probably 15 to 20 infected animals. In a small herd like Jerry's that was almost half the cows.

"This could be a nightmare," Lindsey said.

"I have to get on this problem as quick as I can. That's going to mean a call to the cattle dealer. One of the cows won't even be able to be sold for meat. She's too advanced. The other one looks fine and maybe I can get back a small piece of what Jerry paid for them, not even a quarter, I bet."

"God, Frank. Why is this dairy business so awful? One thing after another and the next thing is always worse than the one before it."

"I hear you. Feels like that right now for sure."

Lindsey got up from the computer chair and they wrapped their arms around each other. So many times this simple posture had given them both the strength they needed for whatever calamity had befallen them. Frank could feel Lindsey's effect on him. She was telling him she'd hold up her side and he could lean on her. She was telling him she was strong enough and she was easing the fear he might have felt if he was facing this alone. He pulled away just enough so that he could see her face when he spoke. He had to know what her reaction was.

"So why do I still want to do this?" he asked her and himself but she buried her face into his chest and gave him no answer.

Chapter 18

GRASS
SOUP

THE SOUND OF A HIGH PITCHED WHISTLE caught Frank's ear. He looked for the source and found Jerry, outside on a bench in front of the barn. Cradled between his fingers was a fat blade of grass and he was blowing across it, coaxing a violin string pitched noise to come off its surface. Aubrey, he noticed, was trying to get the same result but her small delicate hands, those beautiful fingers, an exact replica of her mom's, were not nearly strong enough yet.

Frank went over to hear the grass string ensemble. He looked down once he got close and saw this had been a very busy twosome. In addition to teaching Aubrey how to play a piece of grass, Jerry had been doing art lessons. His drawing of a cow was pretty good given that it was drawn with a stick in the dirt. Jerry and Aubrey were huddled tightly together so Frank could join them on the bench. He couldn't resist asking if he could get the artist to interpret his latest work.

"This is where the cow starts chewing up all that grass," Jerry said, pointing to a large pouch in the middle of his drawing. "She needs a lot of water too because that helps her make the grass nice and small and easy to digest."

"Does that grass taste good?" Aubrey wondered aloud.

"Seems to," Jerry laughed. He'd seen blades of bright green hay that he had felt an irresistible need to taste so he was speaking from experience when he said. "It's nothing people would like though."

"Did you ever notice how the cows always are moving their mouths like they're chewing?" he asked Aubrey.

She honestly admitted that she hadn't really paid attention to that. The little calves were her main focus and they didn't chew like the adult cows.

"That's the cow's way of chopping, like your mommy might do with a knife," Jerry explained. "Does your mommy make soup sometimes?"

"I don't think so," Aubrey admitted again, starting to get a little shy and uncomfortable with all the negative answers to Jerry's questions.

"No problem. Moms don't all make soup. My mom did though and I remember she seemed to be chopping for a long time when she made soup. So that means the cows probably have to chop a lot to make grass soup too, don't you think?

No more no's were going to pop out of her mouth so Aubrey just nodded and smiled.

163

"These cows make grass soup and then that lets them make milk for their babies." Jerry continued.

Aubrey was slipping away from the science lesson so Jerry changed the subject.

"How's our favorite cows, Ada and her Baby Angel?"

"Baby Angel licked me today and her tongue was so long," Aubrey reported.

"Do you think she thought you tasted good," Jerry joked. Aubrey giggled and looked at Frank for permission to go check on her pet.

"Make sure there's no poop in her stall and keep away from all the other babies, OK?"

"Yes, daddy."

"I'll be right there. We have to get home early tonight. Mom didn't make soup but I'm sure she made something good."

Frank moved to Jerry's vantage point and examined his picture. "When did you study cow design?" he asked.

"Actually, I've been looking at a lot of things I've got around the house, mainly about cow stomachs," Jerry admitted.

"Why?"

"I didn't like what I saw with Francie and her daughter, that Johne's disease. I've been in this business for a long time. I've never seen a cow starve to death like that. Breaks my heart to see that happen to a good cow. They look to us to take care of them and we're letting them down if we can't fix that disease. I'm pretty sure they didn't bring this thing on themselves. It's got to be something that's developed from the way we've used them."

Francie was too far gone to sell and the cattle dealer would not risk infecting the other animals with Johne's so he hadn't bought her. Instead she had literally wasted away in front of Frank and Jerry's eyes, daily fixing them with a pleading look to feed her and make her better. They found her thankfully about a month after the first diagnosis, lying stiff on her side in the secluded enclosure they'd had to make in the pasture, starved to death.

"I hope to never see another cow die like that. That's for sure," Frank said. "Did you find out anything else? I thought we tried about every cure the vet suggested and then invented some others. Is there anything else we could have done?"

"From what I've been reading, no. It's incurable. They've tried vaccines but nothing seems to work. It seems to involve a cow's stomach not working right anymore and the intestine walls become coated with the infection and thickened. Then the cow can't absorb the food it's eating so it starves to death."

Frank knew Jerry was blaming himself for buying the cows from an outside farm, probably a dairy farmer that went out of business. He'd been offered what looked like healthy animals at a very good price at a time when his stock of new heifers was too low and some of his oldest cows were done. He kept his herd self-contained up to that point and now in hindsight knew why that had been a winning formula.

There were few tests that he could have required that would have definitely diagnosed Johne's even if he had known to ask for a test on that particular disease. He'd never heard of it and had never needed to. So far, his herd had paid a fairly small price, two cows gone, a mother and her calf who probably contracted it within minutes of birth.

"The good thing is, I think we caught it with those two cows," Frank offered. "I haven't seen any other cows with any symptoms. We got Francie and Fernie away from the rest of the herd really fast once David told us what to do."

"Yeah, I'm hoping we dodged that bullet. Just remember it in the future and keep away from outsiders," Jerry said, offering a rare comment that indicated the possibility that Frank would be around to make decisions like that going forward.

"Do you realize how bad that Johne's disease is?" Jerry asked.

"Well, yeah, cows die from it," Frank said.

"I'm not talking about the fact that the disease will kill individual cows. It's the bigger issue. Those animals are the link between sunshine and food. We can't eat the grass the sun grows, believe me I've tried, so we need these animals to eat it, make soup out of it. Then we get to have milk, butter, cheese. Can you imagine if cows couldn't do that anymore, feed themselves, let alone the rest of us. That's what scares the hell out of me."

"It does seem to be a bad omen," Frank agreed. He'd been thinking something along the same line but didn't realize Jerry did too. Were cows failing? Did men do something to make them fail as a species, use them up, somehow screw up their metabolism so that they couldn't do what they've been doing for thousands of years, giving people a chance to prosper?

"Have you read anything about the food we're giving them, that stuff they're putting in the corn when they grow it, or maybe the kind of hay they've developed is not as good as the old stuff. Maybe their stomachs are rebelling?" Frank threw out some of the thoughts that had passed his non-scientific mind.

"Don't know but I do know it's not good. There's nothing good about these cows starving to death, no matter what little bacteria they want to blame it on. That bacteria has probably been around as long as the cows but it never killed them. Now our herds are failing because of something they're lacking and they depend on us for everything so we better take responsibility for them. I just don't know how," Jerry finished.

Neither did he, Frank nodded. The direction of the conversation was not ending on the positive note it had just held. He said goodnight to Jerry and headed over to pick up Aubrey from her favorite spot, cuddling Baby Angel's head in her lap. Well if love could cure everything, that baby was in good hands, Frank smiled.

Chapter 19

1926

THERE WAS NOT A TRACE OF BLUE on the spruce in the front yard. It stood more than 25 feet tall, had grown a foot a year since the day Jerry planted it. He'd chosen a spot in the back of the house where the tree would eventually shade the kitchen during the hottest summer days. The blue spruce had done its job but now those days were ended.

The gypsy moth infestation of the 1980's hadn't touched the evergreens, only devastated the insects' first love, the oaks. He'd lost some old hardwood trees in that last round. The conditions in the previous years had allowed the state to spray a fungicide that attacked the moth, one of the few things that killed them. The fungus needed a moist environment so the lack of rain this year had been a boom for the moths who loved the dry weather and a bust for any chance of the fungicide surviving long enough to work. The state decided not to waste its money.

It seemed the moths had gotten the order, full speed ahead, no holds barred. They had eaten every needle on towering pines in the forest across the road, Jerry saw. But first they had laid bare every inch of more than eight massive oaks. Those trees had harbored countless critters in their more than 100 years of existence, fed a multitude of squirrels and chipmunks, hosted birds among the many levels of its branches. Jerry thought about the single-purposed caterpillars that contributed nothing to the natural world, only thinking about taking the best and gorging themselves till they looked like they'd burst on the abundance of the wood supply.

When he first saw the start of the blue spruce under attack, he'd been crazed. He got Frank to try to save it, wrap aluminum foil around the trunk, tape it and spread Vaseline all over the foil. That kept the worms from climbing back up and finishing their meal on anything left that the larvae stage hadn't eaten. Frank tried to get the tree wrapped but he'd had to cut back all the lower branches first and by the time he got the barrier up, the tree was already full of black bodies covered with yellow spikes.

The gypsy moth caterpillar was no easy target. It came armed with sharp yellow spikes that hurt to touch and caused a skin rash. Jerry had taken his thickest rubber gloves and attacked the hordes climbing up to feast on his apple trees. They had attacked the fruit trees, blueberry bushes and even touched on some of the grape leaves though those didn't seem to appeal to them much.

The caterpillars destroyed a number of trees and bushes for two years on his property and if they did it for a third year, there would be no recovery. The trees would be lost forever, Jerry knew. He wondered if the area orchards were being decimated too and hoped they had a way to kill the pests.

He'd watched the devastation from his window seething with both anger and sadness. There was no word for what he felt about this invader. They were brought over to North America to make money for a guy in Massachusetts who thought he could raise them to produce silk fabric. That hadn't worked out, the moths had gotten loose and multiplied and the country had been left to deal with the repercussions.

Jerry's seat was next to a bookcase that was virtually unchanged from his father and grandfather's days. He glanced over out of boredom and pulled out the USDA Yearbook of Agriculture 1926.

The United States Department of Agriculture report for the year was almost 1,300 pages long and glancing through the index, Jerry read areas related to the dairy industry, average cow production, skim milk, butter and whey products and the dilemma of what to do with it. The dairy farms of 1926 were producing a fraction of what his cows produced and the country back then had too much milk product. Many crop reports were of oversupply and dropping prices. Some crops had experienced drought conditions and others had been lost but if there was one thing the book told Jerry it was that the country could feed itself.

Against the backdrop of the 1926 report, the emphasis on many years of developing cows to make them produce more didn't seem to fit. There didn't seem to be a need to push the animals individually until he started to decipher the math on some of the reports, cost of feed per individual animal divided by the production made economic sense. The process was an application of a business model for the industry of dairy cows, he finally realized.

Frank showed up just in time to hear Jerry's revelation. Running a factory was the farthest thing from his grandfather's mind when he came out to this farm, Jerry related. Grover Duggan fought in the First World War. He didn't die from being gassed. He returned home to wed and have children but the gas had weakened his lungs.

"He took care of the military horses and thought he'd have some here. He worked with the Army's cavalry horses and all the others they used to pull artillery. The manual on horse care is in the attic in his wooden footlocker," Jerry recalled.

"My grandma Vera got a look at Jersey cows at a farm up the road and she added those to the mix, had to have one. One of those leads to two and two to four etc., you know how it is. Dairy herd grew out of that one cow. Some of these girls are direct descendants of that cow," Jerry noted.

The land had been farmed back to Colonial times. Remnants of the original settlers' cabin lay down a small canopied lane in the southernmost corner. The duplex farm house was built during the mid-1800's when the town was a booming industrial area producing supplies for armies. Bits and pieces of small mills remained in the woods where they once operated by water power, numerous rivers coursing through the landscape. Foundations and stonework raceways that rerouted the waters to power the mills were also still easy to find.

Grover bought horses and cows, plowed the fields and gradually developed a farm that could sustain itself. With growing numbers of families moving further out of the city centers, he'd started to supply milk, his horses pulling wagons of metal cans around to homes, dropping milk into pitchers.

Barns and outbuildings had been built, more fields cleared and Fair View Acres had taken shape. His grandfather's life benefitted from the move and he lived to what was an old age for a veteran. Jerry's father had grown up knowing he would probably be called on to take the helm sooner than later and was a young man well versed in all the farm machinations when he lost his dad.

"My dad loved farming, more than his dad had," Jerry said. "My dad's sister, Debbie, she went off to be a hair dresser, never came back to the farm to visit much. His other sister, Rachel loved horses as much as her grandpa. She had a little boarding and riding place about half an hour from here. My dad, though, he couldn't stand to be away from the farm for a day."

Jerry's dad, Charles, went off to the Pacific theater in World War II and his wife, Ellie, hired help and leaned on family and friends through the three long years Charlie was away.

"Soon as he could get home, my dad was glad to be back to the hard work and freedom. My sister, Tricia, and I were born working this farm, I swear. We both loved it." Post war years were good for the farm with the population booming and young families needing milk, Jerry said.

"All that came to an end for him right here at this table," Jerry said. "My dad died in the middle of his lunch, just a soft sound came out of him and he was gone. I wasn't there but I walked in right after and my mom had her arms around him, trying to catch him and lay him down on the floor, keep him from falling out of the chair. He was a big, barrel-chested, ruddy faced guy."

Jerry was 13, on the cusp of adolescence, living an exciting life full of new hormones, dreaming about his first car and filling the passenger seat with a girl. He didn't add that information to his story.

The picture burnt into Jerry's mind of that day included remembering his dad had been wearing his favorite shirt, the faded red plaid. Now they'd say that shade of red was a warning. It was an almost exact match for his father's complexion that should have been a good indication of a pending heart attack but not too many people were paying much attention to those kinds of warning signs back then.

"How did your mom ever manage?" Frank asked.

"She was never one to sit still and linger on anything," Jerry said. "Not that she didn't love my dad but she was a strong woman. She didn't lose a lot of time waiting for someone to tell her it was all a bad dream."

He and his sister watched as their mother led them away from despair over losing their father to a life filled with purpose and hard work. She pushed them, that was certain, but never without a dose of appreciation in her eyes to compensate. The three of them locked into a flow to keep the farm going. Ellie got a job in town as a teacher. She helped with the farm work at both ends of her days. Weekends she was barely off her feet a minute, maybe to eat a light supper.

Jerry always knew he'd take over the farm, not just because he loved it so much but so that he could give his mother a break, he said. He'd been schooled in Fair View Acres. His dad fed him opportunities and he gobbled up every chance to run all kinds of machinery. He'd started helping with the milking at 12. He knew the herd, their issues, strengths and pedigrees.

He could be counted on to do the milking but his mom always insisted he have someone else in the barn even if all they did was watch. Tricia was better than just a fire watcher. She was a cow-lover like her mother and her grandmother before her. Her favorite job was the cleaning and feeding of the young stock. They had to submit to her heavy dose of spoiling.

Jerry grew up pretty fast after his dad died but not without time to be a little wild with his high school friends. His dark brown head produced curls much to his surprise when he let it become fashionable long in the '60's, His natural acumen for mechanics had him building hot rods and racing country roads.

Another up-till-then untapped aptitude kept him out of the jungles in 1967 when his draft notice came. His stint was spent mostly in England, because he had a knack for language, something that took him totally by surprise. A test determined he could learn languages easily and before he knew it, he was eavesdropping on a Cold War conversation in the safety of a base in England, Bedfordshire in the Midlands. He spent almost all his enlisted time there and returned home aware he'd literally dodged the bullets by the good fortune of being able to quickly understand new sounds.

Jerry thought back on stories of the farm, its development and growth, the good times and the bad and nothing in his memories resembled a business plan that centered on increasing profit margins or minimizing poor "equipment," the least of which would have been a low producing cow. He even remembered one cow who was kept for many years. She was called a free martin. She was probably a twin whose brother died before birth.

She appeared to have male parts in some places but was missing others and she could never get pregnant. His father had kept her on anyway, along with many other creatures whose use was minimal but entertainment value was high. Chloe, the freemartin, was a very sociable cow and since she had no work to perform could be counted on to look for human attention wherever she could find it.

Jerry read as much of the USDA report as he could stand and was putting the book back into storage where it's chances of ever seeing the light of day again very slim.

"Want some interesting reading?"

"What you got?"

"A USDA yearbook from my grandfather's days."

"Anything we could use in there?"

"Yeah, a dose of reality. You saw the blue spruce out there and what's left of the apple trees and blueberry buses. Gypsy moths will kill all of them if they aren't stopped. Those spruces and pines, those trees can't reproduce their needles. I'll have to pull that blue spruce down before it crashes into the house on a stormy night. USDA book here back in 1926 said this would never happen. You could count on our government."

"What was the government doing back then?" Frank bit.

"They were developing a parasite to wipe out the gypsy moth. It was the biggest project of its kind. Let me quote, 'An enormous amount of time and effort has been spent in protecting the nation as a whole from the ravages of these pests and the progress made up to the present time indicates that the efforts put forth are producing substantial results,'" Jerry read, followed by a sharp, high-pitched guffaw.

"If USDA was a private pest control company, they'd be out of business," Jerry said, "but we still have that bunch convincing us that they will take care of our land and countryside. We should trust them to make sure we are fed from this great agricultural land we live in."

"It's not something I've ever thought about before," Frank admitted. "I don't get involved in politics much maybe just a little veterans stuff to try to keep up with the latest on my benefits. I'm guilty of thinking USDA is helping everything grow across this country and if not, fixing things."

Frank had taken care of burying Francie. It had been one of the worst jobs he had ever had to do on the farm. When Frank mentioned to Jerry he was surprised there was nothing that could have been done to save her, Jerry had expressed pretty much the same opinion Frank was hearing today. The government surely wasn't going to find a cure now if this plague had been around for more than 100 years. Another small creature was taking down a much larger one and there was no finding a way to stop it, Jerry told Frank.

His litany of complaints on how the USDA had failed to address problems for dairy farms was long enough to get Frank to lose track and interest. If he wanted to keep any kind of optimistic attitude about moving into this business, it wouldn't happen from adopting Jerry's anger over the past.

"We have let our government become too involved in controlling our farms instead of letting farmers alone to sell food to their neighbors," Jerry said. "I've seen that for years from my vantage point here at ground zero."

"Why haven't farmers stopped the USDA from doing things to hurt farms instead of help them," Frank challenged Jerry's negativity.

"We're all sitting here on our little spreads barely able to make it to a lunch counter and talk about the problems we face, let alone organize an effort to fight City Hall," Jerry countered. "We're to blame, though, you're right. We knew every step of the way what damage was being done and we're watched it happen instead of fighting back."

"Jerry, you know I've got an appointment Wednesday with the guy from USDA to talk about how they might help me stay in this business so tell me there's some hope that I can do that," Frank said with a slight pain in his voice.

"I don't want you to get any false ideas about it. Personally, I never wanted a lot of help from the government. They aren't here in the barn with me. They sit in an office building and now'a days they're farming by computer. If you talk to them and they encourage you to try to find some state or conservation group to buy development rights to this place, that's nothing I would agree to. That means asking their permission for everything that happens here that involves any kind of permit. Like they know something I wouldn't know!"

Frank had been reading about the concept of the government, federal, state even local towns and conservation groups buying up development rights to farms. On the surface it sounded really appealing like a free gift of cash. He wondered what Jerry knew that made him be so negative about it.

"Isn't it good that there's millions of dollars going to farmers to stay farming?" he asked.

"Maybe you'll stay in farming but they'll own your land in the end. Your family won't get the same deal and they'll hardly be able to pay the taxes when you die. I don't see any long-term thinking and planning when I hear about those deals, just a quick fix. There has to be a better plan for farms long-term than anything I'm hearing from any government offices. What I hear from most of them sounds a lot more like excuses."

"This farming stuff nationwide is big business, not like my grandfather's days. You are going to have to try to make money farming. That takes it away from some agribusiness and they won't take lightly to that. Be sure you know it. The government is more interested in helping capitalists make money than a farmer make milk. I can't contribute enough money to my Congressman's campaign to get his attention but you can bet those big businesses can."

"I won't be taking enough away for anyone to notice," Frank replied.

"You are a threat if you start to push back on the direction food distribution is going in this country. There's a lot fewer food producers, a lot fewer food distributors and a lot more profits in the hands of those in a position to benefit. They notice any efforts to change that, believe me."

"That's a bad strategy from a battle plan perspective," Frank said. "One grenade gets you all when you stay bunched up too tight. More scattered farms all over so that a drought over here or a flood over there doesn't wipe out all the available food, that's a much better plan, don't you think."

"What I think hasn't mattered in a long time," Jerry said. "What I see out this window is that insatiable appetites have a lot of power, like those gypsy moth caterpillars. They can't be stopped by the government. They care nothing about anything other than making themselves fat and happy. If they add nothing and destroy things, like those beautiful oaks, that contribute to everything around them, that's just too bad."

Frank reached home just as the first big rain drops that had been predicted started falling. He put the loaf of bread on the kitchen table. He'd run into town for a few things on the way home because of the storm warnings, possible power outages and the familiar advice to stock up on essentials just in case. The shelves of the small convenience shop he'd gone to were showing the public's usual reaction. There was hardly a gallon of milk or a loaf of bread left.

Instead of feeling annoyed, he realized his plans to be successful in the milk business were aided by this tendency for the main food items to be the ones everyone ran to horde. From the looks of the shelves, making milk should be a good place to find a constant, reliable market, not some trend that might dry up. The research he and Lindsey had been doing though, told a different story. Dairy farmers were the last ones to benefit from the product they produced and had been for many years.

At dinner that night, Frank remembered something he'd been wanting to tell Lindsey about his unexpected visit from a fellow National Guard unit member and his idea for more help at the farm.

"Did I tell you about David Mello from Reserves, stopping in at the farm yesterday? He had his kids and their friends, eight of them I think I counted, and he popped his head in the barn around 3. They were visiting a relative up this way. He's heard me talk about the farm and he warned me if he ever was nearby, he'd love to see the place."

Lindsey thought she knew what might have happened given a chance to show off the farm to a friend but she asked for Frank's version so she could enjoy hearing him tell her.

"Did you give them the grand tour?"

"I was a little surprised and not sure what I should do, where I could bring the kids so they wouldn't get hurt or really dirty. David's wife was there too and she said the kids were all really hoping to see everything especially the animals and they all wanted to know if they could milk a cow."

He described the impromptu tour he concocted in short order, taking the kids to see the goats first, letting them climb the hill with him to collect the herd.

"I told them we were going to find the beautiful girls. They all had to pick up a good size stick and just keep it in their hands just in case one of the cows became a little too curious. They looked like a little army with their sticks in the air marching up the hill with me."

"The girls, I swear, heard them coming and they lined up just at the crest of the hill so the kids got an eyeful of beautiful Jersey cows. I thought they were beautiful but I think that every time I see them."

Lindsey was smiling at the description, picturing the girls, backed up against the blue sky of yesterday's sunny day. She wished she had been there.

"We walked the herd into the barn and I had them all put on a glove, those blue ones I use for the medicines and AI stuff. They were all way too big for their hands but the kids were all loving it."

"Did you let them milk the cows?"

"Guess who?" Frank laughed. "Of course it was my girl Ada who was in the first stanchion and I thought, if there's a cow that would go along with this program, it would be her. One of Dave's little boys put his hand on her rump and said she sure was big.

"Ada, I swear, turned to me and asked me if he was going to hurt her. I gave her the mental reply, no way, and sure enough, she let those kids milk her, let her milk out so they could be all proud how good they did. I know she understood what was going on, couldn't ask for her to be a more cooperative. God I love that cow!"

Frank stopped his recount of the kids' reaction and Lindsey saw his focus shift just like it probably had yesterday.

"What happened after that?" she urged Frank.

"It was Dave. I looked up at him as the kids were all going crazy with the milking thing. He looked like this was doing much more for him than the kids. His eyes were just shining and I swear I could see his heart almost bursting through his shirt. He had it tough during his active duty, saw stuff he wishes he could erase, I know. I think he was trying to fill his head with yesterday's good stuff to replace it and I was so glad I could do that for him. I wanted to give him as much of the farm as he could take. I wished there was more I could do but I had to get going with the milking. I hope he comes back for another dose."

"I've had some days, like yesterday, that I feel like a millionaire. I think I want to have that farm so I can do that kind of thing more often, let people enjoy the place and the animals. There are so few real farms like Jerry's place left. Dave is working only part-time for a temporary service that has him going all over the place. It's not a good fit. He needs something with less pressure to always learn a new route and more money. I was wondering if he might help me out at the farm, if I can find a way to pay him, that is."

"You are such a good man, my love," Lindsey said in support of that idea. "I'm not there every day like you are but I know exactly what you're talking about because I want to be there more. Every time I go I love the feel of the place. I can't even put a finger on exactly what it is I like so much. It seems like it's everything, all packaged together," she added. "It fills your heart with good feelings to be on that farm. I can't tell you why. It just does."

"Remember Tuesday when the temperature at the end of the day had dropped a little bit but it had been really sunny and warm all day," Frank said. "It was probably the mix or those temperatures and all the things blooming over there right now. There's a honeysuckle bush that loves that time of day. It just blows off smell like a volcano. I was done pretty much everything I could do in one day so I was moving slow. It's hard to do it justice but I felt like I needed time to stand still for at least a little while."

"I have a herd of happy cows, a couple goats, cats and assorted birds and other critters living pretty large over there. I can stand in a sunny spot, close my eyes and just soak up good smells. It's not like that every day and if it was, it probably wouldn't be as noticeable. I don't know what or who is trying to squeeze little farmers like Jerry out of business so they can live better, I just know it stinks."

They were both quiet after Frank's outburst of storytelling lost in scrutinizing the morals of the story.

"I'm not going to spend a lot of time dwelling on the negative," Frank finally broke the trance. "I have a story to read."

Aubrey was in her room with a book all picked out already on her pillow. "Ready for dad to read you a story?" he asked, as he grabbed her up in one fell swoop and tossed her on her bed. God, she was beautiful, just like her mom, he thought.

"I got the farm book about the little lamb," Aubrey said. "It's not about cows but I like the baby sheep pictures too."

"Sheep are nice too," Frank laughed, just hoping his future didn't involve finding out just how nice.

The book was a picture version of the "Mary Had A Little Lamb" song complete with a button you could push to make a "baa, baa" sound.

"If this was about cows, it would be just like you, daddy," Aubrey said.

"What do you mean?" Frank smiled.

"The part where it says, why do the lambs love Mary so, and it's because she loves them, that's just like you."

Aubrey's childish lilt sang out beautifully "Why do the cows love daddy so, daddy so, daddy so? Well, daddy loves the cows you know, cows you know cows you know," she ad libbed.

Chapter 20

CRYSTAL
BALL

FROM HIS VANTAGE POINT behind the large barn support, Frank could watch and not disturb. Aubrey and Baby Angel, as she insisted on calling her, were involved in a serious operation to make her bed. Aubrey had a new plastic rake, sized for her frame. Baby Angel had a secure tie-up and a collar that would not slip over her neck.

Frank felt comfortable just steps from any pending injuries to either of the little ones. He wanted to see but not disturb this work. Aubrey was so industrious with her rake. He'd taught her to look for any signs of yellow mustard-colored poop. She knew this could mean her baby was sick with scours. One way to make sure she didn't get sick, he'd told her, was to keep her bed very clean, no poop, wet, cold spots or old food that smelled bad.

Aubrey was checking for any of these things, almost getting down into the sawdust bed to make sure. In between checking, she was reporting to Baby Angel.

"You're going to be very warm and comfortable," she promised to what she fully considered to be her calf. Since first setting eyes on the distinctive and very easy-going calf, she had decided this one was special. Frank didn't disagree. Aubrey had an eye for good stock, he thought.

The line of "A" girls was the best in the herd. Their overall strong constitutions, good conformation, natural inclination to cleanliness and not easily excited temperament were all the things Frank was finding to be the best of the bovine traits.

Baby Angel, daughter of Ada, great grand-daughter of Adeline, his first love, it couldn't be any more obvious, these girls were special to the Maddox family, Frank laughed.

Aubrey was still raking but slowing down and moving toward dropping into the sawdust for a cuddle. He had supervised a petting session with Baby Angel before and knew they both seemed to like it. The young calf was a genetic chip off her ancestor's block. Looking at Aubrey, Frank was right back in the barn as a teen, talking to Adeline, scratching her head. It wasn't any of the other young girls who begged for his attention week after week. It was always Adeline, dispelling any notion that all the young stock were the same even if their appearance seemed to suggest it.

Aubrey's natural intuition to select this particular calf for special attention was a perfect coincidence of the right calf being born at the right time for his daughter to experience the same kindred relationship with a cow that he'd had. During the early years he worked there, Frank had been the one to clean the calf barn. He always went into the barn looking for his favorite in the loose pen. She pushed and shoved her way over to the railing making no bones about knowing she was wanted. He'd scratch behind her ears and tell her she was his girl before moving on to the rest of the work. When he left, it was hardly ever without a goodbye to her.

He liked all the calves and heifers, liked the feeling of being around them. When they turned out into the fields in the spring, he especially liked to be a Pied Piper calling them and watching them come at a trot to his voice. Jerry had taught him to handle the girls, try to put a human touch on them so that they were not scared when the time came for them to be milked. It all had come back to him without trying once he started back here.

Aubrey had taken up a seat with her back to the outside wall and Baby Angel's head was now laying across the very limited area of her small lap. Neither seemed to have a problem with the accommodations. Frank wished he could hear better what she was saying. His curiosity won out and he moved out from his hiding place walking toward the pair as though just coming upon them.

"How's my two favorite girls?" he asked. Aubrey smiled and reported her findings.

"I don't see any mustard," she said. "She ate some grass that I picked for her too."

"That's good. She is growing big already. That's because you are taking good care of her," Frank said.

"Daddy, will Baby Angel give milk?" Aubrey asked.

"Not right away, but when she gets to be a big cow, she will."

"How?" Aubrey was going right where he didn't want her to go.

Stepping cautiously into the world of birds and bees, Frank said, "The mommy cows give milk because that is what they would be feeding to their babies." He crossed his fingers that the line of questioning would end soon.

"Does Baby Angel have to be a mommy to make milk?" Aubrey kept up. "Yes, only mommy cows that have a new baby make milk."

"Why?"

"Because that's how God made them," Frank started then added. "Remember I told you your mommy gave you milk from her body when you were a baby."

"Oh, yeah, she had milk in her body and she held me in her arms and I drank the milk from her."

"How long until Baby Angel is a mommy?" Aubrey moved on to new territory.

"She has to be about 2 years old and that's kind of all grown up for a cow. Then she can be a mommy too," Frank explained.

"I don't want her to be big fast. I like her just the size she is now," Aubrey said, putting both arms around the entire circumference of her baby. "She won't get big too fast but it's important she grows bigger pretty fast otherwise it would mean she was sick."

"She won't be sick. I'll take care of her," Aubrey said.

"Thank you for helping me take good care of these babies. It's a lot of work."

"This isn't work, daddy. I love her."

***

A month later, the bulk of Aubrey's kindergarten class field trip to Knowles Farm was clustered around the small hutches with timid calves making an appearance every now and then. They quickly retreated back into the safety of their plastic igloo-like homes at the sight and sounds of the children at the edge of their field.

Lindsey and Aubrey weren't among that group however. It had taken Aubrey about a minute to decide that those large, black and white calves were nothing compared to Baby Angel. Her attention was on the process going on in the milking parlor. She had been seated quietly on an up-turned pail long enough to know what was happening in there and the big difference between what she saw her dad doing and this operation.

First of all there were 20 cows all being milked at once which was enough to impress her, all those milking machines and all of them on cows at the same time. Frank and Nelson moved along with four and sometimes that was hard to keep track of.

The real show, though, was the apparatus that held the cows, a festival of pipes with moving parts that maneuvered the cows into place, held them and then released them like a carnival ride. Aubrey had been to some amusements parks and knew an overhead harness when she saw one.

"That's like the ride I went on at Disney World," she told Lindsey. "Where they bring that thing down so you don't fall out."

"It does look a lot like that," Lindsey agreed. "Those cows can't move and look, the lady is starting to clean them just like daddy does."

A slightly built, young woman was dipping bright blue rags into a cleansing solution and giving each cow's teats a wipe before applying a dip. She moved through the 10 cows on one side. Returning to the first 10, she then started pulling down on a wired lift that brought the whole claw up to waist height and suspended it there while she attached all four inflations securely. The ease and lack of struggle between the human and waiting cows was apparent. A steel butt pan behind the cows tucked up right to their tail. It helped prevent them from kicking back at the milker. The weight of the equipment was being born by the machinery so the human component had two hands free to get things done.

Lindsey wasn't sure if Aubrey had noticed but there was one other big difference in this operation. The cows backside up against the butt pan all but insured they couldn't poop while being milked. Lindsey had been lucky since she wasn't in the barn as often as Frank but there had been days when a cow had really splattered Frank. She saw the aftermath of the clothes he brought home and knew the reason.

It was one of the few things Frank really hated at the farm, taking a manure bath. He wasn't a germaphobe by any stretch but that went over the top for even him. She couldn't wait to tell him there was equipment that would all but guarantee that wouldn't happen.

She also couldn't help but wish he had something like this in Jerry's milking parlor. It looked expensive, she thought, wondering how this relatively small dairy farm had been able to afford it. By the same token, it wasn't selling just milk. This farm was a community resource with almost every school bringing groups here for tours, an area that many organizations rented for functions which were catered using products from the farm, and an ice cream parlor with a reputation for some of the best and most unique flavors.

There was a lot to report back to Frank here. Lindsey was making mental notes. This farm was not struggling. It was being supported and cherished by a large local population. It did have a big advantage in that it was less than two miles off a major interstate but had the feel of being far from the urban congestion. She wondered how long it had been like this. After the field trip, she and Aubrey stopped at Fair

View partly because Aubrey couldn't wait to confirm her suspicion that her baby was far prettier than anything she had seen at this other farm.

"Those big black and white baby cows don't have a beautiful face like Baby Angel's," she told Frank.

"Their mommies make a lot of milk, though," he told her, "and that's why that farmer thinks they're more beautiful than your little one."

"I don't want a lot of milk. I want Baby Angel," she said. "I agree," Frank nodded. "I'll stick to this kind of cow."

"They had big machines just like at the carnival," she said, making Frank look to Lindsey for clarification. What kind of amusement ride did they put their cows on, his grin asked.

"It's actually the mechanism that comes down to hold the cows in place," Lindsey explained. "It looks like the harness on the rides because it all moves at once when they release the cows."

"I'd like to see that," Frank replied with an immediate longing to not only see it but get it. "I was just thinking this place really could use a little modernizing in that regard. The pipe line backed up this morning because Wanda is making so much milk. I blinked and by the time I thought about checking the line, it had already overflowed back into the pipe. I had to flush the whole thing out really good to get it cleaned out. There has to be a better way, I just was saying to myself."

"We should make a point of going over there," Lindsey agreed. "There's so much you would be amazed to see, how the milking equipment goes on and the big one, how the cows can't shit on you!"

"What, no way," Frank almost shouted. "Jerry is going to have to get that equipment, whatever is it. I'm so done with being sprayed."

After Aubrey finished telling Baby Angel how much prettier she was than some Holsteins, the family walked over to tell Jerry about the visit.

"Norm Knowles was about the most hard-headed and hard-working farmer anyone knew," Jerry said. "I remember when he decided to start that retail store right there at the farm. Don't know that any of us thought he'd make it a year. Now look at him. I haven't been over there in ages but I've heard what a success he's made of that place. Knocked down the huge old barn and put up a brand new one. Just that is impressive enough."

Knowles Farm did have a huge benefit being so close to both the interstate and one of the more populated areas, Jerry added. Still, he had taken a big gamble more than 30 years ago when he left the co-op system and started doing his own processing. Ice cream had been the big attraction at first but that seasonal market hadn't sustained the farm throughout the entire year.

There must have been some lean days before the public realized the local milk was worth taking the drive to the farm to pick up, Jerry ventured. Knowles must have had a crystal ball to have gone in that direction and be sitting on that pot of gold he has now, Jerry thought.

"No one made a big deal about farms 30 years ago," he said. "I'm glad it's turned around so there's at least someone now caring about losing them all."

"There's a new coffee shop on the corner of Main Street and Route 51 that has a sign saying they are using Knowles Farm milk so he's growing even more," Lindsey said. "They have a website and you can order stuff like custom ice cream cakes."

"Almost everything there seems to be kind of new. The milking parlor equipment looks all state of the art," Lindsey added. "It just about milks the cows for you. There was one woman milking 20 cows at a time and barely breaking a sweat doing it. I think it said they milk more than 100 cows but that wouldn't take long with that set up."

Jerry had been over there at Norm's a long time ago when he'd just gotten started on that plan. None of the other farmers around could see where his new dairy farm plan would go. In a million years, he wouldn't have believed that Knowles was going in the right direction, telling the milk co-ops to stuff it. Just that had been something for the local lunch counter discussions for a long time.

Most dairy farmers were already well aware of the drawbacks to the coop and the inability to control the price paid for milk. Though the co-ops were formed to give farmers a stronger market presence, Jerry and the other New England farmers knew the one-size-fits-all effects of combining their products into a large co-op were not paying any dividends even as far back as the 1970's.

The buyout programs to drop the total milk production were another source of much deliberation. A new buyout had just been announced when Norm Knowles decided the government could keep all its bright ideas about co-ops and buyouts. He wasn't interested in playing. Obviously he saw something we didn't, Jerry thought.

The one thing Jerry envied most about Norm Knowles, though, was his large family. He knew the third generation of his grandchildren were working in the farm business now. Lucky guy.

"Know what Knowles has that I'd give my right arm for?" Jerry asked Frank.

"A lot of money?" Frank couldn't' resist.

"No, a lot of kids," Jerry softly voiced. "Me and Joanie, we thought we were doing good, what with zero population growth and all that kind of thinking back when we were young. Boy, could I kick myself now. We never imaged we didn't have forever and that when we were good and ready, a bunch of little Duggans would just come along."

Frank heard Lindsey's voice in his head, her appeal to let her add a few more to the Maddox clan. He had to admit he hoped she'd forget that idea if he could just put her off long enough.

"There's not only a lot of great cow stock that's gone extinct or will be soon, there's a lot of great farmer stock that's never coming back. This young generation will have to learn from scratch how to milk a cow. They might even start at the wrong end, if I don't miss my guess."

Thinking about his group of friends and how foreign anything related to farm life was to them, Frank agreed Jerry had a point. He also felt a wave of pride that he was exempt from Jerry's criticism. He had made a decision to invest in this kind of training and knowledge and had no uncertainty about its usefulness. If nothing else, he'd know how to feed his family.

Knowing how wouldn't get him to the point of actually owning a farm. He steered the discussion back to Knowles and what he did right besides making a large family a priority.

"Do you think Knowles got any grants or help from some program that this farm might be able to get too?" he ventured.

"Don't know and wouldn't get my hopes up," Jerry replied.

It wasn't an unexpected response. Frank had begun to understand Jerry's frustration. He'd tried to help him get some assistance for the cost of grain. The paperwork was overwhelming and they hadn't been able to submit it in time, not that the deadline was made clear anyway. Can't imagine what kind of time and aggravation would be needed to apply for equipment grants, Frank thought.

Aubrey piped up to change the tone.

"That big farm had a lot of cows and good ice cream but this one is better. Those cows have numbers on their ears and the lady never talked to any of them to tell them how pretty they are, because they're not."

"You are right about that," Jerry laughed. "Our cows are very special and our cows know we love them, so there."

Frank caught Lindsey's eye and they both knew what the other one was thinking. This situation needed more than a pie-in-the-sky hope for a solution. It needed concrete ideas and probably a lot of concrete cash. Now Frank could add another item, maybe a few more members of a hard-working family.

Chapter 21

A.I.

GLADYS HAD HER HEAD right up against Helen's rump when Frank first saw her. His skills at detecting a cow in heat sounded an alarm. There was no milk if there was no pregnancy, he'd learned that lesson as a young man and found it really fascinating during his adolescent hormone-charged youth. Responsible for keeping a herd of cows bred so they would keep producing milk wasn't turning out to be as much fun in his adult version.

If he missed getting a cow bred, he didn't get another shot until next month and that meant a delay in getting her back into full production. She'd give very little milk in her last days of lactation and not produce even enough milk to cover her grain costs.

Jerry's inseminator, Ray Mello, an older man who had been doing that kind of work since he was fresh out of agricultural college, was a wealth of information. He also was more than willing to try to help Frank pick up on all the signs and ways a cow signaled she was interested. Gladys, according to what Ray had told him, was probably not ready for the full treatment yet but should be in a few days. Right now she was restless and looking for action but he wanted to catch her in full standing heat, when her likelihood of becoming pregnant was highest. The cost of each insemination wasn't something you wanted to waste on false alarms. He'd been doing a pretty good job, so he thought, but he did have a few cows who weren't as obvious in their desires. They might just be exhibiting subtle signs of being in heat and he had missed them.

Just like a woman, human or bovine, to be hard to figure out and of course the guys were supposed to just "know." Frank found himself smiling at the thought of the Jersey girls wooing their bulls with a shake of their wide hips. Any good bull worth his salt would be sure to notice but few farms kept any bulls around. The unpredictable behavior of bulls was the stuff every farmer could tell a harrowing tale of. Most probably could point to injuries and scars provided by a bull.

The world of artificial insemination was supposed to be the answer to that problem and the avenue to better quality animals but Ray had mentioned to Frank that the industry was seeing fewer and fewer bulls. That meant a smaller and smaller gene pool for the offspring and cows that could be inseminated by a bull that was at best a distant cousin.

Those were issues for the professional to deal with, Frank thought, I'm just trying to make sure I pick up on who's ready and get Ray over here at the right time. He moved towards Gladys and found he even interested her which was probably a good sign she was on her way to be bred, he smiled. No one else in the herd was mounting her, though. The girls knew best and when they saw the look in each other's' eyes. They seemed to be glad to try to stand in with no bulls in sight, jumping up on one another and making believe they were the right match, not that it produced any result. Frank gave Gladys a wide berth and tried to see if she noticed any of her girlfriends needing some attention which she was more likely to do in her condition. She nosed over to Ada who stood still and let Gladys on her back for what amounted to a confirmation of a standing heat. Ada was getting on in years and this was a very valuable piece of information. So far he'd been concentrating on whether Gladys should be inseminated but now she had just turned his attention to a more pressing issue by indicating Ada's readiness.

Frank's hand went right into his pocket and hit Ray's contact number. His answering machine took the call but he knew he monitored it very closely. He hoped he was in the area and able to come today. To get Ada bred was even more important than Gladys right now not just because she was one of the cows he had struggled to detect but also because he wanted another calf like Baby Angel. Ada's babies were additions of the best in the line and he didn't know how many more she'd make in her lifetime.

Few farmers kept their cows to Ada's ripe old age of 10. They were past their prime, or so others thought, but Jerry had never followed that practice. His way was to keep his cows well past anything the agriculture schools would ever advise. He'd told Frank that one article he'd read recently on typical life cycle of dairy cows was to turn them over after only three or four lactations. The modern farms standard was as long as there were young heifers to replace them, send the matriarchs off to slaughter. Expendable cows were no problem to a large business model, not much different from getting new equipment to replace the old, but that thinking had no place in Jerry's small intimate operation.

His opinion influenced Frank in every other aspect of dairy farming and this area was no different. Frank didn't even give a second thought to calling Ray and trying to continue Ada's successful run as queen of the herd. He hoped he'd be around to see one of her daughters taking over the role.

Ray's name flashed on Frank's phone interrupting his thoughts about the herd's longevity and he answered.

"Hi Ray, are you able to swing by? I'm pretty sure Ada's ready and willing."

"Are you sure this time?" he joked. "Ada's been a challenge."

"Gladys was having her way with her pretty much. Is that a good sign?" he replied.

"Might be and you're lucky. I was just in your neck of the woods and not so far out I couldn't turn back that way. Maybe a couple hours, I should be over there. Get her in, right?"

"Yeah, sorry, I'm not forgiven for letting Greta out and making you wait for me to round her up, am I?"

"Your bill on that score is getting lower the more times you get it right.

You should be out of debt in a few years."

"Thanks. I'm putting a lead on Ada as we speak. She'll be here waiting."

"See you in a bit."

Frank thought about Ray and his positive attitude in the face of challenges in the dairy business. He was one of the few people he'd met lately who seemed to be able to keep his chin up. His own farm was struggling to stay afloat. Help was hard to find and Ray had taken on the morning milking, he'd told Frank, indicating he had to cut down a bit on his AI hours. How he found time to do both jobs at his age. Frank could only wonder at and hope to match him.

The breeding program was one area that required paperwork and if Frank was averse to anything it was too much paperwork. He tended to glaze over and take short cuts because he reached the end of his patience fast if required to push a pencil for long. He made himself go over to the chart on the wall and list Ada's heat in the right place. She actually was right on schedule, 21 days from her last bleeding off that luckily he'd also forced himself to write down.

The area of cow genetics was a surprise to Frank. He hadn't given it much thought before but in breeding there was always the potential to improve the herd or hurt the animals. Cows like Julie had shown him that a calf too big to fit out of her mother's womb could be fatal.

From his vantage point under many udders now he'd also seem the disadvantage of sagging udders that caused problems attaching the machinery as well as wounds from cows even stepping on their teats.

Ada already had good udder depth, Jerry called it, but he wanted another daughter from her so bad, maybe they should consider a sexed semen that improved the chances for female offspring. It came with no guarantees and costs more but just like many other aspects of dairy farming was a crap shoot you hoped to win.

Doing the math, Frank calculated the average Jersey gestation of 278 days and came up with a late spring birth, good for lifting production after a winter reduction. He'd heard Jerry talk about the half-frozen calves he'd sometimes brought into his kitchen to warm by the wood stove. If he had his way, all the calves would be born in nice weather, not in the deep cold of a winter night.

When Ray pulled in, Frank met him at the barn door with a hand-shake and sincere thanks for coming. He had done as promised and had Ada secure in a stanchion in the milking parlor. She was such an old hand at this insemination thing that Ray expected few surprises.

The process, nonetheless, was quite involved at least on Ray's end regardless of the recipient's attitude. Ray donned his outfit, a head-to-toe covering that aimed to keep some parts of him clean. His left arm gloved in a rubber tube almost the all the way to his armpit, he first inserted it into the cow's anus and started cleaning out the excrement, sending it out of her.

Then, holding the thawed sperm sample in a long tube in his other hand, he sent that one up the cow's vagina, feeling with his left hand for the right spot to release the load, where the uterus began, and the fertilization would be complete. He'd been at this long enough, he was very precise with his drops and if a cow didn't get pregnant, it wasn't because Ray had missed.

"You should be getting at least one more out of old Ada if this takes," Ray quipped. "She is a great cow. I don't see many like her anymore in my travels. The Holsteins are everywhere and they just don't have the personality of these Jersey girls."

"I don't have much experience with the Holsteins but I sure could use the extra milk they give. The size of these Jerseys suits me though and I agree, I would miss the temperament of these cows," Frank said.

"You and Jerry making any plans for this place into the future," Ray asked.

"We have started to talk about the place and whether I might be able to stay around, maybe start some new projects to get more income but we haven't come up with anything solid yet," Frank said.

"It's a small circle now, this dairy business around here and we all have known one another for more years than anyone owns up to," Ray said. "Your ears should be burning most days."

"Yeah, I figure you guys are getting a good laugh out of my blunders around here," Frank joked.

"Not even close," Ray said. "I wish Benny Scarpetto, the supply company rep, was still here. He just passed, I found out, about a month ago. He used to drive the supply route, big red truck everyone knew. Covered the same area as I cover. We always ran into each other on the farms. There was no one better to compare notes with on what was happening."

"Sounds like you two had a lot in common," Frank noted.

"We got together, stopped at a lunch counter, and brought each other up on the things we'd come across. Probably 30 years we watched farms all over this area, watched lots of them go out of business for all kinds of reasons."

Frank was all ears on this topic, wanting to pick Ray's brain on what he'd seen over the years, not to mention, wishing Benny was here to add his perspective.

"There were the places that we were glad to see go, like the mess of a dump that a big convenience store chain had. Polluted the water all around the place. They had trailers full of dead cows rotting and leaching out the most foul smelling run-off. That run-off went right into the stream that fed the reservoir so they got shut down hard by the town and state. Think even the feds got involved."

"We saw all kinds of dairy farms struggling and then finally closing. One beautiful big place had a barn almost twice the size of yours. Fire took out the barn and the timing just happened to be right when the price of nice flat open fields for house lots was sky high. I personally always wondered just how that fire started. Next thing you know, the white perc pipes are everywhere and the Colonials and being built."

"How about the ones who stayed?" Frank asked. "What do you think they did right."

"They didn't do anything right. If they stayed, most of them became like Jerry, a barebones existence, never enough money to take a break, let alone afford a decent living. I can give you names of families, their kids ran from the farms as soon as they were old enough. They ran right to the nearest city, found a job and bought themselves the first set of new clothes some of them every owned."

"New England farms are small. We don't have a 1,000 acres of flat fields anywhere around here. It's all rocky patches of open farmland, connected by swamps and usually on the side of a steep hill, just like Jerry's place here. That makes for a hard scrabble operation," Ray told Frank with a hint of pain in his voice.

"Like I said though, I wish Benny were still here because he was such a good judge of character. When I said I thought some farmer would fold before the year was up, he'd always call it. No, he'd say, that guy can't quit those cows or that land. He felt the connection the farmer had with his place and he knew it didn't matter how hard it got, it would only be a serious ailment or death that would take that guy out."

"I would bet he'd see that in you, Frank. I think Benny would tell me you're one of the stubborn ones."

"I'm not stubborn," Frank came back, "I do know I like this work, the animals, the outdoors, the independence."

"Not everyone is a natural brain surgeon and not everyone is a born farmer," Ray replied. "Heck, not everyone can do this AI stuff, imagine," he joked. "Jerry is a farmer and so was his father. You are too, I wager, and I'd bet Benny would agree."

"If I hadn't come back to this farm, I might disagree with you, but not now that I've been doing this fulltime as an adult. It does feel like I have to be a farmer. It's what I am," Frank said.

"Nothing to be ashamed of," Ray came back, seeing a look of apology on Frank's face. "If the government hadn't made such a mess of the dairy business by helping keep the price of milk stable, I bet dairy farms would have survived better and they'd be modern, state-of-the-art beautiful places. Too many farmers bought into the co-op and thought it was a way of banding together to keep the milk price high," Ray said.

"The truth was, these little isolated farms were no match for big business, and that's what milk is. There's a lot of room for profit on these girl's product. Just think about cheese and all that pizza, now with the stuffed crust," Ray joked.

"My wife and I are trying to see where there is a profitable market for milk but I don't want to be a cheese maker. I don't want to make yogurt or ice cream. I just want to make milk and get it out to the people who want to make those things out of it. That's about all I can handle, time and energy-wise," Frank offered.

"Things are changing with people paying a little more attention to the quality of their food," Ray said. "You might be timing a run at keeping this place alive at the right time for the public to get behind you."

"I really hope so," Frank said. "I sure would like a chance to at least try but if I'm wrong, it could be a big mess for my family and I don't want to chance that."

"Heard you were in the service, went overseas for a tour," Ray said. "I did a little tour too, over in Korea. It didn't kill me and this farm won't kill you. You've already faced worse."

"I don't want to put myself in that position again but I hear you. I know what I can take thanks to those days in the Middle East," Frank said. "I never thought a simple thing like dairy farming would be like going back to war."

"Those of us who have been around a while are rooting for you, kid. We look at you and see how naïve you are but we also hope you can prove the oddsmakers wrong. If you make a go of this place, Benny will be cheering for you up there. There are a lot of people who have simple values and a love of their own land. They have their fingers crossed that you win this fight," Ray said.

Frank took in the heartfelt words and made a mental note to try to do justice to the moment when he told Lindsey about it tonight. The fact that someone he didn't even know was not only watching, but pulling for him produced a flood of feelings, a thunderbolt of positive energy to Frank's soul.

Before this conversation he thought he had to try. After it, he knew.

Chapter 22

VENEZUELA

LORRAINE STUCK HER HEAD into Celeste's office asking if she'd brought lunch today.

Celeste's answer was apparent. She stood up, grabbed her pocketbook and followed Lorraine to the Clark Building on campus where a small café offered light fare, salads with fruit, wraps with avocado and tasty dressing. It had just opened and become a favorite with a lot of the university staff and students so the women hurried, hoping to beat the lunch rush.

A mixed green salad with strawberries, mandarin oranges, feta cheese and walnuts topped with a balsamic vinaigrette dressing was in Celeste's hands and Lorraine opted for a turkey, bacon, cheddar wrap in a sundried tomato wrap. They saw some of their fellow fans of this lunch option at a table and joined them.

Lorraine had worn her Celeste creation to work and the women seated at the table remarked on how beautiful it was.

"I am so jealous," said Jeanne Dusablom, a business professor. "I just could never have the patience or skill to make something even close to that. How long did it take you?"

Celeste smiled at the compliment and tried to make a mental addition of the hours she had invested in one garment.

"More than I could ever recoup selling it," she laughed, "but then again, I don't consider my time on the clock. This did take a while because I couldn't spend a lot of time all at once on it. I started it right after the surgery and it kind of sparked me to get out of bed and at least make a stab at doing something."

The round of comments putting a pat on the back of Celeste for her sewing made her blush but it was exactly what she needed, the sense that she was the same, the same seamstress she had been, the same fabric artist that had drawn these kinds of comments when she let people know that she'd made her own stunning outfits. She wasn't one to brag but she knew the comments fueled her desire to keep on creating.

Everyone was turning to the main event, the lunch at hand, and that day's fare was getting another round of praise.

"I love how fresh all the salad ingredients are," said Sally Greene, an administrative assistant in the physical education department. "The kids are all going wild for this stuff, especially those athletes. There are so many of them on really strict diets. They don't eat meat, dairy, sometimes even eggs so they are glad this place just opened."

"I have such a new appreciation for good food now," Celeste offered. "It's a little scary how much I feel I need to watch what I'm putting into me. The young kids are really on the right track, I think, demanding better food and making sure nothing goes into them to kill them."

"There's a new farmers market in Wakeville on the Town Hall lawn now too," Lorraine added. "I checked it out last week. They only have a few vendors but they hope it will grow. The only thing I didn't think was good was the weather is such a factor with the outdoor markets like that."

"Why, what does the weather have to do with anything?" Jeanne asked.

"If it's not a beautiful day where the trip to the market is like an outing to a festival, people don't come, one farmer told me. He said the set-up to sell directly to the public sounds like a good idea but he's making his living one tomato at a time. If the crop is picked and ready for market but the clouds come out before his truck is unloaded, he might as well just pack it in. He'll barely cover the cost of his time to bring it all there."

"I didn't realize that," said Jeanne. "Still it's so great there are more local farmers growing the food right here and getting it into people's hands." "I don't know if any of you follow the international news but we've been following the mess in Venezuela from a business standpoint," she added. "They have a severe food shortage right now and that country had tremendous wealth just in their oil resources. People are lining up for food distribution and they're happy to get anything to eat, doesn't matter what it is, high quality, low, favorite dish or not, they are starving. Worse than that, they're paying any price for any quality food, just something to eat."

"How did that get so bad? Aren't they the ones that send the free oil to the Kennedy kid for our poor to have heat in the winter? You'd think if they can give away oil, they could keep their country fed," Lorraine stated.

"Their oil income is in the toilet and inflation over there is triple digits," Jeanne explained. "Another big factor is there are shortages of basic stuff. The government is deep into controlling food products over there but failing miserably."

"Sounds like our government. They're here to help up until they get it so screwed up it is totally broken and then they just say, oops, we can't fix it now that we've made such a mess of it."

Celeste and Lorraine both were about to jump into the discussion with all they'd been hearing from Frank about the government intervention in "helping" keep dairy products fresh and available.

Jeanne continued the economics lesson before they could reply. "They're trying to grow more food in the countryside and distribute it nearby. It's supposed to make the communities self-sustaining but so far they've got fallow fields that aren't even ready to be planted and big plans but no results," she finished.

"Don't think we can't get into a situation like that if we don't keep an eye on our government do-gooders. We've got people in positions of power in this country who don't have any reservations about lining their pockets with profits at the expense of anyone. If they can make a buck on controlling food for their profit, we'll be looking at bags of rice and thinking we're lucky to have that," Lorraine started.

"There are so many more people pushing for higher profits on their investments," Jeanne countered. "You're in the university's retirement fund. Those companies working to let you get out of the rat race are only doing it by turning a profit whatever their product is. Food is one of those areas. That creates for a lot of people who need to have their cake and eat it too, not to be too corny," laughed Jeanne.

Celeste spoke up to try to steer the conversation to concrete issues they had firsthand information about.

"We've been buying some milk from a farmer out in Fairford. He's been telling us how bad the dairy business is with government controls. He can't improve the farm because the price of milk is set nationwide. If he spends more to make better milk, he has no way to recoup it."

"We think we have a free marketplace in America," Lorraine added, "but it's not free when the government has its fingers in it. They've controlled milk prices for so long, we have barely any farms left in New England and have to truck in milk from New York and Pennsylvania. The government took all the potential for profits out of dairy farming a long time ago. We're lucky we don't have to queue up to get milk products. I don't want to bet on what might happen in another 50 years."

The women's conversation dissolved into separate threads and the group headed back to their varied offices. Celeste and Lorraine were left at the table.

"Can you imagine people in America not having enough food?" Celeste said. "We have the best country and probably the best land in the world to feed us but I don't like what I hear about Venezuela. It makes we worried about our future."

208

"They have a great climate to grow food. They have wealth and resources," Lorraine agreed. "If it can happen to them, it's not that far of a stretch to think it could happen over here if we let too much of the food supply get into too few hands and if we lose all our farmland."

"Just when I was really starting to like this new fresh food I've found," Celeste lightened the conversation.

"Hope you're around to eat lots of it for many more years," her friend smiled.

***

Their weekly trip to the farm a few days later turned into a more serious conversation with Frank, sparked by the lingering effects of that luncheon. "Do you think we could run out of milk in New England?" she asked Frank. "We were talking to some of the people in other departments at the college this week and they were telling us about Venezuela having food shortages. I was wondering what you thought."

"Not run out of milk but get a poor quality and it could even start to cost you more," Frank responded. "That's what I've been seeing as my wife and I look at trying to get a plan for this farm. There will be lots of milk because there are places making plenty and cows are so plentiful just not here. I don't think the milk is anything great, though. It gets processed and moved and that's just not a good combination for something perishable like milk. It's best right out of the cow and into the person."

Lorraine wanted to know everything that Frank might be thinking and planning and didn't hesitate to ask. Celeste wondered if

Frank would be able to get a word in edgewise as her friend fired question after question at him.

"Do you want to expand this farm?" Lorraine asked, "because I'd love to help you. I do marketing and fundraising. Those are my specialty and this place would sell itself with the right pictures. Maybe start a Facebook page with those beautiful cows. Do you want to sell raw milk, because I think that's the thing that people who know good food really want."

Frank let Lorraine's stream dry up before he tried to answer. Smart man, Celeste thought.

"The raw milk thing is something I have a lot of reservations about. There are cows I would rather see their milk pasteurized. The testers do a thing called a somatic cell count and Jerry's herd has years of low cell counts. I still have some ways to go to keep it that way. If the cell count is high, it's much better to pasteurize the milk," Frank explained.

"Remember that time we stopped in and you were having trouble with a cow and we asked you about the corn you feed?" Lorraine started. "Well, I just started to look around for somewhere else to buy raw milk and I couldn't believe the price they were getting for it. Four and five dollars a half gallon!" she reported. "You should think about that. Regular pasteurized milk doesn't taste as good. We did the taste test already," she added. These women had started to become welcome visitors. They were both enthusiastic about the farm, the cows, the milk. Frank had gotten into the habit of looking for them, hoping they would show up, which they very consistently did, and talking to them about the outside world that they had a tight connection to. He was spending so much time just on the farm that he knew he had somewhat lost touch with civilization. It was evident that a woman with Lorraine's energy would be a huge help in getting a marketing plan together and the USDA business plan came to mind. Frank and Lindsey had looked over the form but had hardly been able to make any headway in completing it. There were too many unknowns.

What price could they expect to get from the farm product? Raw milk would bring a much higher price, they agreed, but they both felt some part of the population would never drink raw milk even with a lot of nice cow pictures on a Facebook page. They had priced a small pasteurizing unit and estimated selling that for about double what the farm was getting paid by the co-operative. They couldn't get a solid estimate though of what the costs were going to be to do the pasteurization at the farm and then deliver the milk.

The other big question they'd had was where would they sell this milk. They'd looked at the products on the shelves of every store they went in. The large national chains were loaded with their own store brands or major food labels. There was no sign of local, small dairy milk in those stores. One small market chain had a New England brand but didn't stock a lot of the product.

They both wondered what the possibility was of getting any of their milk onto a supermarket shelf and all but counted that out. Instead, they hoped to start a delivery route, harking right back to Jerry's grandfather's days. Knocking on each one of the farm's neighbors doors sounded like about the only way to test that plan.

"You really should get a website up as soon as possible," Lorraine went rushing ahead. "That is so important. You can reach the world if you do that and I can definitely help you design it and get it up and running. Then we can start a blog. People would love to hear about everything that happens up here," she rambled just getting started.

Frank and Celeste exchanged grins and turned their attention back to the explosion of ideas coming out of Lorraine.

"I think you believe this farm could sell the milk locally," Frank started, getting his words out as Lorraine took a rare breath.

"Just watch. I have no doubt there are people concerned with their food quality that would queue up for this milk," Lorraine said. "It is going to be a lot of work though to get the message out."

With that last statement Lorraine's brain finally went to the other obstacles that had nothing to do with customer base but all to do with the reality of Jerry and the current condition of his farm.

"There are a lot of changes people would want to see in the farm," she added. "Just a real nice coat of bright white paint would go a long way."

Frank was sure painting the entire barn was not in his scope of work but he was glad for the show of support and he told Lorraine. Having her experience and connections as an ally in this effort was going to help tremendously. Like reinforcements to the battlefield, he let himself feel a little of the weight lifted. She was a powerhouse. Put to good use, that power was just what this thing needed, he thought.

"Do I have your e-mail address?" Lorraine was moving on. "If you send me some of the business plan information, I would love to give that some thought and tell you what I think would work."

"I'll write it on this paper towel," Frank offered, tearing off the first sheet to wipe his hands and taking the next one to write down his address. "I'm putting my wife's down too because she is much better at checking her mail. Copy her on everything."

"I'm sure we can help," Lorraine smiled. "We love this place."

"Thanks," was all Frank could offer before excusing himself and heading back to his current project, repairing the multitude of broken windows needing replacement and caulking before winter. Painting them was not on the list.

Chapter 23

HOMECOMING

THE TIMING OF CHRIS' CALL WAS PERFECT. Frank had reached a point where he couldn't talk about the future of the farm anymore without bringing him into the discussion. Selling their family home was a big piece of this puzzle. He didn't want his little brother to feel like he was being pushed out of the only home he'd known.

In his mind Frank hoped his little brother loved being in the Coast Guard. It was crucial that Chris be happy in his chosen career if there was any future to Frank's farming one. Of all the possibilities he and Lindsey had scrutinized, living at the farm instead of commuting the five miles added a lot more than just time to each day.

Jerry had tried to describe what would happen if they lived there. In the middle of the night, you'd be up in the barn checking on the latest mother waiting to give birth. Almost as though called by some voice, you'd find she needed your help. What or why you woke up, you'd find yourself asking for a little while, he said. After a while if you didn't catch the important middle of the night messages, you'd start to ask yourself, how you could have slept through that.

Frank understood. He was moving in tune to the demands of the place already and often found he'd stumbled upon a situation at a crucial moment as though his feet weren't his own but moving to some other force. Being on the property 24/7 would make that a constant.

Lindsey was supportive, even enthusiastic and optimistic about the prospects of becoming a dairy farmer's wife. She would be no minor partner either, Frank knew. She brought every ounce of intelligence, compassion and intuition she possessed to the barn every time she was there.

Chris' message asked Frank to call at 11 p.m. East Coast so that he was free from his West Coast duties. Frank cringed. He hated to be up that late when the 4 a.m. alarm was going to be heard so soon after. He took a nap after supper hoping it would help. Lindsey nudged him at 10:55.

His brother sounded great, told him right up front he loved being a Coastie. He described the medium Endurance Cutter as an old tub soon to be replaced by a state of the art cutter, the OPC's the Coast Guard was building. He hoped to have a new boat under him as soon as they got them. He kept up a running monologue about the daily events, some ex-citing moments on the sea, all of it explained in a detail Frank was only catching or understanding bits of. The big thing he was hearing was his brother's commitment to the service and the energy he was investing to be a great Coastie.

A cutter deployed to the Central and Western Pacific, Coast Guard Cutter Kukui, he hoped would be his next step. It patrolled places with exotic names to lure Chris farther away from his roots.

That gave Frank a perfect segway and he took it.

"So, I've gotten involved in old Jerry Duggan's dairy farm. I think I mentioned it a while back."

"You still doing that? I thought it was just till he got back on his feet.

How long is your hitch?"

"Well, there's some possibility, I might want to take it over."

Frank waited but didn't get a quick reaction from Chris. He let his brother digested exactly what "taking over" Jerry's place might mean.

"Know what," he finally said. "I remember you going over there when you were younger. What were you 14, 15? You didn't say much about it but I could tell you liked being there. You were in a really good mood when you came back and hardly picked on me."

"I never picked on you," Frank laughed. "Nothing you didn't need, anyway. Yeah, I never really minded being at that place, other than the manure stuff, you know."

"How would you do that, take over for the old guy?"

"Well, that's the big sticking point. Lindsey and I have looked at some information about farming programs. There's a USDA young farmer program that I might have qualified for but I need to have three years working there. I'm not sure Jerry will last three more years, to be honest, and we can't last just working there and not owning it or at least making money somehow from it."

"Dairy farming in New England is not where it's at, Frank. You need to get out and see the world, other than the Middle East, that is. Boy it's beautiful out here in California. I've gotten out to the mountains and deserts around here. It's all at your fingertips and it's all much more impressive than a New England farm."

"I'm glad you're happy, Chris. Sounds like you're on the right path for your life but I've been trying to find one for mine and this is the best one I've found so far. Lindsey says she knows there's a dairy farmer's heart in me."

"Hey, never mind about me right now. Isn't it your dime? What's up?" Frank said.

"I wanted to make sure you guys were around. I'm hopping home for a week next month. Can we make some plans? We can talk more about the farm thing when I get there."

"We definitely will be here. Can't wait to see you. Call me when you get all the details on what day, flight, all that stuff. We'll be there to pick up."

"Thanks, can't wait to see you either. Be safe around those cows till I get there. Wouldn't want you getting your head bashed in before I get to try with my new military training."

"Bring it," Frank urged.

***

Four weeks later Frank was checking the arrivals listings on the display at T.F. Green Airport. Chris' plane was on time and arriving at Gate 20. He headed to the waiting area at the base of the escalator joining the group of others, some holding signs, welcoming family, friends, and business associates.

Frank hadn't seen Chris since he shipped out to the other side of the country and he realized he was a little nervous. He hadn't corresponded that much with him and felt a little like he was waiting and maybe going to be surprised by the person who stepped off the plane.

Chris appeared at the top of the escalator and gave out a "Frankie!" that took some of the edge off. His little brother wasn't that different if he was still yelling his name that way, like he wanted something.

He was likely to be the one who was going to be asking Chris for something, Frank thought, but maybe there was something else behind this visit that Chris needed and he could oblige. They hugged as soon as Chris got level with his brother and both instantly started an appraisal of bulk.

"Coast Guard not feeding you much," Frank teased, seeing his little brother in fighting trim shape, wide shoulders tapering to a slim waist, a new straightness to his back that Frank noticed developing as soon as the Guard had gotten a hold of him. There was a deep russet gold to Chris' face as well as every visible inch of his body that could only come from the West Coast, Frank thought. He felt proud to be the one welcoming this guy and being the one to call him brother. He realized he missed him, this last piece of family that he'd somewhat been losing touch with. He mentally made a note not to be so long between communications with Chris.

They heard the rumble of the bag conveyors starting and Chris' duffle was luckily one of the first to come around the carousel. They headed to the short term parking lot and then toward their childhood home. Chris kept up a good banter about the things he'd done and seen taking Frank off of the hot seat about what he was doing and or thinking about doing.

The ride went quickly for both of them and they were soon turning into the driveway of the only place Chris once had ever called home. Frank looked at it with what he thought might be his brother's eyes. The place had gotten a color change thanks to Lindsey. It had always been a white Cape with green shutters and now it was a soft yellow Cape with white shutters.

Frank liked the change, thought it brought out the lines of the house, the black side dormer roof making a better contrast against the yellow. The house needed a lot of care that neither of them had taken any notice of after his dad wasn't there to remind them anymore. Lindsey had stepped in ready to take over that job. She saw the things his dad would have told him needed attention, Frank had to admit, and he was more than glad to oblige her feeling like maybe his dad could see.

Chris remarked on the color change but said it looked good. Lindsey had taken care to fill the flower beds in the side yard and had a welcoming door decoration. Frank helped Chris unload his bags from the trunk and followed his brother as he burst through the door yelling for his niece.

Aubrey barely knew Chris in person but she knew of him as Uncle Chris. She had been excited to meet the stuff of stories that her dad told about a brother that he had countless adventures often ending in a pretty funny way. She had already decided this guy was all right and gave him one of her biggest smiles and a hug.

Lindsey loved Chris almost as much as Frank from the moment she met him. He was not at all like her husband but she saw that those contrasts made him such a great sidekick to Frank, his spontaneity and humor, his adoration of his big brother and his ability to let Frank know he was the greatest guy in the world. Lindsey could never dislike a man who did that. She'd made a ham dinner because it was one of Chris' favorite meals, pineapple sauce on the ham, broccoli with cheese sauce, mashed potatoes and Portuguese sweet bread. It was a dinner his mom had made many times and she had heard stories about the enormous volumes of fixings these boys put away. She hoped hers was up to the standard.

Chris could smell the dinner and knew exactly what was on the menu. He grabbed Lindsey in a bear hug and said, "Thanks. Did you say you had a single sister?"

"Sorry she just got taken, married off now. You're too late," she replied. "Well actually, the West Coast has some pretty good options," Chris blurted out, looking like it was not intentional.

Both Frank and Lindsey looked at him for the rest of the story and he turned beet red and said, "There's this girl I met."

Frank's face was pulled out to the corners in a huge smile that encouraged Chris so he finished the story.

He'd gone to a friend's home not far from where he was stationed to celebrate Easter. The family dinner was huge, not just his buddy's family but it seemed like every one of the kids dragged a friend along just to cram more people at the enormous dinner table set up outside under grape arbors. There was no comparable dinner in his life experience, Chris realized, to equal this feast.

"You should have seen this place, the land, the house, it was all right out of the Lives of the Rich and Famous with a definite California theme," Chris said.

He'd felt a little unsure of what to do as everyone was starting to take their seats and his friend was lost in a conversation with someone he obviously hadn't seen in a while and had a lot to catch up on. He was standing off to the side of the main ring of activity when one of his friend's sisters, a California girl if ever Chris had imaged one, all gold skin and hair with a pair of cobalt blue eyes, rescued him. He smiled what she called a shy New England boy smile and he saw that she was not making fun of him, she was complimenting him.

She sat beside him during dinner feeding him information not only about what they were eating, lots of new food stuffs like roasted vegetables with a spicy glaze, beef from the local ranch dredged in a chipotle rub, but also about the backstories on everyone around the table.

He enjoyed the food but even more so the company. His mind knew he would require more and hopefully large portions of it. Her name was Sarah and she agreed with his plan to see her again. They'd taken every small window of opportunity to see one another when Chris was on dry land. "We are pretty serious and I'm going to ask her to marry me. I think she'll even say yes."

"Wow, I'm glad to hear that," Frank said, smothering his brother in his arms. "I have nothing but the best of reports for this marriage thing especially if it's to a great person."

"Yeah, well I kind of came home to tell you about it and warn you. We might do it kind of quick like if she says yes, it would be day after Christmas and you have to my best man."

"Oh God, not another wedding and this one would be where?" Frank asked.

"San Diego. I haven't even officially asked her yet but I think she'll say yes and I bet this affair will be a totally California-style bash you won't want to miss. They really know how to live out there."

There was no way Frank was going to miss his brother's wedding. Even a herd of dairy cows needing him constantly would not be insurmountable, just difficult. He resigned himself to starting to work out a plan as soon as Chris had an answer to his proposal.

"Wouldn't miss it for the world," he told his little brother.

"Frank had a slight issue at my sister's and he wasn't really there," Lindsey chimed in. "It will be nice for him to get to go to another wedding and hopefully, he can have a better time."

Chapter 24

THE
BROTHERS

HIS LITTLE BROTHER HAD INSISTED on borrowing some old clothes and joining him in the barn and Frank had obliged. Looking over at Chris' ankles showing clearly out from the edges of his worn jeans, Frank was enjoying the sight of his younger but taller sibling slinging cow shit into a wheelbarrow. Chris hadn't wanted to actually milk the cows but was fine with all the prep and clean-up.

They were different in many ways, he knew, but like the intertwined yin and yang, they formed a whole circle. Frank thought about his earliest memories of Chris. They were kids splashing in the same bathtub, talking each other to sleep from their respective bunkbeds, sneaking snacks from what mom thought were her secret hiding places and mostly just laughing together. If he was pressed, Frank might have been able to come up with a time they had fought, but it would have been very long ago and very brief. As brothers went, they were tight as a drum. Chris was asking him about the next chore, acting very confident, telling Frank to bring it. He pointed to the calf barn and warned Chris they were about to step it up in terms of manure moving. They entered the barn and he pointed to the large empty iron tub hanging on the track.

"It's called a manure trolley and you fill it, slide it along the track and dump it into the spreader. Takes about three fillings to clean this place," Frank explained.

"Sounds like this may be the deal breaker," Chris smiled. "You really do this every day?"

"Usually, I let Nelson have a go in here before I show up. It's one of the advantages of being the boss," Frank laughed. "Then I come in to spread the sawdust."

"You seriously think you want to do this every day for the rest of your life?" Chris asked.

"Actually, no," Frank said. "I want to do it most days, have some days off like a normal person and even take a vacation. They tell me that's never been done by any dairy farmers but I'm going to be the first one."

"Jerry doesn't look like he's taken many vacations," Chris noted. "He's one tired looking, used up guy."

"Wonder why no one wants to get into dairy farming. People who grew up on the farms with barely enough money to put clothes on their backs go running from it as soon as they can and people who've never done it see only the manure and the work. I think I'm one of the few people alive who can see something else."

"What," Chris asked. "What do you see in this?"

"It's great to work with the animals, see life born and thrive, see the farm even in the worst winter storm, it's a beautiful sight. In the spring I felt like I was waking up just like the land, every nice day energizing me and then getting out here and making things grow. There's a lot to like."

"Just don't think about the manure and heavy lifting, right?" Chris teased.

"I'm young now. I'm sure it will get tiresome, but while I'm filling that bucket, I'm planning all the next things I want to do around here. Before I know it, I've been lost in my thoughts and the work is done. Then I get to go do everything I just mentally planned."

Chris looked around at an antique scenario surrounding him, the general condition of the barn unchanged in more than 50 years. Iron work pens were still in decent shape for their age, he thought, notching one for the days before planned obsolescence. The bucket and the manual work needed to clean this place, though, needed to come into the 21st century, he told Frank.

"Believe it or not, the past two years have been good financially for this place. Milk was selling at $24 or more a hundred weight. Jerry bought that tractor last year with some of that money. It's used but a huge upgrade from the 1940's vintage he had before. There just is never enough money and not for long enough to cover everything that's needed around here," Frank said.

The price of milk had just dropped down to $15 a hundred weight though nothing had changed at Fair View Acres. Not one item, feed, sawdust, energy, had decreased in cost. The only thing that had gone down was the price they were going to receive for the milk the farm produced.

"The milk price dropped because we are having issues with Russia," Frank almost shouted. "Can you believe that? Here I am trying to make a simple thing like milk on a New England farm and I have to be involved in international diplomacy issues or my profits go down. No offense little bro, I know Uncle Sam pays your wages but the government seems to have really messed up this milk business."

Chris smiled a knowing smile that indicated he knew all about working for the government. He touched a round metal door knob and watched the simple mechanism operate probably for the millionth time, functioning just as well as the first time.

"There are some things that don't need work around here," he said, eyeballing the handle, "but wouldn't you want to bring this place a little more up to date?"

"Lindsey and I have been researching all kinds of ideas for that," Frank said. "I'd like to process the milk here and get a local route, deliver it, maybe add some eggs and vegetables, really, go back to Jerry's grandfather's original plan. It worked for a long time. I think it can work again now that people realize they need good local food."

"So spit it out, Frank," Chris said. "Do you want to sell mom and dad's place?"

Chris' visit had been mostly about his life, his wedding plans, his exciting Coast Guard adventures, but Frank had been hoping he could find the nerve to tell him about his hopes for taking over the farm. They did involve the possibility of selling their home and he had been petrified to say it out loud to Chris.

"Thanks for that," Frank said. "I didn't know how to mention it."

"I have to say selfishly, I never want you to let our house go," Chris admitted. "I'll be on the West Coast for a while, maybe not coming back to New England that often and maybe never living here again but mom and dad are still in that house for me."

"Don't have to explain," Frank stopped him already broken up about the mention of their parents and the implications of what he was telling Chris, that he would sever the biggest tie they both had to them, the home they grew up in.

"I'm not asking you to let me sell the house," Frank said. "I'm not ready either but when I try to figure out how to make a go of the farm here, I know I have to live on this property, not commute."

Frank knew Lindsey kept close track of the local real estate market, following the sale reports online and she'd estimated their parent's property probably would sell in the mid $300,000 meaning Frank and Chris would have close to $150,000 if they sold it. That would only put a small dent in the price of the dairy farm, though, and the remainder would be beyond anything the farm income could pay. They hadn't been able to see a clear path to making the purchase of the farm work but Frank was glad that the sale of the house, one piece of the puzzle that had been included in the calculations, wasn't something he had to continue to keep from Chris.

"Just sit on that thought, if you can," Frank asked Chris. "Don't think I'm forcing you to go along or even that it's something I need to ask you to do. There might be other ways to get this thing done. I'm meeting with a USDA guy in about a month to see what programs they have and what we might qualify for."

"I'm glad I'm home right now to take a close look again at the old place. Funny how much you forget when you're away," Chris said. "By the way, I like what Lindsey did with mom's Hoosier cabinet."

Frank had wondered what Chris thought. He noticed his brother walk over to their mom's favorite piece of kitchen furniture and put his hand on it. It had once been painted a cream white but Lindsey had transformed it to a bright royal blue. The brown metal top had produced countless pies and baked goods in their youth. Standing at the cabinet, her arms white up to her elbows, their mom had shouted instructions while she tossed flour and rolled dough. The picture of that was ingrained in both their minds.

Now that counter was replaced by a new composite countertop with a white background speckled with bright colored chips including one blue chip that matched the paint color. It wasn't used much for baking anymore. At Lindsey's direction, Frank had altered the base, taken out half the lower drawers and made the baking cabinet into more of a desk. Aubrey loved it and sat at it all the time, coloring and lately doing some school work. What had been the breadbox remained but now resembled a roll top desk that stored all her crayons and paper. The upper cabinets were stocked with paper goods and an overflow of household items. The flour sifter held a large bag's worth of cat food. Frank had refitted the mechanism so that the food came down through what was once the sifter and into the waiting cat bowl.

"Did you ever notice that nothing stays the same?" Chris asked. "I see it being away, see how many things are different every time I'm back this way. I know it's useless to try to keep everything the same and I wouldn't want you to stay locked in our childhood just because you live in the same house. I really like how Lindsey changed the cabinet and the best thing is seeing Aubrey sitting at it."

"Just promise me you'll keep me in the loop on all the things going on over here. I support you, Frank. Do what you need to do because I'm where I need to be. I know that."

Frank felt the world lift a little off his shoulders and shot his brother a smile of appreciation.

Chapter 25

DARK
HORIZONS

JERRY HAD LONG AGO LOST TRACK of how many mornings he'd woken up stiff with aching joints but even he had to admit this pain was different. The intensity and the location of the pain was seated deep in his bones. He didn't like the feeling.

He'd ignored most of the health issues that had crept up on him over the years. This new one was a lack of stream and now the blood in his urine. He was a prime candidate for prostate cancer holding out hope that it would either cure itself or that it wasn't as bad as all that.

The doctors who finally got a look at him when he arrived by emergency vehicle after his accident weren't fooled. They'd run every test possible making a pincushion out of him and then announcing their discoveries like they were news to him.

The hernia had been there since his late 50's, not getting worse but not getting better. He had always tried to be careful how he moved to avoid setting off the pain and had managed it pretty well, he thought. His doctors convinced him to have it fixed but they'd also convinced him he never wanted to go back anywhere near a hospital after he was discharged. The condition of his prostate wasn't a big surprise either. It had been years that he'd spent standing for long periods of time over the bowl, sometimes holding on to the sink as he almost fell back asleep waiting to urinate. Then there was the increasing frequency of those episodes, he realized.

Now, it was an ache in his hips and back. He'd always prided himself on his strong, good back, no lower back pain like so many other men he knew. He'd shoveled, lifted, pushed and pulled with that back a thousand times more than most people. For the first time in his life, he was in not just pain, but excruciating pain reaching down into his hips. Doctors wanted to probe and he'd relented allowing them to do a biopsy. The results confirmed an advanced stage of prostate cancer. They'd suggested radiation but Jerry knew that would mean frequent trips to the hospital, side effects yet to be determined and most of all, admitting he had cancer. Now his health would be a factor in the future of his farm. He hoped Frank could come up with some plan that kept the place going. He'd offered a number of options for his part, letting Frank lease it as he tried to build up some revenue to buy it, continuing to transfer ownership of the cows to him and giving him the best price he could arrange.

There was Denis and Tricia's interest though that was going to limit what he could do on the price, he'd told Frank. They had been essential financial supporters but it wasn't without a payback cost. The farm had always had a large land value that Denis felt comfortable he could recoup when it was finally sold so he'd been more than willing to subsidize his wife's family but he wouldn't give it away.

Jerry made the phone call to Tricia about two weeks ago that spelled out some of the big news, first his hopes to sell or lease the farm to Frank and then the news about his health. Her first thought was to jump on a plane and come East to fix everything. Jerry had to be very reassuring, making promises for frequent updates to finally convince her to stay put.

He'd already been found out by the astute nurse, Lindsey, which made it easier to tell Frank. She'd come into the house late one night after finishing the milking and found him doubled over in pain, not able to move. He'd tried to minimize it and put her off but she wouldn't be fooled. Her professional grilling of just what he was feeling and how long it had been going on produced a long list of confessions about the prostate cancer, hernia and the permanently damaged collarbone as the highlights.

Of all Jerry's issues, the cancer was the one that Lindsey knew was the worst. From her days in the nursing home, she'd seen older men at this point in a prostate cancer battle and it had been a short and unsuccessful fight. Jerry was exhibiting signs of a very advanced cancer that had moved into his bones, the kind that could have him dead in a year. She doubted he had many options for treatment.

They'd decided they'd tell Frank together. Only they hadn't found the right time yet and he was moving at a furious pace to try to put a plan in place before the cold winter months set in.

Jerry walked out to the barn on a rare 70 degree Indian summer night in late October hoping to find them both just about finished with the clean-up. His timing was good and when Lindsey saw him and the panicked look on his face, she'd taken her cue to get to the news.

Frank didn't say much just looked at Jerry, a multitude of emotions splaying for seconds across his face, everything from anguish to anger. The first wave of frustration with Jerry realizing that he hadn't taken better care of himself for years was outweighed by his more deep-seated second wave of emotion, a love for this man who had given his whole life to something without thinking about himself.

"Gee, Jerry, I'm sorry," Frank had finally blurted out. "What can I do to help?"

"I'm not telling you this news because I want you to do anything for me, Frank," Jerry said. "You need to have the whole picture and know you might have a shortened window of opportunity if you want to make a go of this thing. That's my only reason for letting you know any of my health issues and because your nosey wife over there is too curious and head-strong for me to have been able to keep it from her."

Lindsey put her arms around Jerry, something she had never done before and Frank joined her. Holding both these people in his grasp, Frank breathed in their strongly contrasting scents, felt the softness of Jerry's worn flannel and the firmness of his wife's arms and back and closed his eyes.

The bad news put Frank back in Bagram, in the far distance a loud explosion and then the feeling of waiting for the news of the repercussions.

Jerry disentangled himself from the circle and made his way back into the house. Instead of dropping his clothes in a pile at the daybed and sleeping in the kitchen, he made his way to the bedroom he'd used before Joanie passed. It had changed little, her decorating touches still intact, the same curtains in the windows and the thing he had come here to find. When the world had become too much for him alone, he found her again here in the bed they had shared, tucking himself under the same old woolen blanket. It had a soft satin edge that was worn threadbare in places.

He let himself come here for solace only rarely but today qualified. Pulling the blankets up he took hold of the edge, tried to breath deep and relax and mentally sent Joan a message that he may be seeing her sooner than later.

Chapter 26

THE
A GIRLS

THE FIRST HARD FROST OF THE SEASON killed what was left of the small garden plot Lindsey had planted. It also sparked a reminder from Jerry to Frank to keep up with the manure spreading. No telling when you'd find the manure pile frozen under an icy mix or even an early snowstorm, he warned. Keep spreading it on the fields every day so there's never much accumulation when the weather prevents you from driving in the fields.

Frank had never minded the field work. Driving the tractor set his mind off on so many tangents and he even found himself working out solutions to the hum of the engine and the creaks of the attached equipment. Today was no different but as he pulled the spreader around a surprising memory surfaced, one that had up to that point been lost to him.

He was back in his younger days, a member of the high school varsity baseball team. It was the weekend of the state baseball finals. His team, a scrappy group that by all rights had no business making it this far, was up against the perennial powerhouse. Down three runs in the bottom of the ninth, his team had mounted a valiant comeback cutting the lead to just one. With two outs and runners on second and third Frank stepped to the plate with the possibility of driving in the winning run.

Fouling off a couple tough curveballs, he worked the count full. All he needed was a base hit here to win the game. The next pitch blazed towards home and Frank could see that it was going to be a strike, but for some reason his mind couldn't force his body to swing.

"Strike three," the umpire bellowed as the opposing team began to swarm the field. Frank stood there momentarily numb to what had just happened.

After the game his teammates tried to cheer him up by telling him it wasn't his fault. They wouldn't have been down by three runs if they hadn't made crucial errors earlier in the game. He showered and changed quickly not interested in who was making plans for any activities later. None of it was registering with Frank. He just needed to be somewhere else.

He wasn't sure how his car found its way to Fair View Acres that day. He couldn't even remember making the drive.

What he would always remember though was the look that Adeline gave him when he first walked into her pen. It had been maybe six months since the last time he had been to the farm, but there was instant recognition in her eyes. The big black eyes of that Jersey cow seemed to understand him more than any person could. She was glad to see him, he sensed. Her consistent expectation was that he had come back to provide just for her.

The grain was stored where he remembered and he filled a small black feed bowl, laying it down so she was the only heifer who could eat from it. She was never one to refuse extra grain but he knew she was listening too so he started to tell her about the game, how he'd struck out and let the team down. It helped to unload on her and she had no problem listening to his confession. The grain finished, she tucked her large golden head up under his hand and he scratched it.

He stayed a while just feeling her soft cow hide but knew he'd have to break away again. His days were filled with other things now and he had come here on autopilot, not as a planned return. It had worked to ease his broken heart. He thanked her, told her to be a good girl for Jerry and grow up to make lots of milk. Then he snuck away again.

Jerry was in the middle of a chaotic day at the farm. The tractor had broken down and he had two cows on antibiotics, meaning they weren't contributing any milk towards his much needed production numbers. He'd lost Frank's youthful energy and had found a replacement through the Jehovah's Witness temple but realized already this help was nowhere near as capable as Frank had been.

Jose, his new helper forgot to close the gate to one of the fields and the cows had gotten loose. Trying to usher them back was taking much longer than he had available. The group was laced with first calf heifers, one of them not at all inclined to have her meal interrupted for that stuff she'd finished with in the next field over. It was times like these that made Jerry wonder why he ever wanted to be a farmer.

As he was walking by the heifer barn Jerry saw the car in the driveway and knew it was Frank's. He'd last seen those tail lights heading away from the farm. He slowly entered keeping quiet and out of sight, curious as to what had brought Frank back today. There he was pouring his heart out to Adeline. Careful not to rouse any attention, Jerry slunk back behind a beam in the corner where he could observe the expressive interaction without being noticed.

Although he never told him, Jerry had seen a farmer in Frank shortly after he began coming there. It wasn't just that he seemed willing to do the messy work or put in the long hours that would scare most people away, Frank had a way with the animals that was the key. He was as good as anyone he'd ever seen relating to the cows. The animals were always the best judges of character and Jerry saw right away how quickly they came to trust Frank.

The exact opposite was true of his new man. Jose was afraid of the cows and disliked being around them. They knew it and they in turn had judged him to be unworthy of their trust and cooperation. That was a disastrous combination. Jerry knew he'd have to let him go before either he got hurt or one of the cows did.

When an animal as bright as Adeline assessed Frank to be a star in her eyes, Jerry knew not to second guess that, just be glad you had that kid on your team. Even though he hadn't always been easy on Frank, giving him a harsh dose of farm reality when needed, he also had made weekly reports to his best friend, Walt. Those were always laced with so much more positive than negative that they started joking about the kid as Farm Boy Frank.

He hadn't seen Frank at the farm now in about six months which was not all that unexpected given he was a teenager occupied by sports, friends, and all kinds of other distractions. For some reason though Jerry had always held out a hope in the back of his mind that one day he might see this boy grow into the great farmer that he believed he could be.

Jerry watched as Adeline licked Frank's hand. He saw him gently caressing her head, the best listener he could have ever hoped for, while pouring out the musings of a teenage soul. Jerry had done the same on similar occasions when a Jersey's eyes were the only thing that would suffice. When his wife's cancer had progressed to the point she was hospitalized, Jerry had run to the hospital as often as he could but he had few people helping at the farm in those days. His trips were arranged between milkings. That left no time for feeling bad for himself or for preparing himself for the end.

Joanie's service had been late in the morning giving Jerry time to clean up after he did the morning milking. He'd survived it was about all he could say he remembered of it and then turned back to the farm without his partner.

During the milking that night, his girls had let him unleash his sorrow.

"She's not coming back," he'd told them, then buried his head on the closest cow's neck and produced dark, salted-brine streaks on her coat.

***

Frank smiled as he pulled the tractor into the shed remembering that day back in Adeline's stall and was amazed that until that point, he'd totally forgotten it had happened.

The night milking was starting and Nelson came into sight indicating he was putting things in motion, cleaning equipment and filling grain buckets. Frank joined in and they settled into the work. Things were going along well tonight and it looked like he'd get to head home early, Frank dared to think. That hopeful prospect was soon halted.

Frank's mind was slow to grasp what he was seeing. A thin skeletal cow had just come in with the last batch of four. He knew he was looking at a cow with advanced Johne's.

That cow was Ada, the pick of the herd, but that couldn't be. He was planted at the milk room door. If he didn't go over and confirm that the markings on her head were Ada's and that the walking carcass attached to that face was hers, then this would all just go away.

When Nelson walked in, his presence necessitated movement, either to confirm his worst nightmare or to somehow fix it, make it not be what he saw and knew.

"Is that Ada?" he managed to almost whisper.

Nelson looked. There were two cows still standing in the milking parlor, one as thin as a rail with a white blaze on her forehead, the other the large, dark Holstein cross, Pam.

"This one, yes," Nelson put his hand on her back.

"Nelson, didn't you see?" Frank asked.

A blank stare was the answer. Nelson did see, but not react, see but not feel what Frank was feeling, the horror of the fate that awaited this best in Jerry's girls, the finest of his dairy cows.

Frank wanted to scream at Nelson, the seldom felt anger finding root in him. It wasn't Nelson who was responsible, he stopped himself. Even if he had noticed early on, it wouldn't have been anything different. Ada still would have gotten to this point once infected with the deadly condition.

He was to blame for not seeing her symptoms and how she was declining. Now she was maybe a month away from death and there wasn't going to be anything he could do. She'd go on trying to give milk even as her body refused to feed her, all the stomach regurgitation not working properly to let her feed herself, let alone make milk.

He'd let Nelson finish the milking most days now, had rushed out of the milk room to start the clean up so that he could get done faster. He hadn't thought of the possibility that a sick cow was the last one straggling in, that was why she was the last one in, providing further confirmation of her weakened condition. Ada wouldn't have had the strength to be with the first pushy girls hungry to be fed. She would have been falling to the last in line. It all was so clear now to Frank he wanted to kick himself.

He walked to her, his favorite girl and as he got closer to that face, his heart again took a lurch for the worse. The picture, burnt into his mind of her Baby Angel nursing for all she was worth, was the next anguish he faced. Johne's cows usually gave the disease to their calves with the first colostrum they feed them. It wouldn't be evident until almost two years later but it was there, in them, a silent killer.

He held Ada's face, just like she always enjoyed, the dog-like petting that he so relished doing for this girl who he knew was the best and the brightest.

How was he going to tell Jerry? Or Aubrey?

Not that it was going to make a difference in her outcome, but after she was milked, he walked Ada over to a corner of the rear lean-to and put out a big chunk of hay, added some extra grain and made sure the water trough was flowing. Anything to try to make her life a little easier, save her expending energy she didn't have.

Jerry's read of his expression when he was barely two steps into the farmhouse kitchen was at its usual acumen and there would be no beating around the bush.

"What's the matter?" Jerry asked.

"Ada. She has Johne's."

"Are you sure? Did you call the vet?"

"I'm pretty sure but I'll call the vet right away," Frank wanted Jerry to yell at him, ask him how he could let this happen but he didn't. Jerry's face was punishment enough, worse than any tongue slashing. A sorrow was plastered there that went into every crevasse of the man's soul. When he'd lost Joanie, he probably hadn't looked much different, Frank realized.

Neither of them spoke further and Frank walked back out, phone in hand, the vet's number ringing as he walked to clean the heifer barn. There really wasn't an emergency, he told the receptionist, just when the vet could get there, he had a cow for him to test for Johne's.

A week later the diagnosis was confirmed. Ada had deteriorated pretty far. Francie had died a slow, wasting death, trying with every breath to fend off the specter and continue to live. Johne's had a cruel consistent path. Frank had seen it.

He couldn't wait to get home to Lindsey for the comfort of her presence and the hope that somehow she'd make it better, see some way to ease his pain.

"It's not your fault," she said, in response to his blurting out the grim news to her. "You know, you didn't cause this disease. The vets don't even know why some cows get it or how to cure it so don't think you failed that cow. You've taken great care of all those cows. That herd would be sold and maybe slaughtered by now if you hadn't gone over there."

She held him which was the most helpful thing to him and he again thanked God for her in his life. He was certain he couldn't be living this latest nightmare without her beside him.

"It's not just Ada who will die of Johne's," he told Lindsey. "It could be Baby Angel too."

"Oh God, no," Lindsey sobbed. "Don't tell Aubrey. Not now. Maybe she won't have it. It's not certain that all babies get it from their mothers."

"The ones who nurse from them have the highest chance and I know for a fact, I saw them. Her baby nursed right away after she was born."

"Don't say anything to Aubrey about Ada or Angel," Lindsey made him promise. "Don't give up on them."

Chapter 27

KILL
GROUP

THE INFLATION TUBE SPLIT on Linda, only the third cow of the morning milking. In a bygone day the litany of crucial equipment breaking would have put Frank in a foul mood. He hadn't noticed it when he assembled the equipment and made a mental note to try to catch that kind of thing before it was too late. Now the cow had already begun letting her milk down and wanted to keep doing it until she'd milk out fully. This was just the kind of interruption in milking that Frank had learnt led to problems down the road. The cow's chance of developing mastitis was reduced by a quick, consistent flow of milk, not this five minute interruption while he found and then installed a new rubber tube without a gaping hole in the side of it.

Once back on the cow's teat, Frank paid attention to see that she had a new and strong flow started again. It seemed like she did. Linda was that kind of cow, luckily, not a newcomer to milking, probably in her fifth lactation. She was mostly problem-free so in that sense, he had been saved from a worse fate, Frank reasoned. It was then that he also realized how far he'd come from the man who would have been throwing things and swearing at something like this.

Since Afghanistan, there had been very little that made him angry. He'd recognized it for some time and was not proud, more appreciative, of the calm he had acquired.

It was definitely a condition that had been a result of one of the worst days of his life. The patrol in the Khost Province near the Pakistan border was burnt in his mind. He had no illusions that it would not be there forever. His group had engaged the Taliban out on the road and were dug in for a shootout. Air support was going to be at least an hour away. They had to take other measures.

Keeping the enemy occupied with a strong narrow focus, his team leader sent six as a kill group to flank them and end the engagement. He was in the kill group, his shooting skills making him a frequent choice.

He moved out trying to find any cover in this land of undulating hills mixed with nothingness, barely a rock big enough to hide a grown man. The Taliban were not likely to be fooled by the maneuver but the American force had the number advantage and could do a good job keeping the enemy occupied.

As his team moved, Frank spotted a higher promontory near a mound of grey rocks. He instinctively moved toward it. From here he quickly zeroed in on the target he planned to hit. The stony cover had the rest of the group moving along on their bellies. He kind of liked that

245

position as he lowered himself to that level. His success from this vantage was better than average.

He watched and assessed and when the opportunity presented itself, took a shot he knew hit its mark. The rest of the group added punishment to what was a small enemy force and the fight was over. The fallen that day though had included one special friend he'd dared to make. A soft spoken Southern kid who was leaving behind a young wife and child, Frank knew. Why him? Why not me? I have no one waiting for me. There was no arguing with fate. He'd learned that lesson not just that day but over all of the days he endured fate's whims.

He almost always thought about his father when he was in any kind of fire fight. His dad taught him to hunt when he was 13, taking him with him on what was considered a duty—to keep the deer population in check so they didn't destroy the garden and landscaping and to fill the family freezer. He'd watched and listened to his father's instructions and waited for the day when he could try to take the shot. When it had come, he'd missed a kill shot and the injured deer fled, leaving a more than adequate bloody trail to follow. They'd searched for more than two hours but hadn't found her. The weight of that animal left to suffer a slow painful death was heavy on Frank.

He took to bugging his father to go to the shooting range as often as they could. When he was there, he was all business, having made a vow to himself, not to repeat his bad shot.

His father set up targets in the farthest corner of their woods, targets that Frank spent many free hours punishing, practicing shooting day in and day out. Frank swore he was not to going miss the next time he fired his gun at a target. There were guys in the military who swore a home-grown hunter was the worst for marksmanship because they had been taught all wrong to begin with but that wasn't Frank and he was glad to prove them wrong and do his father proud.

Not long after that day, what turned out to be the last kill group he was assigned to, Frank had his first conscious thought about his mental state.

Not one to look for a fight, he was also not one to back down if pushed. He didn't let a slight pass without an offer to settle it. He'd almost been tempted to take pride in his temper, hoping to be angered. His father, the methodical machinist, had worked hard trying to teach him to be calm but it had continued to elude him.

It was months now at the farm and he hadn't let anger, including the aggravations that had previously been certain triggers, derail him. Nothing was worth getting mad about anymore. It wasn't something he had made a vow to attain, it just was a fact. He couldn't muster the emotion anymore.

In the barn with the herd attentive to his every emotion, he'd seen the change as a Godsend. The old Frank might have spooked these girls on a daily basis but the new Frank was very good at keeping a mellow mood. His quiet acceptance of challenges was going to be called on today, he knew, with the list of fixes needed.

The farm not only capitalized on his newfound calm, it challenged his creativity, the MacGyver factor that he had always liked to bring. With no money for most repairs, he was constantly scavenging a makeshift solution and often liking the result good enough to be glad it hadn't been done the easy way with new material.

Adding up the accumulated satisfaction he found at the farm, he smiled at the variety and unexpectedness of the best moments and outcomes. He envied Jerry, having had so many years to enjoy this life.

Even days with their challenges like today, weren't a reason to quit but instead a reason to acknowledge how right the work and demands felt.

He was in a good position for a kill shot at this target, he thought. He could take this mission and make a success of it with some support from a group like he'd had back in the battlefield. That's where his daydream on the similarities of the two situations started to unravel though. There didn't seem to be anyone else moving out to accomplish this critical victory, not even anyone who saw it as a war worth fighting and winning. He believed that any remaining dairy farms in this part of the country were worth fighting for. He wasn't sure how to battle the many things that were defeating that objective though and he was late to the fight. There were hardly any farms left to save.

The similarity in the complexity of the situation and Afghanistan were striking to Frank, the lack of new, constructive ideas to move beyond a mountain of mistakes.

The necessity that he continue in this war and fight to win were as strong as those he'd had serving overseas so he bent to his next task, calling the supply company and ordering new inflations. He didn't like the odds, he realized as he waited for a human voice to take his order over the phone. He was reminded that he had intended to find the company's website and try to get the farm supplies ordered online. So many things in this war could be made easier with new technology and a few more fighters. Instead he was involved in a war without allies and there were too many enemies, maybe even his own government. He didn't know where and how they would ambush him next.

Finding a little time to spare, Frank walked to the top of the high pasture just before the afternoon milking and took a seat on a large boulder under a 40-foot oak that had been spared the gypsy moth infestation and still had a thick canopy of leaves. He hit the Google search on his phone knowing reception up here was the best. The search was "pasteurization equipment for dairy farms" and he scanned the offerings, skipping the ads and clicking on the company that had small scale size in their equipment line. A goat operation unit might be the right size, he realized. The largest in that line would handle about a 30-cow load if he bottled every other day. He wanted a slow pasteurization process, not a high temperature, short time system because of the taste the higher temperature imparted to the milk. It was going to be a luxury, however, because it could take only 15 seconds with high temperatures to pasteurize milk. If he used the slower process, he was going to have a 30-minute process at a lower temperature that was going to take up valuable limited farm hours.

He'd have to make a selection of a pasteurizer and send a request to one of the companies to get a price quote. Used equipment was sometimes available from a few companies, he noticed, and he liked the thought of picking up some lightly used stuff that he felt confident he could tinker into working.

He and Lindsey were spending every available minute doing research on dairy operations, what kind of equipment was available, what market could they tap if they tried to sell directly to the local community and how could they market the farm to quickly build a customer base?

Frank had started listening to Lorraine more as she offered plans for the farm. As a professional fundraiser for the college, he saw her as an expert at generating money for a cause. She'd been working to convince Frank there was a large enough population of locavores who would embrace the sale of local milk. Lorraine's plan revolved around a raw milk operation but Frank was not inclined to sell raw milk for a few reasons.

He hoped to draw the most buyers he could for his local milk and didn't want to meet resistance from customers who didn't want something "unadulterated," meaning not guaranteed free from all germs. He could never make that assurance about raw milk just the assurance that his cows were vaccinated from the diseases that had brought about pasteurization.

His latest idea was to try to keep a portion of milk available raw. That might mean milking in two different batches. He could milk the raw milk cows first, he formulated. Those would be the cleanest and healthiest cows who would provide the best quality milk for the raw market. Their somatic cell counts were low enough to meet the raw milk testing standards, he knew.

He thought he could bottle that milk before putting the rest of the herd's milk in the bulk tank and pasteurizing it. The timing of exactly how that would work still eluded him but it surely meant more hands working in the barn, he realized. As he drew the plan for "his" farm, he often thought about his parents. They'd be happy to see him pursue this effort, he thought, and he felt they were helping especially when positive developments came together.

During an online search one weekend afternoon, he and Lindsey decided they would go back to glass milk bottles for their product. The design on the bottle would be Baby Angel's heart-shaped head and a drawing of the barn with its peaked roof in the background. They'd gotten as excited as kids thinking about how great the bottle would look. The price of the glass bottles was a little steep but it was an investment toward ensuring their farm product had a quality appearance. It became one of the definites in the business plan they were developing to submit to the USDA office.

There were plenty of things Frank was willing to try, but ideas that Lindsey found that sounded like making the farm into a playground instead of a farm, he resisted. Doing a corn maze, if there even was a field that the farm could dedicate to that income producing effort, ran counter to his aim to make the dairy farm a success as a dairy farm, not an amusement park. If nothing else, Frank's argument often just came back to not pinning the success of the farm on something that families might like today but could be replaced with any other new attraction in the future.

On some issues Frank and Lindsey were united and firm. The farm couldn't continue to sell its milk to the co-op and accept the drastic highs and lows of the milk pricing system. Congress offered nothing to New England farms and with the particular challenges of land values, topography and climate. They vowed the only plan they would develop would be one where they broke away from the national dairy system.

Lindsey researched all the small independent area dairies to see if any of them would take on another dairy but none were expanding and they had all the producers they needed. That led them to a plan where they developed their own customer base and then tried to work out the system for delivery.

The work of filling out the USDA Farm Business Plan Worksheet had mainly fallen to Lindsey, the member of the team able to muddle through the forms like she did for the IRS returns. Even she had some moments of throwing up her hands in frustration at the minutia of the forms but Lorraine's help had gotten her through. Once she had what they thought was a reasonable plan, they submitted it and attempted to find a meeting day that worked for Lindsey's schedule and the farm demands. An appointment a month later at the Farm Service Agency office to review it with a loan agent was finally agreed to.

They also agreed on a few ground rules. One, they wouldn't divulge anything about Jerry's health or any cases of Johne's. Those were two aspects of the reality they dealt with that both felt were best kept private for now.

Chapter 28

U.S.D.A.

THE LAPTOP SCREEN remained a dark info-less black. John Horsemann sat back in his office chair and accepted it would be another typical day with computer issues stopping any attempt to make much use of these work hours. Nothing new. The USDA had pushed an update through for a new Share Point this weekend. Odds were it was going to cause as much damage as it offered of improvements.

His morning's appointments were in his Outlook calendar and that wasn't playing so he wracked his brain to remember just what it was he was supposed to do today. He had agreed to sit in on a meeting with the young guy from Fairford on that loan for the dairy farm purchase. That situation was interesting to John, bringing him back full circle to the days when he was taking just the opposite route, meeting with USDA personnel to work on the closing of his family's farm and the dairy buyout amount that would send his herd to slaughter.

He'd been in the agriculture business too long, he smiled, when instead of closing farms down and spending money to kill cows, the USDA and state farm bureaus over the last few years had developed plans to spend millions of dollars on loans and grants to keep farms. You just never could tell how things would turn out, John reflected.

His last days at his family's farm had been a blur of frantic activity, the negotiations with USDA on a price in the dairy farm buyout finally being something he could live with, the loading of the cows onto the cattle transports, the empty barn and the quiet descending on him like a great relief. He had moved on using his experience working the farm to his advantage, securing a position with the federal government agriculture department and then moving up through the ranks. He sat in a comfortable state USDA office, taking home a GS 15 salary and safe in the knowledge of his retirement benefits waiting for him to collect. Not a bad life, he grinned.

He had disliked dairy farming and the filth and was bewildered by the farmers who had come to his office over the years. They were willing to do most anything to get or keep their farms and the dirty work linked to that life. Go figure, he mused.

This new guy, Frank Maddox, was right up there with a dream of dairy farming. He is in for some education, John thought. So many land owners seemed reluctant to partner with the government but this guy needed them and they needed to reach their farmland loan goals so he had scheduled a meeting with the loan agent and John had offered to sit in.

He knew the farm Maddox was interested in buying or at least running and he also knew the county commission chairperson, Alfred

Tocci, was very interested in getting his hands on Duggan's farm, had been for years, hoping the aging dairy farmer would just give up. Tocci's vegetable and fruit business could use the prime farmland to expand its operation and the largest field had Tocci salivating with the prospect of a new corn maze. John felt he would be needed in the meeting with Maddox to help explain the limits of the government program and hopefully send him on his way. The old man who owned the land had been around too long. He hadn't taken any of the dairy buyouts for the past 30 years, too much Yankee in him for that program. According to John's sources, he was trying to talk young Maddox out of using the USDA program to help him get the farm. Not sure how he thought Maddox would have any chance without them but he was all ears to gather information from either of them on other options and try to close this new farm deal option.

Hopefully he could help Tocci get his hands on the property. The man knew how to operate a farm in today's world. If there was a program that he could qualify for, John knew he'd have an application in on the first day it opened. Those were the kind of farmers he liked to encourage, not the rebels who wanted to go their own route.

Another rumor he'd heard about Maddox was he wanted out of the co-op and wanted to install a processing unit at the farm and develop a local route. Talk about taking a step back in time. He had no doubt Duggan's dad did exactly the same thing. Look where that got him, John shook his head.

He wondered just how strong Maddox's resources were. He may have some backing from an outside source, maybe even was thinking of doing something online with crowdsourcing. Those had produced some surprise outcomes, he'd seen. Those private conservation programs might have something out there he didn't know about, though he made it his job to know their programs almost better than they did. Know your enemy, he figured.

The meeting with Maddox was around 1 p.m., John guessed, not having the benefit of a functional government laptop to confirm that. Maybe he'd start keeping a paper copy of his calendar since the electronic issues were starting to annoy him. His 62nd birthday was 17 months away, but who was counting. He was feeling more and more certain every day that would be his retirement date. Nothing left to keep me here, he'd determined.

The good thing about the computer glitch was they wouldn't be able to pull up Maddox's application so John already knew this meeting would not move the prospects of USDA loans any further. It would only be providing him with a lot of information and additional time to react to it.

In the parking lot Frank looked about as nervous as Lindsey had ever seen him. He was cleaned up nice, had his stowed-away GI training showing which they hoped would be helpful. All the research they'd done had uncovered an initiative by the government to help veterans get into farming. They hoped it might offer another program for their plans.

The hesitancy on Frank's part was the jumble of paperwork still to surmount coupled with a shrinking time table. He would not divulge Jerry's medical condition to the USDA agents, but it weighed on him and was going to become an issue if there was no flexibility in the requirement for three years of management of the farm before he could qualify for any ownership assistance.

He'd decided he was even going to throw out his two years as a teenager working on the farm. Yes, he was young but he now had fully realized what an impact the work had had on him and how much aptitude he'd had early on, how easily he'd absorbed the farm and animal's needs.

He wasn't a sales man, had never considered any job that required him to sell something because he lacked any inclination to bullshit. He hoped that wasn't going to be his downfall on this endeavor. Lindsey wasn't much better at the selling work but she was a fierce proponent of her husband's dreams. He'd been amazed at the intensity of her efforts to help them get the farm. When he told her thanks, she came back with a very direct statement about him deserving this chance and the world needing him to do this.

She would bring it if he hesitated to state his case strongly enough to the loan agents this morning. From their discussion leading up to this meeting and even continuing in the car on the way over, Frank saw Lindsey setting her mind on being a dairy farmer's wife and raising their daughter, and even another newcomer, to follow in their dad's footsteps. She was as passionate about the project as he was and more willing to show it.

He was always one to stay reserved in his show of emotions and was taking that same path in this process, not letting on how much of his sleepless nights were spent figuring out all the possibilities that might make the farm a reality. He'd usually fall deep asleep from exhaustion just about 2 a.m. only to be jolted awake a couple hours later by the alarm clock. Then he could look forward to rolling out of bed and face a day full of work on only a few hours rest.

They walked into the lobby of the small Farm Service Bureau office and saw the reception desk but no one was sitting at it. They moved in that direction and waited for someone to arrive. After about five minutes and no sign of anyone, Lindsey walked over to a door and knocked, calling out hello.

She was answered by a woman appearing and asking if she could help them. They had an appointment about a farm loan, Lindsey explained. Apologizing for the computers being down and the calendar not operational, she asked for the name of the person they were scheduled to meeting with.

Lindsey had the names seared into her memory and produced John Horseman and a loan agent, Henry Mitchell. Indicating they were both there, the woman asked them to have a seat and she would let them know they had arrived.

She disappeared beyond a door and Frank and Lindsey sat in the waiting room. They soon realized they may as well begin to read the stock of outdated magazines as the woman didn't reappear for a long time.

Finally, she came back and told them she'd located John and Henry and they would be with them shortly. Another 10-minute interval and Henry appeared at the door calling Frank's name. He stood up, walked over and offered his hand. Henry fit the vision Frank had developed about his loan agent, a youngish college agribusiness grad who had an outdoorsy bent but wasn't into getting hit with any flying manure. He had heard the reservation in Henry's voice on every phone call and read between the lines in each e-mail. A dairy farm in New England had small chance of success and really, why bother was the under current in Henry's answers to his questions about USDA loans and the young farmer initiative. Milk was plentiful. It could be produced far away and trucked in. The milk business was no place for smart, young people. If you did have to farm, make it a specialty organic vegetable or fruit operation or an edible herds or even exotic mushroom farm, not a smelly, dirty dairy farm.

Frank and Lindsey, however, were more firm than ever in their determination that what they wanted to do was make milk, very good, fresh, local milk. Teaming up with Lorraine, the fundraiser by occupation and a passionate fan of their farm, set that goal in stone. The business plan the USDA required was focused on building a customer base similar to a community supported agriculture farm, another suggestion from Lorraine.

In their optimistic expectations about the outcome of this meeting, Frank and Lindsey hoped the USDA office would offer strong support and want to maintain a dairy farm, one of very few left in this area of New England. They needed compromise on the requirements they couldn't meet including waiting three years for Frank to have the experience to qualify for assistance. It wasn't likely Jerry would have that long.

Another big compromise they hoped to discuss was the need to take USDA required courses for new farmers. If those couldn't be done online to a large extent, Frank knew he'd have little chance of working the farm all day and taking courses. The time away from the farm seemed to only lead to more work when he got back because his eyes were the ones that noticed what needed to be done. If a cow was starting to come down with something, a calf had scours, a piece of equipment was about to fail, Nelson had little capacity to notice. Frank had tried his best to tell him to keep his eyes open and report anything he saw, but there'd been few reports from his main helper.

They also were realistic on their limits. They couldn't sustain a plan to take over a business without quite owning it and getting the financial benefit of their efforts. They had to have a way to work the farm and support themselves, even put money in Aubrey's college fund.

They decided against giving away any medical information on Jerry's condition instead pinning their hopes on the lack of any other viable candidates who wanted to save a dairy operation.

Lorraine's initiative had been intense. She had laid out a marketing plan for both a home delivery and farm pickup operation that would offer the pasteurized product at twice what the farm was getting paid by the co-operative and a raw milk product that she estimated could command a premium price of almost three times what Jerry was paid for a gallon of his milk.

If her plan worked, the farm would be able to support Dave Mello as a fulltime employee, though Frank still hadn't gotten a firm commitment from him to work at the farm. He'd made it clear he wanted to do the work but couldn't make a decision that would hurt his family and that might be too risky to try.

If not Dave, Frank hoped that the salary they'd estimated for him would still attract a fairly well-educated worker who would have the type of integrity and work ethic that would let him take a day off without being terrorized by the prospect of contaminated milk and sick animals.

Henry walked them through a maze of cubicles and sat them down in his tiny space. He began right away with a statement that their application couldn't be brought up online where it was stored because the federal system upgrade had not gone well. The most they could accomplish today would be a discussion of their business plan and a rescheduling of a review of the application for an operating loan and purchase assistance.

Frank felt like he'd been hit with a baseball bat. How could they expect him to take another day off and make an almost two hour trip into this office only to be told he'd have to come back. He was inclined to stand up and walk out the door immediately but Lindsey was asking a question.

"Can we do this without coming back to the office because it has been a little difficult for both of us to get the time off and to get the coverage at the farm and someone to take care of our daughter?"

"Well, did you bring a paper copy of your plan?" Henry asked, already knowing they had brought nothing in with them and that it wasn't likely given that they had no indication it would be needed. "If not, then it wouldn't be possible to finalize anything but we can probably make some progress on the application through e-mail and phone calls," Henry offered.

John sensed that this couple would not be here long so he stepped into the cubicle.

"Hi, I'm John Horsemann, area director. Sorry about those computer issues. Unfortunately, they're almost a constant problem and we just have to do our best to get through it."

"We had to make a lot of arrangements to get in here today," Frank spoke up. "This is an hour from the farm and I don't have a lot of help so any time I'm away means I'm falling behind."

"That's too bad," John retorted before he'd had a chance to stop himself. "I mean it sincerely," he quickly added. "We don't like to be out of commission either but it's one of the things that is a reality that we have to deal with."

"So in that regard," he added. "Can you tell me what you think you want to do with the dairy farm?"

Frank didn't hold back and Lindsey was often inputting energetic additional information anytime she thought Frank hadn't elaborated adequately.

John saw the enthusiasm and laughed inwardly. Boy, youth doesn't change, he thought. These two are seeing success in a farm plan that I know is a useless effort.

When Frank ran out of steam, John said he thought he had a good idea of the plan and that he would review it with the loan agent before they came back. The date of a return though was hard to determine with all the jobs Frank had put aside to make it here today. It was finally decided to get back into the office in two weeks.

In the car Frank and Lindsey tried to be optimistic about how the meeting had gone. Lindsey said she thought the USDA director was really interested. Why would he take part when he didn't have to?

"I hope he's on our side and we can get some help," Frank said, eyeing the road ahead and just consumed by the weight of what he had waiting when he got back to the farm. "and I hope he realizes this dairy farm could be lost very easily and real soon if they don't have any way to help us keep it going. Neither one of those guys seemed to have any grasp of the urgency of doing something to keep this place going."

"It's Jerry's favorite expression, I think, you can't be a little pregnant or a little bit a dairy farmer. Those cows need milking every day, twice a day or this farm is gone. This place could be lost like crazy fast. Maybe I just didn't catch it, but nothing they said made me think saving one of the few dairy farms around was a priority."

"I didn't hear anything that made me have a warm and fuzzy feeling either," Lindsey admitted. "Maybe they will need to be brought in on Jerry's health so that they can move this as fast as possible. What I really didn't like was describing how the government process works and all the approval levels and the time it will take to get through those. I couldn't add up all the names of offices that had to review our plan but it seems very involved and thorough but also very slow."

"We have USDA and computers that don't work when what we need is FEMA for farms, emergency management" Frank blurted out.

They rode a long way in silence both lost in imaginings of outcomes they hoped and dreaded. Frank got Lindsey's OK to take the time to check in at the farm before he brought her home so that he'd know as soon as possible what he was coming back to.

What hit Frank when he got back to the farm was a bigger setback than any he expected and one he couldn't have ducked.

"Nelson hasn't come back yet," Jerry said, as he saw Frank's head in the kitchen doorway and the question on his face.

The crucial farmhand had missed an early milking on a Monday morning before, probably the result of some hard earned fun on his rare day off but for him to still be missing in action this late in the day was unusual. Frank had milked alone in the morning, annoyed by his absence but fully thinking he'd come wandering in at some point.

Jerry didn't have any phone number other than Nelson's cell phone and that had been dead all day, going to voice mail. That message box would be full of Jerry's messages by now. They both knew what the loss of the trained help would mean and how long it would be to get anyone up to the level where Nelson was, able to milk the herd and give Frank a needed respite from that activity. There was also mandatory Reserve time away where Nelson was able to cover with help from a seemingly endless pool of friends or relatives.

Now the New England winter was only months away from battering the farm. Frank had hoped to find Nelson handy with a hammer or at least able to carry roofing shingles up a ladder. The entire corner of the calf barn needed major repair and wouldn't survive the winter. He also knew he couldn't continue to load the manure into the massive iron trough and lug that thing out like he had been doing. He had designed a new doorway big enough to drive the skid steer through. Then he'd be able to mostly push the calf pen waste into the center aisle and pick it up and out without exerting half the effort.

Those two jobs alone were crucial happenings in Frank's mind before the first snow and both would be so much harder without at least one able bodied assistant. The work of milking by himself would push his resources. During Nelson's days off, Lindsey came over as often as she could and even Jerry had resumed some milking duties though always staying far from any backside of a cow and not doing any heavy lifting.

It had taken Jerry almost three years to teach Nelson enough about the dairy operation that he felt safe with him completing a milking session alone or with a cousin. Training another person who probably would speak limited English and have virtually no experience with mechanical systems or cows was going to take a lot of time.

Both Jerry and Frank kicked themselves for not having seen anything amiss with Nelson but were sure they'd missed signs if only they had been paying more attention. The realization sank in that Nelson could be anywhere from New England to Mexico, and based on the variety of license plates he'd showed up with on his vehicles, he could be in any state in between.

He'd seemed happy living in the other side of the duplex but when Jerry and Frank went over to see if there was anything that could offer a clue to Nelson's whereabouts, they found virtually empty space. Maybe Nelson had been planning to leave for a while, Frank thought. Maybe he'd felt some responsibility for Ada. He certainly had seen how upset Frank was and maybe that had hit him harder than Frank realized. He thought he had checked himself and not come down too hard on him for not noticing her condition but maybe his words had been harsher than he recalled.

As more days passed without any contact from him, Jerry finally called the church that had been his source for help when he hired Nelson. The person who answered the phone didn't know Nelson or where he might have gone. He did agree to put out a word to his church members about an opening at a dairy farm. He promised to give anyone interested in the job Jerry's phone number.

The pool of applicants for a dairy farm job was well known to Jerry. He'd been lucky to find good help through the years, one in particular a young man, Luis, much like Nelson, strong back, quick smile and always seeming to agree with him though not actually following through. Luis had solidified the connection with Jerry to the church group and when he left, he had found his replacement there. That had been the hiring process for Jerry's help for the last eight years. Nelson had been one of the best and had stayed the longest.

Frank called Dave Mello. He was working for a temporary agency and offered to come for the afternoon milking on his two days off. Once his temporary work was done, he was interested in talking to Frank about a fulltime job if plans for the farm were moving along. He sounded like he really wanted his life to go in that direction, get his wife and kids out to the country. Frank didn't offer too much encouragement to him, though, hesitant to later have to burst that bubble with a dose of reality.

The meeting with USDA had solidified itself in Frank's mind as they'd searched for Nelson this past week. Help from any government program was going to be a painstakingly slow process with a battle to get needed concessions. He didn't meet their requirement for the amount of time he had spent farming, the minimum three years, and he couldn't reasonably expect to attend classes that USDA required given the time and distance to the school. There were other unseen issues that Frank had caught an inkling of from Jerry, like that other farmers might be more entrenched in the USDA's good graces and more likely to receive government assistance.

***

Just before Thanksgiving, an early storm put a foot of snow on the ground and took out power. Frank was into the night milking when the lights went off. Without the benefit of Nelson or anyone else to help, he powered up the generator. That would only provide for the pump, bulk tank and some of the electrical outlets but the lighting was reduced to half. He could barely see well enough to be sure the cows were prepped right but he moved through the milking, putting the herd to bed with lots of good hay dropped in front of them by a man too exhausted to do much more than break open the bales.

Frank walked into Jerry's kitchen at the end of that day. He didn't even have to say anything. His worn appearance was a mirror image of Jerry's on many days and his father and grandfather's before him.

Somehow they had found ways to keep this farm going. It wasn't going to continue. They both felt it more than knew it and it wasn't for lack of wanting it to be otherwise.

Chapter 29

LAST CALL
PRELUDE

THERE WERE A LOT OF PREPARATIONS to make but Frank went through his list mentally. They were all done. He'd driven up to the high back part of the field about dusk yesterday. The cows were down in the farthest pasture enjoying a new grazing area.

He'd dug the hole with the Kubota and a shovel, tucked into the woods somewhat but along the edge so he could get to it.

Those were the easy things. The hard ones all had somehow come together too. Lindsey had caught him in their barn, cleaning up what had obviously once been an animal stall, hay rack, rolling rail door, a nice big roomy space and on the south side corner. It hadn't been used in the years he and Chris had lived there and he would have had to have asked his mom and dad about the last use of the stall because he didn't have any memory of livestock being housed in there.

When he'd put together this plan, it seemed to him to have been waiting for its next occupant. As he cleaned out the accumulation of things that had gravitated into the unused space, its good qualities were all being revealed. It was no worse for the lack of wear. The wood all around was in great shape. No other animal had chewed away on the edges. Once he got to the floor, a task that had taken him about four afternoons of hard labor, the subsurface was some kind of firm material topped with loose sand, perfect to add a layer of sawdust and be ready.

It was good that Lindsey had found him at his work because he hadn't figured out how he was going to tell her about it. He needed her buy in and support and wasn't worried about getting it but the fact was he was set in this plan and had come to the decision without asking her first.

"Looks nice back here," she said, as she walked into the barn. "What are you cleaning this out for?"

The woman could read him like a book so he kept his head down and mumbled something at first, like "nothing special."

Not put off, she came around where he couldn't help but look her in the eye.

"Franklin Maddox, what's going on?"

"I was planning on bringing Baby Angel over here," was as much as he could admit to right now.

"Why? Aubrey's fine going over to see her. She doesn't have to be over here. That kid is too attached to that cow already. This will really put her over the top," Lindsey offered. "We don't need to be caring for cows in two different places. We're pretty busy already, don't you think?"

"Well, I'm not going to keep working at Jerry's," Frank blurted out. "His health isn't good enough for us to ease into this farm transfer thing. It's not going to work."

From the first time he looked into them to now, Lindsey's eyes never failed to destroy him. The look was a direct feed from her heart into the pupils. The instant message that flashed was a surprised sorrow, deep and almost overflowing her capacity. What it wasn't was angry so he knew she was in the same place he'd already been to, examining every other option.

"I don't think we should give up that easily. I know Jerry's got more medical issues than we knew about and really, he's let them go so long, he has a hard road back but you know, if he puts his mind to sticking around, there's a lot of fight left in him."

"It's not just Jerry's health. It's the cows' health. You know Ada has Johne's and she's failing fast. Every day I see more of her ribs. It's the way she acts that's the toughest thing. She has a desperate look in her eyes and she looks at me, wanting me to make her better. I've tried everything. I know there's nothing I can do for her. She and all the other girls who might come down with that disease don't' deserve to go out that way. Not after all they've given to people. I can't do it anymore."

"When a dairy farm is struggling, it just takes a little to topple it. Jerry's seen it a million times," Frank said. "There's no easy way to get out with the cows needing to be milked all the time. He'd get word of another farm closed and it surprised even him to learn it was gone that fast."

Lindsey had apprenticed at the farm to know how demanding dairy farming was. The cows had to be milked every day, twice a day. You couldn't just leave for a few days and pick it up again. It was constant and exacted a huge toll if any crucial thing was neglected, milking properly every time, feeding, cleaning, looking for signs of problems.

"What does Baby Angel coming over here have to do with all of that?" she had to know.

"I guess I just want to try to save at least her. Maybe over here, away from any contamination from the other cows who had Johne's, just maybe, she'll be OK. If she's grown up and is Johne's free, maybe I'll breed her. Maybe she'll be like her great, great, grandmother and start a whole new herd. That's far enough down the road that we have a little more time to think of a plan."

"What's going to happen to the cows without you?" Lindsey asked.

"It was Jerry's call and he made it. He's going to sell the farm, maybe not right away, maybe after he sees where his health goes. I can picture him staying on at the place and finishing his days there if the news is not good, and then he'll ask to be laid somewhere on that land. His family is all up in the cemetery at the top of the hill."

"He's got most of the cows he still owns sold to a farm in Pennsylvania. Seems like a good place. He didn't get a great price for them because of the Johne's thing. It's hard to make sure the cows don't have it."

"And your cows?"

"I sold most of mine to the same farm too. Just not Ada and Baby Angel."

"Where's Ada going?" Lindsey questioned.

"She couldn't be sold as a dairy cow so I would have had to sell her for meat, not that there's anything much left of her."

Lindsey stopped based on a look on Frank's face that was bringing her to tears. She wasn't sure how but she was seeing the picture of Frank's plan and didn't want to know the full details.

She walked to him with open arms and he let her hold him but not for long. There was still a lot to do and this conversation, now another hurdle behind him, was not going to change anything he'd already firmly set in motion.

Chapter 30

DONE

THE LIFELESSNESS WAS PALATABLE. It contrasted sharply against the crisp air of the sunny November day. A stack of trash, six-feet high was building just to the side of the barn doors. Where at least some farm equipment was usually visible, not a tractor, manure spreader or even a shovel was in sight.

Celeste caught the change first. She looked at Lorraine to see if there was any sign that her friend also was noticing the vacant state of the barnyard, not a golden Jersey in the barn or pasture. Her friend's usually non-stop chatter was turned off so Celeste knew the message was being absorbed.

Something drastic had happened at the farm. The two women had taken vacations to visit family, Celeste finally making her way to the

West Coast, getting a chance to hold grandchildren and show off her vitality to her daughter. Lorraine had headed south to visit a cousin in Florida. They hadn't been to the farm to pick up milk in over a month. The last contact Lorraine had received from Lindsey talked mainly about their frustrations with the USDA process. She hadn't gotten the impression that this was anything more than a stumbling block that she felt sure she'd be able to help them through. In Lorraine's mind, this farm was already turned around, a big success selling gallons of fresh milk with local people lined up competing to buy. The thought that she wouldn't see it saved was not even something she'd considered.

They parked their car in the usual spot but Frank's truck wasn't in sight and they were there during the late morning pickup time that had always meant he'd come walking out of the milk room any minute now.

Celeste got out of the car and headed into the barn with Lorraine following close behind. They liked to see the young stock on every visit but the corner where they should have been was an empty square of sawdust flooring, halters strung over the fence railing and overturned water pails. Not a baby calf to be found.

"Where is everyone?" Celeste asked softly.

"Something big went down here since we've been gone," Lorraine confirmed.

"Do you think the cows are all gone and the farm is closed?"

"I sure don't see much sign of anything left," Lorraine ventured. "It's just so fast and we were working on the plan to make this farm so great."

"How can this farm not still be running? I need my milk," Celeste voice rose to a near scream pitch.

They wandered through the entire barn calling Frank's name, looking at the state of abandonment of all the spaces. The milking equipment left haphazardly on the floor of the milk room, the milking parlor sporting large dried patties that hadn't been cleaned up and gates that were always latched, left wide open as though there were no need any more to confine a herd of cows.

After about a half an hour of looking and finding nothing right and no one to speak to, Lorraine said she was heading to the house. They'd only rarely spoken to Jerry but he was the only one she thought maybe was still here. She knew he didn't go far and wanted desperately to hear him tell her the cows and Frank were just away for a day and would be back tomorrow.

From his kitchen lookout, Jerry had seen them and hoped they wouldn't decide to knock on his door. He wasn't inclined to talk about the farm. It was only two weeks ago that the cattle transporter had taken away the last cows. He and Frank had planned on doing a few things to secure the buildings for winter but Frank was already working for a local construction company.

He struggled with hiding in the back room or answering the door and decided the women were due some explanation after being good customers and trying to help.

The man who answered the door was not the positive, upbeat older man Lorraine remembered. Defeat lay as heavy on him. His shoulders were down four inches lower than she recalled and the corners of his eyes that bore more laugh wrinkles than frown lines were slack.

"We stopped in for milk," Lorraine began, as though they hadn't noticed anything amiss.

Jerry hadn't prepared what he would say and so the response to that statement hung in the air for a long time.

"It's all done here," he finally said.

"What do you mean, all done," Lorraine came back but without her bluster. For a rare moment, she held her voice down to just shy of a whisper, taking even Celeste by surprise.

"We sold the dairy cows to a farm in Pennsylvania."

"Why?" Lorraine came back still keeping a monster hold on her emotions and tone.

"We couldn't keep going," Jerry said, thinking that might lead to more probing than we was going to respond to but hoping it wouldn't require a long explanation.

"Frank, is he all done, with buying the farm and the USDA application and all that?" Lorraine couldn't go away without more answers.

"I can't speak for Frank and what he might still do about farming but it won't be this farm now," Jerry offered as honestly as he felt he wanted to be.

"There are hardly any others it could be," Lorraine continued. "I so hate to see this happen. You have such a beautiful farm here and the cows and that milk...."

Jerry needed to say something that thanked these women for caring but made them go away. He had areas that were definitely off limits, his health, Nelson's loss and the Johne's outbreak. The only course left him was a philosophical response.

"Farmers like me and farms like this, a couple generations from now, not a kid in New England will have a chance to see one let alone get any food from one. Right now it would take a revolt to stop the runaway train that this lifestyle in on. "

"I like revolts," Lorraine's voice rose to its usual level. "Why didn't you tell me I needed to do more and sooner. I could have worked on helping Frank before it was too late."

"There's no warning for farms most times," Jerry said. "The end comes up quick. There are no timeouts in dairy farming and if enough things go wrong all at the same time, they're done, quick as that. There's no bringing them back either."

"Where do we go now to get this milk that just saved her life?" Lorraine pointed at Celeste.

"Still a few places but you'll have to go a bit farther out west," Jerry suggested. "Make sure you know who's running the place. You can't make people careful and conscientious so don't go buying raw milk from just any farm."

Silence occupied the next three minutes. For Jerry's part, he was not going to apologize for his entire life. He wouldn't make excuses for any of the decisions that led to the end of this farm, not that he wouldn't have wanted to see a different end. Placing the blame on Frank or the government might have crossed some other farmer's mind but not Jerry's.

"All I can tell you now is that I'm tired. Farming is hard work with a lot of great days thrown in to keep you going but it's tiring. You just get tired," Jerry stated and he closed the door.

Chapter 31

LAST CALL
FINAL

FRANK HADN'T BEEN THE LEAST BIT EXCITED when his name was called as the winner of the main prize at the game dinner, a new shotgun. His days with guns were behind him, he thought, but he'd walked up and accepted it, smiling at least outwardly.

He only remembered he'd won it when he started to formulate his plan, thinking fate had put that gun in his life for this reason. It was a Remington pump action 12 gauge, something he hoped was big enough. He hadn't even looked at it much after winning it just placed it in a locked cabinet, the one where his dad had kept their guns. He realized he'd need to school himself on the weapon and get some target practice.

He brought it to the farm and got out into the wood lot area a few times on days when the weather was just a little overcast, no one looking to have their hay cut, not a good day for much of anything outdoors. He'd taken to the farthest corner of the lot and hoped no one would be curious as to what the shooting was. The hunting season on the state land was going on and he hoped they'd just think someone was close to the line.

Jerry wasn't fooled. He outright asked him what he was shooting at the first opportunity he got. By then, he had made the arrangements to sell as many girls to the Pennsylvania farm as they could and were just waiting for the return on some of the Johne's test, hoping that more could be added to that list and fewer on the cattle dealer's list. It was taking every bit of strength for Jerry to see this through. He was weighing the prospect of putting the place on the market as soon as the cows were taken care of. The word must have gotten out that this place might be for sale and there'd already been the opportunist buyers knocking at his door.

He'd decided to meet with a real estate agency that specialized in farms. They sold mostly to horse people. Jerry had no problem picturing horses enjoying the high pastures.

"Scaring away coyotes up there?" Jerry asked.

"I just don't want to see Ada go to the cattle dealer," Frank offered. Jerry looked away and Frank walked out of the kitchen.

That had been a little over a month ago, the day Frank had chosen because the cows were shipping in three days and Ada and Baby Angel hadn't been included in any of the dealings. Frank wanted them far away when livestock started moving.

Ada was where he'd left her, near the milking parlor, tied to the fence. She'd actually still given a small amount of milk, emaciated and not even making food to feed her own body, she'd still given up something for the milk can.

He untied her and urged her to come with him. She only slightly hesitated, following him with a willingness to trust him that was the crux of his dilemma. There was such an ease, a cooperation from these animals, a dependability and faithfulness that surpassed anything Frank had ever imagined.

He walked very slowly, Ada's pace, just a quiet crawl up to the spot he'd fixed. There was new grass, a beautiful view, usually some breeze Ada would appreciate. They reached the spot and he tied her loosely to the tree branch, stood and stroked her neck and spoke to her.

Then he stepped away slowly, leaving Ada grazing peacefully and went to his appointed spot, the Remington waiting for his return. He didn't want to delay this thing he'd set on so he picked it up and sighted down the barrel. Ada's chest was in his direct view, the spot behind her front leg a direct target. He squeezed and she fell, almost exactly where he'd hoped she would so he could get her body into the bucket of the Kubota.

He made quick work of his hilltop duty, covering up the grave with some boulders he'd pulled close.

He headed back down to finish his next duty. He'd been able to borrow a trailer from a friend and though Baby Angel was growing fast, she still would need some packing to keep her from being hurt on the trip over to his place. She didn't come along as quietly. Her instincts were to kick up her heels at the smell and sight of the outdoors, something she had only gotten short glimpses of so far.

"Don't worry, I have some nice fresh air at my house you can run around in," he told her, the levity of her antics and the joy of seeing her frisky healthiness, blunting the memory of his last moments with her mother.

They both got loaded, Baby Angel tied securely and encased in hay bales and him behind the wheel. He started his truck.

Jerry watched from the farm house. He lifted his hand in a wave and Frank returned it, not sure what else to offer.

The man had given him a chance to do something that he knew would be a memory he'd cherish, maybe the source of stories he'd tell his grandchildren. He dared to hope for a chance to make more cow memories, his little passenger his best chance, but he didn't want to set his heart on it.

***

He couldn't relax that night and finally decided to visit Baby Angel in her stall to calm his racing mind. He used only the light of the bright full moon to enter. He wanted to see if she had settled in and seemed content in her new digs.

She was curled up in the corner of the stall making no sound just opening her eyes and asking him, what's up, when she saw him. That did more to soothe his nerves than any alcoholic or chemical mix he could have used. He rolled back the stall door and entered, bringing Baby Angel to her feet. He touched her coat, the vibrancy of life and potential within her coming right through the fuzzy golden covering which already was thickening to endure the cold winter.

He planned to open up a window in the stall come spring, let her be bathed in sunshine on days she couldn't be out grazing. His small acreage would not afford her a big pasture but he had designed a fenced two-acre portion for grazing then reserved the largest piece of his flat open acres to become a new hay field.

As payment from Jerry, Frank had asked for and received the hay making equipment. He was already viewing every YouTube video on the machinery and how to repair it. He'd tinker with it during the winter and hoped to have it primed and ready in the spring.

The first cuts of his field would bring little in the way of good hay but that would be just to get rid of the current crop of grasses so he could replant it with alfalfa and clover hoping to grow some of the best hay he could produce for his little princess.

He'd brought some of Fair View Acres grain to his house to get started but was ordering a high grade, organic blend. Feeding Baby Angel a mix of the good grain and hay along with providing as much fresh green pasture as he could, he hoped to fight the Johne's threat.

The conventional avenues to find a cure for Johne's had failed. He'd found a Johne's forum online that tried to bring together the most recent tests available, offer information on positive results but the overall outlook still was not good. Like so many other failed attempts by supposed experts knowledgeable in disease or pest control, there were no breakthroughs on a cure.

His medicine would involve an overload of care. His daughter had fairly jumped out of her skin at the news that her baby would be just outside her door now. He had no doubt about her lavishing love and attention on the calf at least until she was old enough to be distracted by other things. By then, he'd know if his hopes had panned out. In his wildest dreams, he would start another Jersey herd, not unlike Jerry's grandma, Vera.

From the love of one beautiful girl, he'd make a new start. Frank wanted a chance to slowly become, if not a fulltime dairy farmer, at least the owner of a small herd of exceptional bovines and he would figure out what to do about that when and if he ever achieved that dream.

He sank down into the thick sawdust bed, the calf coming over, at first standing and expectant but finally realizing this guy had nothing to offer in food. She dropped down next to him and he took to scratching her head. He finally fell asleep there dreaming of looking out from the top of a high pasture.

ACKNOWLEDGEMENTS

TO THE FARMERS who let me work on their farms, I never had the worries or the responsibilities. I only had the pleasure and it was a great pleasure to work for Ruth Mann, Doris and Bill Tomlinson and Chris and Mavis Newton.

To the farmers I interviewed and wrote about who were free with the secrets of their lives, the pains and joys, thank you Henry and William "Rhody" Franklin, Dennis Rambone, Tony DiMuccio, Jane and Louis Escobar and so many others.

To Jason Smith, a veteran of the Iraq and Afghanistan wars, for his exquisite descriptions of the Middle East and the work of the military there. He has a dairy farmer's heart and a warrior's and so gave me the crucial pieces to tie those two occupations together.

To Cleveland Kurtz for being the first person to encourage me to write, thank you for reading the rough early version of this book.

To all the friends, Elizabeth O'Dea, Rachel Rickson, Tricia Wynne, Linda Faria and my family, Paul and Dina Mandeville, Monique Sabatino and my mom, Juliette Mandeville, who read the first drafts and helped me make improvements.

To Yoda, the master, who came into this project late but gave me the eyes to see many more ways to make the message clear. I promise to return to complete the Jedi training for my next book.

To Tommy Card and Cristina Vandall, the best farm hands anyone could ask for and the least expensive, for all your days working side by side with me and loving the animals as much as I do.

To my sons, Tim and Joe, both my life in a thousand ways, both giving so differently, Tim, a farmer and animal lover, who worked alongside me so I could continue to milk cows even as I lacked the physical capacity for all the heavy lifting and Joe, a writer and artist, who brought this book out of the pile of papers I handed to him and asked him to read, and then reread and "just once more, I promise." This book would not have happened without his vast input.

To my other half, Tom, and here I have no words for a person who makes me complete. This book is dedicated to a beautiful cow and not to my husband. He is not jealous instead able to understand how deeply I care about the cow but also how totally I love him.

ABOUT
THE AUTHOR

Lucille Benoit is a journalist and dairymaid. She worked in both fields in three New England states for more than 30 years. A graduate of the University of Rhode Island, she currently makes her home in Rhode Island with her husband and family of three dogs and three cats.

Contact her at lucillebenoit18@gmail.com and visit the Come, Bos website:

www.keepthecows.com

Join in the conversation about dairy farming and cows. Lend your ideas in the battle to stem the loss of farms, keep the ones we have and start new farmers on the journey.